HIDDE

Fifth book by Nancy Temple Rodrigue in the *Hidden Mickey* series of historical fiction mysteries about Walt Disney and Disneyland written for Adults, Teens, & Tweens (age 10 and up).

A HERO ALONE

After battling the wicked Maleficent, traveling back in time to rescue a friend, and struggling to get over a broken heart, Wals finds himself alone with an exciting new clue from Walt Disney. Will he be able to figure it out by himself, or will he require help from an unlikely—and skeptical—source?

CAN A FEISTY CAST MEMBER IN FLORIDA HELP SAVE THE DAY?

A petite brunette with definite opinions might hold the key to solving Wals' dilemma. Can they find a way to work together, or is Wals' story too far-fetched to be believed?

A GLIMPSE INTO FORGOTTEN ATTRACTIONS

Walt Disney expected his clues to be discovered. What will Wals do when he learns that Walt's attractions have been moved, closed, or are slated for removal?

NOW IS THE TIME TO WRAP UP SOME UNFINISHED BUSINESS

Disneyland is the backdrop for this exciting tale of hope, love, & discovery. *Unfinished Business* reunites us with a hard-working, deserving hero and introduces his beautiful partner as they work together to keep the Disney magic alive—both for themselves and for Walt's legacy.

Unfinished Business - Wals

HIDDEN MICKEY 4.5

UNFINISHED BUSINESS
WALS

Nancy Temple Rodrigue

DOUBLE R BOOKS

HIDDEN MICKEY 4.5
UNFINISHED BUSINESS—WALS

BOOK 4.5 IN THE HIDDEN MICKEY SERIES
FIRST EDITION PAPERBACK, VOLUME 4.5, JULY 15, 2017
ISBN 13: 978-1-9383192-7-3

DOUBLE R BOOKS

DOUBLE R BOOKS PUBLISHING
740 N. H STREET, SUITE # 170
LOMPOC, CALIFORNIA, 93436
 WWW.DOUBLERBOOKS.COM
COVER CONCEPT BY NANCY RODRIGUE
 www.NANCY.RODRIGUE.org
COVER ARTWORK BY CHRISNA RIBEIRO
 www.JUHANI.DEVIANTART.com
COVER SILHOUETTES BY DOUBLE R BOOKS
 WWW.DOUBLERBOOKS.COM
COVER COPYRIGHT © 2017 BY DOUBLE R BOOKS
 WWW.DOUBLERBOOKS.COM

1ST EDITION HARDBACK - JULY 2017 - ISBN 13: 978-1-9383192-8-0
1ST EDITION PAPERBACK - JULY 2017 - ISBN 13: 978-1-9383192-7-3
1ST EDITION eBOOK - JULY 2017 - ISBN 13: 978-1-9383192-9-7

PRINTED IN THE UNITED STATES OF AMERICA

Dedication

To my husband Russ Rodrigue.
He has read every word I have written,
offered support every step of the way,
and has been there for
almost every book signing
and appearance I have made.
His behind-the-scenes work
has been invaluable to me.
Thank you with all my heart!

Nancy Temple Rodrigue

Disclaimer

Walt Disney Company Trademarks: *Hidden Mickey 4.5: Unfinished Business—Wals* is in no way authorized by, endorsed by or affiliated with the Walt Disney Company, Inc., Disneyland Park, or WED. Disneyland Park is a registered trademark of the Walt Disney Company. Other trademarks include but are not limited to Adventureland, Aladar, Aladdin's Flying Carpets, *Alice in Wonderland*, Animal Kingdom, Bengal Barbecue, *Bertha Mae*, Big Thunder, Billy Hill and the Hillbillies, Blizzard Beach, Blue Bayou, Buzz Lightyear, Carolwood, Carousel of Progress, Casey Jr. Circus Train, Cinderella Castle, Club 33, *Columbia*, Contemporary Resort, Davy Crockett, Discovery River, Disneyland Railroad, DinoLand USA, *Dinosaur*, *Disney Magic*, Edison Square, Expedition Everest, *Fantasmic!*, Fantasyland, Finding Nemo Submarines, Flame Tree Barbecue, Fort Sam Clemens, Fort Wilderness, Frontierland, Golden Horseshoe, Grand Canyon Concourse, *Gullywhumper*, Hall of Presidents, Haunted Mansion, Hollywood Studio, Horseless Carriage, Hungry Bear Restaurant, Jungle Cruise, Keelboat, Kilimanjaro Safari, Magic Kingdom, Main Street, Maleficent, *Mark Twain*, Mike Fink, Mickey Mouse, Monorail, New Orleans Square, Omnibus, Pirates of the Caribbean, Progress City, Rainforest Café, Schweitzer Falls, Silhouette Studio, Skyway Chalet, Sleeping Beauty Castle, Snow White, Soundsational Parade, Space Mountain, SpeedRamp, Star Wars Land, Stitch's Great Escape, Tomorrowland, Tom Sawyer Island, Tree of Life, Wilderness Lodge, Walt Disney Studio, Walt Disney World, Walt's Apartment, Walt's Barn, and Walt Disney. All references to such trademarked properties are used in accordance with the Fair Use Doctrine and are not meant to imply this book is a Disney product for advertising or other commercial purposes.

While some of the events and persons contained herein are historical facts and figures; other persons named and the events described are purely fictional and a product of the Author's imagination. Any resemblance to actual people is purely coincidental.

The actions depicted within the book are a result of fiction and imagination and are not to be attempted, reproduced or duplicated by the readers of this book. The Publisher and Author assume no responsibility or liability for damages resulting, or alleged to result, directly or indirectly from the use of the information contained herein.

Acknowledgements

I WOULD LIKE TO THANK THE FOLLOWING PEOPLE
FOR THEIR HELP AND ENCOURAGEMENT:

SAM GENNAWEY – AUTHOR OF *THE DISNEYLAND STORY*
FOR HIS INFORMATION ON THE CAROUSEL OF PROGRESS

TIMOTHY CRUMRINE
FOR HIS IDEA ABOUT THE COMPASS

JAMES D. KEELINE
FOR HIS MINE TRAIN PICTURES AND HISTORICAL INFORMATION

LYNN BARRON – CO-AUTHOR OF *CLEANING THE KINGDOM*
FOR HIS DISNEYLAND BACKSTAGE INFORMATION

CAROLYN HOAGLAND
FOR HER HELP WITH THE *KING GEORGE V* LOCOMOTIVE

THANKS ALSO GO TO
OUR PROOFREADERS AND EDITORS

Dear Readers,

When I finished writing *Hidden Mickey Adventures 5: When You Wish*, I thought I had nicely wrapped up the Adventures series. Everyone seemed to be on their way to their own happy endings.

However, my fans had one name on their lips: Wals. What happened to Wals? They knew he had received a clue from his friends Lance and Wolf at the end of *Hidden Mickey 4: Happily Ever After?,* and that Wals had been on his way to Walt Disney World in Florida. That was where Wals' story appeared to have stopped. But, what happened in Walt Disney World at the Carousel of Progress? Did he find the next clue? What happened next?

I am pleased to present to you Wals' complete story. You will meet a feisty new character who is amused by this good-looking stranger's odd quirk of saying out loud what he assumes is just his thoughts. With her security guard brother and a no-nonsense best friend, Wals finds he has more cut out for him than he ever imagined.

The clues in *Hidden Mickey 4.5: Unfinished Business—Wals* take you to never-before explored places in the *Hidden Mickey* universe. Discover these new settings that were dear to Walt Disney and his wide world of fans. Travel with Walt himself as he moves through some of his newest creations and newest acquisitions. Go back in time to attractions that have been dearly missed for many years.

Written in the same clue-driven narrative as the very first *Hidden Mickey* novel, I hope you enjoy this exciting, heartfelt new Adventure.

Nancy Temple Rodrigue

CHAPTER 1

Walt Disney World — 2009

So much for being invisible.

"Hi, can I help you? I've seen you here a couple times today." The pretty cast member couldn't understand why the man just stood there looking, what, guilty? The Carousel of Progress drew a different assortment of people. Some came because they had never heard of it before. Some came because of the nostalgia. Some just liked to sit in a quiet, dark, air-conditioned room with few other guests. Since he had been lurking near the entrance again, obviously perplexed, she couldn't quite fit him into any of the categories. "Any questions about the ride? Any observations? Comments? Complaints? Want a sticker?"

That seemed to work. Wals looked at the proffered Mickey sticker torn from a long roll taken from the cast member's waist pack. A reluctant grin tugged at his lips as he reached for it, his eyes on the smiling mouse's face. "Um, thanks. I'll add it to my collection."

"So, you collect stickers?" She tore off another three Mickeys and handed them to the red-faced man. "My name is Rose. Did you want to see the show again? It will start in about five minutes. There's a fascinating history behind this…" She broke off when his widened eyes shot to her face. He had gone from being uncomfortable to shocked in mere moments.

"Rose? What? Really?" His wide brown eyes darted down to the oval name tag pinned to her costume as if to verify what she had told him was true. "No, no, no!"

A hasty step backward ran her into a projection from the building that stopped her retreat. The easy smile on her lips became frozen. "Well, yes, sorry. I was named after my grandmother, not that you asked." A quick look around showed she was alone for the moment, something she regretted not checking earlier. She did a mental calculation as to how long it would take her to reach the nearest Cast Member Only door and the safety of backstage.

Flustered, Wals ran a shaky hand through his hair. He knew he was acting incredibly creepy. An explanation, an apology was due this innocent woman. But, how could he explain what he had gone through— the time travel with Wolf, the life on Tom Sawyer Island, fighting Maleficent with a Lakota brave named Mato, all for a woman named Rose? A short, audible chuckle broke from his throat. He scarcely believed it himself. "I…I'm sorry. I knew someone named Rose…a long time ago." *In a galaxy far, far away.* "It just took me by surprise, that's all." He tried a self-deprecating smile like he had seen his friend Lance Brentwood successfully use. But, he wasn't Lance and she didn't relax.

"Okay, I guess." *Drat, there still isn't anyone around. Where's Security when you need them?* "Did you want to see the show again?" Anything to get him away from the entrance…and her.

Wals looked up at the brightly painted round building as if he had forgotten where he was. "Oh, right. The Carousel. Yeah, I've already seen what I need…" After shaking his head as if to clear it, his smile became natural. "Let me start over. My name is Wals. Wals Davis. I'm from Huntington Beach, California. I work at Disneyland."

Her frozen features thawed. His expression had transformed his whole demeanor. The creepy/stalker image he had been projecting vanished and the nice guy she had previously pegged him for returned. He still gave the impression of being somewhat lost, but harmless. "Oh, really? That's a relief. I mean, great. What rides to do you work on? Gosh, I haven't been to Disneyland since I was little."

Relaxed now, more himself, Wals could turn his attention to the woman in front of him. Her short auburn hair framed a pixie-like face, full lips, and warm, oval eyes. *Gosh, you're so beautiful.*

The amber eyes he was still staring into filled with amusement.

"Why, thank you. I can't take much of the credit, though. That would go to my parents. And my grandmother is lovely." Rose's hand went to her lips as she tried to stifle a laugh. "You have no idea you just said that out loud, do you?"

"This day is just getting better and better. I'd probably better leave before you call Security."

"No, no, that thought already came and left." At his raised eyebrows, her slender shoulders gave a dismissive shrug. "Well, you were acting awfully…" Remembering her cast member training, Rose blushed when she realized she was on the verge of insulting a guest. "I mean, uh, you didn't look like you were having a magical day."

This caught Wals by surprise. He began to laugh and shook his head. "Oh, man, I think we had the same trainer at Orientation! You know, you could have just told me to get out."

Her high color quickly faded as she took up his unspoken challenge. "Well, now, that would have been rude. I could have told you to *please* get out."

"And I could have exited the same way I entered…"

"Pushing, shoving, screaming, scratching, biting, fighting. So, Wals, you work on the Jungle Cruise."

"No, never. You?"

"Nope. Always wanted to, though."

Wals nodded as he looked around the unfamiliar Tomorrowland. "Me, too. I work Westside Ops." At her questioning expression, he saw the need to clarify. "Frontierland, New Orleans Square, Critter Country, mostly Canoes and Pirates. Well, there was that stint on the Casey, Jr. Circus Train."

Rose folded her arms over her chest and casually leaned back against the same wall she had run into because of nervousness. "I didn't hear the same loving emphasis on the words Casey, Jr. as I heard in Westside Ops."

"Ah, the lady is observant. Yes, I was stuck in Fantasyland for about ten months. I think a friend of mine arranged it, but he'd never admit it."

"Nice friend."

The wretched memory returned of being stuck in the small cab of the Casey, Jr. train on endless loops. The women he had worked alongside had a gotten perverse, giddy joy out of his misery. All of this faded, though, as he thought about Lance, Wolf, and his other friends on the opposite coast. "Yeah, he is a good friend, actually. Strange sense of humor. You have to put up with a lot to remain his friend."

Rose understood. "I have a few friends like that. Like the one who was supposed to relieve me fifteen minutes ago." With a tilt of her chin she indicated the building closer to the Tomorrowland Transit Authority ramp. "She's over there at Buzz Lightyear's entrance waving right now."

Wals turned to see a raven-haired woman blowing them a kiss as the last guests in view disappeared inside to take their turn blasting at the space aliens. Her expression immediately returned to Disney Professional as another group approached her position. "She seems busier than you are over here."

"Yeah. That's why it's so hard to get her to follow the rotation."

"But, you won't complain."

"Nope." Rose gave him a wide smile. "That's what friends do. And, here's Anne. She's the third rotation."

Wals stepped back a few paces as Rose's replacement arrived, suddenly unsure of what he wanted to do next. The women exchanged whatever information Anne would need for the next shift before Rose walked over to where he had retreated. He expected her to give him a word or two of brush-off before she disappeared. What he received was a pleasant surprise.

"Would you like to go on break with me? There's a nice little place backstage where you can see the trains go by."

"I'd like that. I haven't been backstage here at Walt Disney World yet."

"Great. Then you can tell me why you've been on the Carousel of Progress six times in the last two days."

His wide smile slowly faded. "Great."

"**H**ave you always worked in Tomorrowland?"

A sip of her cola covered the amusement at his changing the subject. Let him have his moment. She'd get back to her questions soon enough. "No, I've been in quite a few different areas. I like Frontierland the best and hope to rotate back there in a few months. I dance as one of the fairies in some of the parades."

That's not hard to believe.

Her eyes crinkled again. "Why, thank you."

"You heard that, didn't you."

"Yes, I did."

"Sorry. Hmmph, I seem to be saying sorry to you an awfully lot."

She waved him off. "Not a problem. I think it's cute."

A whistle sounded as a train emerged from behind Space Mountain and neared the Main Street Station. "Which train is that?"

Again a diversion. "That's one of our steam trains. I thought you had them in California."

Wals gave her a quick glance to see if she was serious or teasing. He wasn't sure. "Yes, we have trains. I just wondered which train that one was. I know you have four engines."

She took another sip to hide her grin. "That's the *Roger E. Broggie*. You can tell by the red cab and green body. All five of the passenger cars are yellow. Did you know all our trains were found in Mexico?"

"Really? All of them? Usually there was more of a search."

"When they were looking for trains, they heard about a railroad boneyard in Mérida, Yucatán, Mexico. There were four usable engines and a fifth to use as parts. I think the whole purchase came to just over $32,000." She broke off when someone approached their table. "Hey, Rob."

"Pick up another stray, Rose?"

Wals wasn't sure if he liked the smirk on this guy's face. After working on the Canoes for so many years, he knew he was in good shape. But, this guy Rob must have outweighed him by twenty pounds—and it wasn't fat. Rather than start something that would probably end badly for him, he remained silent.

Rose didn't notice the tension that had arisen. With an airy wave, she tried to shoo him away. It didn't work. "We're just having a chat. Rob, this is Wals. Wals, Rob. Wals works at Disneyland."

"And enjoys long walks on the beach, warm puppies, and world peace." Wals couldn't help himself. This guy was glaring at him for some unknown reason and it ticked Wals off. Must be a special friend of Rose's. He wondered *how* special.

Rose cracked up and put a hand on Wals' arm. "Oh, that's too much! 'And world peace.' If you tell me you can twirl a baton, I'll die right here!"

Rob watched the innocent banter between the two. "Anne called me, that's all. I need to get back to Fox Patrol."

Security. That figures.

"Yes, I'm Security. Problem?"

Rob was ignored. "That came out loud again, didn't it, Rose?"

"Yep! No problem, Rob. I appreciate your thoughtfulness. We were just discussing the history of the railroad." As expected, Rob's expression glazed over.

"Well, you are the expert on that subject, as we all learn at the dinner table, all cast parties, and every break you take."

"Hey!"

"Well, you do go on and on..." Wisely Rob caught on to the daggers in Rose's eyes. His hands went up in self-defense. "Not that it isn't fascinating. Hey, look at the time. I need to get back to...somewhere..."

Rose let out a small chuckle as Rob turned on his heels and left. When her attention reverted to Wals, she could tell he didn't know whether to be angry or amused. "He means well. Loyal to a fault. Just kind of..."

"Dumb?"

"Well, I was going to say protective."

Wals took a long slug of his drink. "If you say so. How do you know so much about the trains? Is that your specialty or do you know everything about Walt Disney World?"

Was he being polite, sarcastic, or sincerely interested? Only one way to find out. "I try to learn as much about the Magic Kingdom as I can. I find History fascinating. I focused on the trains when I was a Conductor. How about you?"

"I was never a Conductor."

Her laugh showed she caught the joke. "You know what I meant! Do you know much about your Disneyland?"

"I'm not sure where all our trains came from, but I do know some history. In our positions as cast members, we need to if we want to answer guests' questions. Sometimes they seem to know more than we do and we don't want to give a wrong answer."

"Boy, that's the truth. Your Disneyland is older than the Magic Kingdom, so you probably have more to research."

"It's not so bad working on the Canoes. You can basically only interact with the guests in the row nearest yours. They're usually too busy trying to figure out how to paddle correctly."

Rose lowered her lids and stole a glance at his muscled arms. He must have worked on the Canoes a long time. A warm blush stole up her neck. "Yes, uhm, right. So, why are you so interested in the Carousel?"

Not sure why she became embarrassed, Wals tried to figure out how to deflect her question—legitimate as it was. "It used to be at Disneyland, and, uh, I missed it, and wanted to see it again."

Now her arms were folded across her chest. "Right." It was drawled out so long it sounded like it had three syllables.

Okay, that didn't work. Wals fumbled with the folded piece of paper in his pocket, the paper that had sent him here in the first place. How much should he tell her? Would it help or hurt? This new camaraderie they had developed was enjoyable and he didn't want to mess it up. Hearing the impatient *click, click, click* of her fingernail on the tabletop brought him to a decision. He had to trust someone and, after so many viewings of the attraction, he knew he needed help. "Don't you need to get back from your break?"

Her head tilted to the side. "Really? You still aren't going to tell me?"

Wals held up a hand. "No, I'm not putting you off this time. Really. It's... it's just that it would take more than the two minutes you probably still have left of your break."

"Fair enough. Actually, to be honest, I'm off duty. I've been off since we came back here. Ha, you look like you don't believe me."

"You must do things differently here. We would've had to clock out."

"I'm a Lead."

"Okay," he nodded. "That makes sense. We have a little more leeway than our minions."

That earned a chuckle. "Don't let Anne or Louise hear you call them minions." She stood and gathered the empty cups.

"Are you leaving?"

"Ah, you sound so disappointed." Her bright smile teased the worry out of his eyes. "No, I thought we'd take a walk around the Park while you tell me your story. We've sat here long enough."

Boy, this one's a handful!

"Yeah, that's what my dad says all the time."

"I really need to quit talking to myself." With a lighter step, Wals fell in next to her and let her lead him wherever she wanted.

Instead of leading him onstage, as the public area of the Park is called, Rose led Wals through the Utilidor, which delighted him. "I'll be right back." Once she changed clothes at the lockers, she rejoined him. Taking him by the arm, they re-entered the Park using their cast member ID's. She headed for Adventureland. "Now, Wals, tell me a story. The real one."

CHAPTER 2

Flashback — Disneyland — 2008

"I'm sorry, Wolf, but we have a bit of an emergency right now." Lance quickly walked through Adventureland, coming in from the New Orleans Square side, as Wolf fell into step beside him.

Wolf frowned as he glanced down at his silent walkie-talkie. "I hadn't heard anything since I got back. What is it?"

Lance glanced around to make sure none of the guests were near enough to hear him. "There was a big problem a couple of nights ago. I'm still not sure if it was a backhoe, or what, but someone set something heavy on top of Schweitzer Falls to continue some work they were doing. Apparently, it was too heavy for the aging Falls, and," he stopped to look around one more time, lowering his voice, "the Falls collapsed."

Wolf merely grunted at the news. "That's too bad. Is that why you can't go with me to Columbia again?"

Giving his security partner an unbelieving look, Lance slowly shook his head. "Yeah, that's why. This isn't a good thing, Wolf."

As they neared the boarded-up entrance to the popular ride, Wolf shrugged. He couldn't see why Lance was so upset about the Falls. "So, they'll fix it. They always do when something goes wrong."

When Lance stopped in his tracks, the unimpressed guard ran into him. Lance lowered his voice even more. "You don't understand, Wolf. There's a capsule Walt had hidden somewhere in Schweitzer Falls. Another branch of a Hidden Mickey quest that

19

Kimberly and I don't know much about."

Letting that sink in for a moment, he was rewarded when a look of recollection came into Wolf's sharp blue eyes. "Oh, that's right. I forgot all about that one. I'm the one who put it there."

"Great. Then you should know right where it is." Lance was more relaxed now and inclined to chat. "We were alerted to the problem when Kimberly was in the War Room last night. Sometimes she can't sleep because of the pregnancy..." He clamped his mouth shut at the get-on-with-it look on Wolf's face. "Anyway, one of the green lights on the map of the Park was now blinking yellow, indicating something was wrong. When she called the Park, they were surprised we knew already—even though they really don't know who 'we' are." Even after working as a Guardian for a few years, Lance was still amazed at the intricacy of the system Kimberly's father—and Walt—had sent into place so long ago. "After rather reluctantly telling us about the collapse, Kimberly immediately put a stop on the work—which they knew we would do— so I could check it out. They didn't like it, but there's nothing they could do. You know what's funny?"

His mind on his upcoming trip, Wolf had been only half-listening. Now he realized he was supposed to give some sort of an appropriate response. He merely grunted, knowing that would be enough to satisfy Lance.

"What's funny," his partner repeated, knowing Wolf wasn't really listening, "is that I walked over those Falls when I was chasing down the second El Lobo hidden in the ride."

At the mention of the carved wolf-shaped rock formation, Wolf's attention shot back to the problem at hand. He and Lance had found the original El Lobo in the jungles of Columbia when Lance had been on his second Hidden Mickey quest, the one apart from Adam and Beth's. Knowing he had to go back there soon, Wolf became more interested. "What about El Lobo?"

"Ha, I knew you weren't paying attention." Lance's observation was rewarded with the same narrowed-eyed frown that had stopped quite a few teenagers from doing something stupid. Unperturbed, he continued his explanation. "I said I had walked over the top of the Falls and, in the darkness, never saw the **W E D** that had been engraved into a couple of the rocks up there. You know that's our indicator that we're in the right place..." He broke off when he got the same get-on-with-it look he had received moments earlier. "Which you put there, obviously. My, are we a little testy today, Wolf?"

The blue eyes narrowed even further. "Would you care for me to reiterate what I've just gone through and what's coming up next?"

Lance held up placating hands. "No, no. Sorry. I know you have a lot on your mind. I was just teasing. You know, you *really* don't have much of a sense of humor. Wals and I were just talking about..." At a low growl, he wisely stopped and went on with his former line of thought. "Long story short...."

"Too late for that." Wolf's mumble was clearly heard as they pushed aside one of the barriers that blocked the exit to the Jungle Cruise.

"Long story short, your undiscovered capsule is buried some-where in the debris and we need to find it before the backhoes and dump trucks carry everything off. I still think it's amazing. Another piece to another Hidden Mickey quest has been hidden here all along."

"Amazing. And what do you mean we? I just came by to see if you wanted to take the pendant back to Columbia with me."

"You won't help me?" Lance's propensity for not getting dirty was well known by all his friends. But now his curiosity overcame the necessity to move quickly on the missing capsule. "When are you flying out?"

Wolf looked at Lance with a smug gaze. "I'm not flying."

Lance's eyes got wide as he finally understood what Wolf was going to do. "Oooooh. So, you aren't just going to bury the pendant again under that El Lobo." As his friend's head slowly shook side to side, Lance tried to work it out. "Right. We already found it so there's no point in that.... Wow." Running a hand through his hair, he gave up on the intricacies of time travel. "You know where to go? How to get there?"

"I know how to get there. Apparently I've done it before." With a frustrated gesture, Wolf remembered the words of the local native De Tribu who met them deep in the jungle last time. *You've been here before. The future*, he had said. "It's confusing, even for me. But, I know what I have to do to get things back on their right course. In fact, it could be very interesting for you if you came with me. You might get to meet Walt." As an added incentive, he dangled that fascinating possibility of a carrot in front of Lance.

It worked. Lance was torn. He always wanted to try that *thing* Wolf did, but knew Kimberly would kill him if he did. And meeting Walt? Wow. After a few minutes of mental deliberations of the pros and cons, he had to finally, reluctantly, realistically shake his head no. "Not this time, buddy, but thanks for thinking of me. Perhaps someday we all can go with you. Maybe after the new baby. Since he met your brother, Peter would love to go back to see the rest of your family."

"Let me know," was all Wolf said. He, too, knew it would never happen.

"So, are you going to help me look for the capsule? You should know about where it is." They reached the edge of the silent Jungle Cruise dock. Three boats sat motionless in the slip, waiting for skippers and passengers. Since the water had been drained, it looked odd to see the boats propped up with wooden beams to keep them centered between the two docks.

Wolf looked down at the mud in the riverbed. The water hadn't been drained long enough for the bottom to dry. "I really didn't come with you for that reason."

"Two hands make for quick work." Lance was still hopeful. Kimberly had requested a couple of shovels be left on site. There should have been some there anyway, but they wanted to make sure Lance wouldn't have to improvise with whatever he could find.

Wolf let out a chuckle at Lance's feeble attempt. Well remembering who was on the business end of the shovel when they had to dig in Columbia, he was sorely tempted to turn around and go back to his security patrol until it was time for him to leave. Instead, he gave a small sigh. "How much time do you have to find it?"

Grinning internally, Lance didn't let it show on his face. "Only a little while." Kimberly had actually shut down the site for two days, but no need to tell Wolf that little tidbit.

"Fine." After his grumbled acceptance, Wolf lightly jumped down from the end of the unloading dock into the muck. Saying something unpleasant under his breath in Lakota as his spotless shoes sunk up to their laces, he headed for the opposite bank where the mud wasn't so deep.

Lance let himself down a little more gingerly and followed in the footsteps of his partner. As they turned the corner and went past the motionless Trader Sam and the baby elephant, Ellie, Lance started his favorite trivia game again. "So, Wolf, tell me: Who were the first people who actually lived at Disneyland?"

Wolf was following the rail between the mechanical piranhas. They didn't seem quite as menacing when seen on their wires, stopped in various positions on the rollers. The water buffalo and the huge python didn't even glance in the men's direction as they headed for the huge mound of fallen earth, framework and pipes. "You mean Owen and Dolly Pope? Nice couple."

"Now, how would you know that? They could have been as mean as snakes?"

"If you are talking about the first animal handlers, they were really nice. They had quite a job getting the horses and mules ready for all the sights and sounds they'd have to face every day. If you remember, I knew them." His backward glance caught Lance walking almost on tip-toes to avoid the mud.

"Oh, yeah, I keep forgetting how far back your history goes here. Do you know the burro story?"

"Which one? The miniature burro that Walt loved? He didn't believe it when he was told it snapped at people until it tried to bite him."

Slightly deflated that Wolf knew this tiny tidbit of history, Lance mumbled, "Yeah, that burro story."

"I thought you were going to ask me something difficult, like what ride in Fantasyland was supposed to be a roller coaster?"

Lance gave a quick grin. "You mean the entrance to Storybook Land."

"Nope. A full ride."

Stumped, Lance's attention was drawn to something else. Coming to a stop, hands on his hips, Lance let out a low whistle. "Wow, look at that mess! I'd hate to be the guy who'd been running that backhoe."

Not stopping to admire the destruction, Wolf pointed upward with the shovel he had picked up off the bank. "Hmmm, now where did I put that marked stone? I know it was up there somewhere. It's been a long time."

"You don't remember? Oh, great. You're no help. The light on the map indicated it was about in the middle on top."

Wolf stepped back a few paces into what would have been the

path of the oncoming boats. Taking a visual measurement and walking forward again, he dug in with his shovel, silently getting to work in what he thought was the most promising area. The capsule would be well covered with debris.

Ducking out of the way of the flying dirt, Lance wandered over to Wolf's side and finally started to dig. "So, are you going to tell me the answer?" After an hour of scooping out the never-ending dirt, he leaned on his shovel.

"Answer to what?" Wolf didn't even pause.

"Which ride was going to be a roller coaster. I'm so tired that I can't even come up with a smart retort," as he wiped the sweat off his face with his sleeve.

"Mr. Toad. Now get back to work or I'm leaving."

Daylight was fading when Lance's shovel finally hit something that wasn't a rock or pipe. They had been at it for hours and began to wonder if the capsule had somehow already been removed. This new sound made him think that they had finally found it.

Squatting down in what looked like a small cavern in the middle of the pile, Lance carefully pulled dirt away from his find. When the familiar gray color of the hard plastic capsule revealed itself, he let out a happy yell. "Got it!" He quickly learned that was unnecessary as Wolf stood right behind him, looking over his shoulder. It was a longish capsule, almost a foot in length and about six inches in diameter. Holding it up to his ear, Lance gave a careful shake. Hearing something rattling around inside, he let out a curious "Hmmm," and held it out to Wolf.

With a tired shake of his head, he had something else in mind. "Give it to Wals. He earned it." Seeing Lance's attention was only on their find, Wolf's shovel pointed at the hole they had created. "Shouldn't we fill that in?"

"Fill it in? Why?" Lance looked from the capsule to the excavated hole in the mound. "You think anyone would notice?" He had been testing how tightly the end cap was attached. There was no reply. His partner silently glared at him, impatience written all over Wolf's dirt-streaked face. "What?"

"You don't think someone would notice a large cavern dug into the middle of what was previously just a pile of dirt? I thought you didn't want to be obvious."

Lance was more intrigued with the hidden capsule than what

any of the workers might think about the hole they had made. After a moment's thought, he could see Wolf's point. It was also plain to see that Wolf did not intend to fill it back in by himself. "Fine." With a dramatic sigh, the capsule was gently set on the grass of the river-bank. "I'll help you fill it in. You didn't happen to see the rock with the **W E D** on it, did you?"

"You don't need any more souvenirs." Wolf's huge shovelful of dirt barely missed Lance. There was a satisfied, unseen grin as Lance leaped out of the way and then picked up his shovel to help.

Head down, Lance's attention was focused on their important find as he continued the disgusting, back-breaking work of filling in the cavern. Darkness had fallen, both men quiet, each with their own thoughts.

Lance suddenly chuckled as he threw another shovelful of dirt into the smaller cavern. "Hey, Wolf, listen to this skipper joke I just heard the other day. 'Those of you entering the Jungle Cruise, please notice that there are two lines, one on the right and one on the left. If you want your family to stay together, stay on the same side of the line. But, if there's someone in your family you want to get rid of, just send them to the other line and you'll never see them again.' Isn't that great? Wolf?"

He hadn't even realized he had been working alone, that his partner had silently gone to the island that had affectionately been named Catalina by the cast members. Behind the attacking na-tives, well hidden by the overgrown brush and vines, was the smaller rock statue of the open-mouthed wolf. In sight of the pass-ing guests in the boats, however, was a tall thatched hut, a drape of some indistinguishable fabric hiding its entrance. Wolf hadn't gone to El Lobo this time. He had ducked inside the hut and quickly removed his dirt-stained security uniform. Tilting his head back, he gave a low, calling howl.

Knowing what was coming, Wolf took the red heart-shaped di-amond pendant out of his pants pocket and put the chain in his mouth. The pendant slowly swung near the side of his chin as he exited the hut and stood waiting in the darkness.

Not sure where his missing partner had gone, Lance was star-tled when a sudden, stiff breeze blew down the empty riverbed and blasted past him. Recognizing what was happening, he threw himself to the ground, protectively covering the capsule with his body until the violence around him stopped and the air returned to normal.

Getting to his feet, he looked around, but already knew he was alone. "Well, I guess that answers the 'when are you going' part."

Once the hole was filled in enough for his satisfaction—which wasn't much longer—Lance picked up the gray plastic canister and turned to retrace his steps to the dock. Remembering something from his past trip, he halted and turned back to head for Catalina. Going through the dense vines, he used his security Mag light to look around inside the grass hut. The last time he checked inside the hut he had found a pile of clothing and had wondered what kind of wild party he had missed out on. On further inspection, he had discovered it was a security uniform—only it was different than the one he was now wearing.

Using his light, he saw that the odd uniform was gone and replaced by another, muddier outfit. He knew it was Wolf's and realized his security partner was now on his own mission back to the past. Thinking it would be a nice thing to take the uniform and have it cleaned for Wolf, he nixed that idea as quickly as it came. He didn't know how soon the Guardian would be back and didn't want his friend to have to find his way naked through the Park, amusing as that might be to Lance and his other security friends. He gave the clothes a small pat, and silently wished his friend a good trip.

The capsule securely tucked under his arm, he let the hut's flap close behind him and made his way back to the dock. Picking up his walkie-talkie, he pushed the button that was only present on his and Wolf's machine. When his wife immediately answered, he relayed the latest news and asked if Wals was still at work in the Park.

"**H**ere's a gift for you from Uncle Walt." Lance grinned at the confused expression on Wals' face as he handed over the unopened gray capsule.

Happily back at work on the Canoes, Wals and the security guard sat at an unoccupied table at the far end of the Hungry Bear Restaurant. Lance could tell Wals was more contented than he had been in the previous months.

"What do you mean? What is this?" Curious, Wals gently

shook the plastic and felt something muffled rattling around inside.

Lance glanced around to make sure they wouldn't be over-heard. "You know a little about the treasure hunt Adam and I went on a couple of years ago?"

Wals shrugged. "A little. I also know you and Wolf were in-volved in something similar. But I've never been told any details." The capsule was furtively moved to his lap in case Lance changed his mind and wanted it back.

Noticing the movement, Lance just smiled as he ignored the obvious hint. "Well, Walt set a few things in motion years ago. We think this is another leg of that journey. And," he stressed, "we want *you* to have the honors—wherever this might lead."

"You have no idea?"

"Nope, none." Lance thought back on his own exciting Hidden Mickey searches. "We never did know where we'd have to go. If this follows suit, it will be a clue you'll have to solve."

"Clue to what?" Wals was getting more intrigued by the minute.

Lance gave him a vague shrug as he stood to leave. "You'll just have to open it and find out. If you run into problems, contact Adam and Beth." A warm smile spread over his mouth. "They're experts at this sort of thing. I've got to get back to work." He glanced at his watch. "And you are officially off duty."

"But I have another two hours to my shift."

"No, you don't." Lance sauntered off with a friendly parting wave. He envied Wals right now. The Hidden Mickey quests he had gone on had changed his life. He wouldn't return to his previ-ous life for anything.

As Lance headed down the ramp of the restaurant, Wals thought about the unexplained power he and Kimberly had at the Park. If Lance said he was off work, then he knew he was off work. With a soft chuckle, he tugged at the sealed end of the gray plastic. "Okay, Walt, let's see what you have planned for me." The cap didn't budge. "Gosh, Walt must've had quite a grip." He set the capsule between his feet and gripped it with his knees. It took both hands to work the endcap back and forth, back and forth, until it fi-nally gave way.

His heart sped up as he anxiously tilted the container. A small lump surrounded by some kind of colorful cloth fell out. Untying a knotted, golden cord and carefully folding back the edges, the cloth proved to be a large silk scarf with various scenes of Disneyland printed onto its light blue background. But, it wasn't the Disneyland Wals knew. This was an older Disneyland with rounded Skyway cabs going through the Matterhorn and oddly-shaped cars poised on the Autopia track.

Once the scarf had been thoroughly examined, he picked up the screwdriver that had been so carefully protected. "Walt wanted me to have a screwdriver?"

Confused, he set the two items on the table and ran a finger inside the capsule. He could feel the edge of paper. "Ah, the plot thickens." The container was tilted so he could better reach the heavy paper curled around inside the tube. When he finally got it out, he actually found two pieces of paper. One was a small off-white page that looked to be ripped out of a book. The larger piece turned out to be a conceptual drawing of the new Tomorrowland of 1959 with sleek and streamlined Monorails. Not only was the sheet signed by Gurr and Hench, it also had Walt's signature of approval.

When he finally set down the incredible art find, he turned his attention to the small piece of paper, comparing the writing to the signature on the drawing. "This was written by Walt." He clamped a hand over his mouth to keep from shouting. "This was written by Walt!"

Now it was necessary to force himself to remain seated and not jump around like a small girl. Hands shaking, he read the words Walt had written so many years ago. "**If you think there's a great, big, beautiful tomorrow, just jump on the Speedramp to Progress City. <u>But</u>, watch out for that hand-cranked washing machine!**"

Heart pounding in his chest, Wals looked back at the small screwdriver. "Carousel of Progress? Looks like I'm going to Florida!"

CHAPTER 3

Walt Disney World — 2009

"**W**ell, our Castle is taller than yours."

"True, but we still have Mr. Toad's Wild Ride."

The triumph on Rose's face faded as her mouth turned down in a disgusted frown. "Okay, I'll give you that one. Don't get me started on losing Toad."

"Ha! Score another one for Disneyland."

"Don't get cocky, Wals. We have the Country Bear Jamboree."

"Yeah, I need to see that before I leave, too. But we have a Matterhorn."

"We have Mount Everest and the Yeti."

Wals stole a glance at her face. "Are you going to tell me yours is bigger?"

Her laugh drew an appreciative look from a passing man. "Well, it is!"

"We had Walt."

That definitive statement seemed to put the final stamp on their on-going debate as to which Park was better.

"Okay, I'll concede. But," as she raised a finger for emphasis, "just on that point. He did come here to scout out the location and buy the property. As huge as our property is..."

"Hey, why am I getting wet?" Wals jerked around trying to spot some kid with a water pistol.

Rose's face was all innocence. "Water? Really?" She had stopped so Wals would be positioned in the line of fire from one of the spitting camels standing guard over The Magic Carpets of Aladdin attraction. When another shot landed dead-center she could-n't control herself.

"You did this. Stop laughing at me!" Her chuckle was infectious as he wiped his dripping face. "Great, now I have to use the restroom. Where's the closest one, Tour Guide?"

With the cast member two-finger point, she indicated a building behind them. "Over there, next to the Island Supply store."

"What is it with you and strays?" Rob approached her as soon as Wals disappeared through the door.

"Didn't know this was your beat today."

With a non-committal grunt, he ignored her sarcasm. "You alright?"

The irritation at his abrupt arrival faded. "Yeah, I'm fine, Rob. This guy seems pretty nice."

"You never know." Rob glanced back at the entry of the rest room. "But, he does look an awful lot like that mangy terrier you found alongside the road years ago. Same wide-eyed I-don't-know-what's-going-on look."

"Your comparing Wals to Rocky?" She doubled over with laughter. After she wiped away a tear, she had to admit, "Well, Rocky did take an awfully long time to get used to things and trust us."

Rob's grin wasn't quite friendly. "You did have Rocky eating out of your hand at the end. What's your plan?"

"Just curious so far. Enjoying the day. He's pretty funny once he relaxes." She, too, checked to see if Wals was coming out yet. "I probably won't be over for dinner tonight."

"It's spaghetti night."

"Yeah, yeah, I know. You'd better take off, Rob. You two didn't seem to hit it off."

"Just looking out for you, little one. I'll be around."

Rose watched him stride away. "I'm sure you will." Her heart filled with affection. "Just quit being so obvious. You know we can see you!" she yelled before he was out of range.

"Wasn't that MegaTron just now? Was he bothering you?" Wals glared at the retreating back of the undercover security guard, his hand unconsciously reaching down to his side. Finding nothing there, his fingers curled into a fist.

"Just checking on me, that's all." Rose saw the movement and wondered what he had expected to find dangling from his belt.

Wals' harrumphed. "If you say so." Noticing she was bothered by their inexplicable animosity, he knew he should change the subject—something he was getting rather adept at doing. "Oh, look, the Swiss Family Treehouse."

"That's why I brought you here."

Glad the diversion worked, he indicated that she should start on the walkway ahead of him. As they toured the thatched huts and ingenious ways the Robinson's had turned bits and pieces of a damaged ship into a lovely, unique home, Wals relaxed. The familiarity of the attraction seeped into him as he rediscovered pieces of his childhood. "Isn't that the pulley that opens the roof of the bedroom? It would be so cool to lie there and watch the stars."

At the tallest point, one of the boys' bedrooms, they paused on the wooden deck to watch the Jungle Cruise boats glide by far below. "We used to be able to do this back home. Then they built Indy and moved the river to make room for the new entry."

"Indiana Jones?" At his nod, she continued. "Never saw that. I heard it's pretty good."

"Same ride vehicles and layout as your Dinosaur ride in Animal Kingdom."

"Yeah, that I knew about. I'd like to see it."

He turned sideways to face Rose. "When was the last time you were at Disneyland?"

She had to think. "Gosh, before my Dad left. I was, maybe, five or six?"

"So, about ten years ago?"

Rose gave his arm a playful swat. "Charmer. Let's just say yes, that's right."

"A lot's changed since then. You probably wouldn't recognize some parts of the Park."

A cloud passed behind her eyes. "Yeah, a lot has changed."

His hand felt warm on her shoulder. "Sorry. Didn't mean to bring up bad memories."

She looked out over the Jungle Cruise river instead of at him. Her voice became quiet. "It's been a long time. Dad turned to some New Age thinking. Found out his moon was in someone else's house. Lives somewhere in Arizona. Sedona, I think." There was a brief pause as she attempted to throw off the old feelings of abandonment. "But, Mom got married again to a man named Steven. He...he turned out to be so wonderful! I even got a brother out of it. Steven adopted me and he's been Dad ever since."

She suddenly pivoted and started down the steep stairs. Wals only had time to briefly glance at the furnishings in the huts. Once back on ground level, she made a quick left turn. "I feel like a roller coaster. Big Thunder?"

"Sure."

"You have any brothers and sisters, Wals?"

There was a noticeable pause before he answered. "No, there wasn't any time for that."

His response hit her as odd. Curious, she tilted her head as they walked. "What does that mean?"

"Ooh, Pirates. Can we come back to that?" After her amused nod, he quietly answered her question. "My parents and my older brother were on their way back from some outing or other. I was home sick. Grandma was babysitting. I remember it had been raining cats and dogs all day. On the Interstate, I was told, a semi hydroplaned on the water, jack-knifed and hit another truck."

Rose flinched. She knew what was coming.

He noticed her movement and nodded. "Yeah. Once they pulled the trucks apart, they found my family."

"I'm so sorry."

"Twenty-three years ago. Still expect them to walk back through the door. Grandma immediately packed me up and moved me into their home. Sold the family house and put the money into a trust for me. It's still there, actually, untouched." He could see her eyes well up. "It's okay, really. I had a great childhood. Gran and Gramps were at every meet during school."

"Football?"

"Water polo." He had to chuckle at one of his memories. "In the water we were all just floating heads. They had a hard time telling which team was which. I could hear Gramps cheering when the other team would score."

"Still with you?"

"Well, Grandma still is." They had reached the tall red and yellow spires of Big Thunder, screams of happy riders drifting over them. Wals leaned on the wooden fence railing and stared unseeingly at the rolling expanse of desert that led up to the entrance.

"She's in a care center. Dementia. Her instructions had been to sell their house in Newport Beach to cover her expenses if something like that happened."

"Dementia? That's rough. Does she know you?"

Wals thought on how to answer. "Sometimes. Most of the time she realizes I'm someone she knows, but not exactly sure who. Do you know the TV show *Whose Line Is It Anyways*?"

Confused by the apparent change in topic, she shrugged. "Uh, yeah, I've heard of it."

"Visiting Gran is just like that. Totally improv. You never know what she's going to say, but you just roll with it and never say no."

"You seem to have a good handle on it, Wals."

He didn't seem to hear her. "One time I visited, I had to go ask the nurse something. I was gone for, like, two minutes. I came back and she was like, 'Well, hello, there!' A whole new day." He visibly pulled himself back to his surroundings. "So, how did we get from comparing your miserable little Park to my original, glorious one to the story of our lives?"

"Miserable little Park, is it?" She, too, knew it was time to talk of other things. "Do you have a veritable desert leading up to your Big Thunder?"

"We have a McDonald's French fry cart."

"Well, you can't top French fries."

"You can with catsup." Wals laugh was cut off when he happened to glance behind them. "Oh, really? Andre the Giant is still following us? Hey, why don't we ask him to ride with us."

"He's supposed to be on duty. On Main Street." Her eyes narrowed. "Tell me something, Wals. Why does your hand drop to your side every time you see Rob?"

I'm reaching for my sword to protect you. "Uhm, do I? Hey, look, the line's short. Let's hurry." He obviously had not said his thought out loud this time, thank goodness.

Wind-blown, hair mussed, they exited the ride, comparing the ride in the two different Parks, laughing as they strolled along.

"I like that goat trick you mentioned. I'd like to try it on your Big Thunder." The idea was to keep your eyes on the dynamite-chewing goat for as long as you could while the train went through a corkscrew spiral at high speed.

"Well, you'll just need to come visit."

Her amber eyes crinkled at the corners. "Is that an invitation?"

The words had just blurted out as they walked and talked, but Wals suddenly discovered he had meant them. He would like her to visit California. Soon. "Yes, I guess it is."

"Well, answer my original question and we'll talk about it." She squeezed his arm. "Surely you knew we had to get back to the Carousel of Progress, didn't you?"

Wals sighed. "Yeah, I know. I was hoping you'd forget, but should've known better." He looked around Frontierland to take stock of where they were. "Tell you what, let's take the *Liberty Belle* around the River and, once I let you know how superior the *Mark Twain* is, I'll tell you why I'm here." Heart pounding, he hoped he wasn't making a mistake. Turning, he suddenly cupped his hands around his mouth. "Hey, Rob-inator! We're going to ride the *Liberty Belle* now!"

A hand came out of the shadows under a clump of trees lining the River. Rob waved that he had heard and flashed a thumbs-up.

Flashback — Disney Studio — 1964

"**Y**ou asked to see me, Walt?"

Walt Disney motioned for his Imagineer to enter his private office. He stood by one of his windows, the one that overlooked the water tower. "Yeah, yeah, come in, Bob. Say, you remember what I told you around, oh, I don't know, 1960 or so?"

There was a slight pause. "That was a few years ago, Boss."

Lost in thought, Walt didn't seem to notice. "I had said that there would only be one Disneyland, but realized we only played to about one-fourth of the United States. That there was a whole other world on the other side of the Mississippi." He returned to his desk, ignoring the piles of papers strewn over the top. His sharp gaze fell on Bob who, used to it, didn't squirm under the intensity.

"I wasn't there, but I did hear about it."

"That was the time when I knew there'd be the big fair in New York. A lot of money spent by huge corporations to build exhibits. All they could think of was to top the other guy and stand out as different. That was where we came in."

Bob nodded and grinned. "That's right. You knew we could use their money to develop a lot to technology to help Disneyland in the future." He chuckled appreciatively. "Once their two years were up at the Fair, you knew the attractions could run another five to ten years here. So, what happened?"

Walt moved around some of the papers and picked up a drawing of a round theater. "General Electric. You knew they were having image problems."

"I heard. Some big scandal. At the time, I wondered why you'd approach them. That kind of thing wasn't exactly our image."

A wide, sly grin took over Walt's face. "That's exactly why I wanted to work with them. They wanted their image back. The concept appealed to them: a theater in which the spectator's seats would revolve around the stationary stages. Each act would show the progress of the American house and their electrical appliances."

"Then what happened?"

"Oh, they sent one of their vice presidents to coordinate their Pavilion. His whole experience had been in heavy machinery. No imagination. In one of the meetings, I showed him these drawings, how the show's household improved from the 1890's to the future. You know what he said?"

Bob grinned. "No, but I'll bet it didn't set well."

There was a disgusted snort. "He actually said that my idea wasn't what they had in mind, that they weren't in the business of selling progress. He couldn't imagine what we wanted with all that nostalgia stuff."

"Ooh. I hadn't heard that part."

Walt's hand smacked down on the desktop. "I let him know right then and there that this studio was built on nostalgia and that we've been doing pretty good selling it to the public." He reached up to smooth his mustache. "Gosh, I was so mad I went to legal to see if we could get out of the contract."

"From the work going on in New York I'm guessing the answer was no."

"You're right there." Walt let out a hearty laugh. "Two weeks later, the president himself came here for a vacation. I told him I was having trouble with one of his vice presidents. Never saw that guy again!" Hands clasped behind his back, Walt returned to the window.

Bob wondered if his summons was over. "I have a question about the Carousel, Walt. I've heard different stories, but, horse's mouth, you know."

That earned a chuckle.

"Where, exactly, did you get the idea for the Carousel of Progress?"

"Have you ever seen the play *Our Town*?"

"Uh, no. Heard of it, though."

Walt turned to lean back against the windowsill. "Ever since 1958 I liked the idea of warm and humorous families welcoming people into their homes of the 1890's, 1920's, 1940's and today. Was going to put it in Edison Square off of Main Street, but, well, that didn't work out like we planned, did it?"

"Well, money was tight. How did Progress City fit into that?"

The look that came over Walt was introspective as he pulled out a different rendering. It showed a city complete with shopping centers, schools, stadiums, and a small amusement park. The transportation was indicated with a monorail system, People-Movers, cars and trucks. An airport runway was drawn toward the back. Trees and parks were shaded in soft greens. A nuclear power plant was put in to run this all-electric city. "I'm planting a seed, Bob. A seed of what's possible. Roy and I purchased some land in Florida." His eyes narrowed. "You know that's just between you and me right now, right?"

"Yeah, Boss. I know that."

"Well, this," as he held up the drawing, "is my vision for an ex-perimental community of tomorrow." There was a low chuckle. "The model that will be built on the second floor of the Carousel will be there for everyone to see. They just don't know I have plans to build that city!"

CHAPTER 4

Walt Disney World

The relaxing sights and sounds around the River had gone by mostly unseen. The Haunted Mansion, the Native Village, the moose and deer, happy kids scurrying over the Island. The only indication of recognition was when Wals had let out an imperceptible groan as they floated past Fort Sam Clemens. Engrossed in his story, Rose hadn't noticed his momentary lapse. *Just as well*, he was relieved to think, *one less thing to explain*.

With a slightly shaky hand, Rose handed back the paper that had been crumpled in his pocket for days. "And you're saying this is a copy of the note you found in a capsule that was dug out of the Jungle Cruise? And you were told it was written by Walt himself?"

Now in a quiet corner of Liberty Square, they were seated close together on a bench. The Hall of Presidents—that Wals hadn't seen yet—was across the way. From the intent look on her face he knew he wouldn't be going through any attractions any time soon.

"Well, all Lance said was that whatever was in the container was from Uncle Walt. I could tell the handwriting matched the signature on the drawing that was also in the container."

Unbelieving, her head slowly shook back and forth. "But Walt's been gone for over forty years. How can that be?"

Wals could only shrug. "I don't know. Lance indicated things had been set in place a long time ago and this," indicating the paper in his hand, "apparently is part of another treasure hunt. I do know Lance and Wolf and Adam have all gone on similar hunts."

37

"Are these more of your friends?"

"Lance and Wolf both work in Security. Adam I don't know very well, but he seems like a good sort of guy. I've worked with his wife Beth on Pirates occasionally."

Rose held up a hand to stall him. "Wait a sec. I keep hearing all these different names and I'm getting confused. You've mentioned Lance the most. Tell me about him. Maybe that will help."

Wals had to think. "What to say about Lance... Well, he's been in Security as long as I've known him. Loves his job. Looks like a movie star. All the women seem to love him."

That piqued her interest. "Ooh, really?"

"He's married! Sheesh."

"I'll try to contain my disappointment."

Wals could tell she was about to start laughing at him. At least the serious mood had been broken. Ignoring the mischievous glint in her eyes, he continued. "Wolf is another enigma. I've...traveled...with him some and, the longer you know him, you never seem to get to know him better."

She batted her eyelashes. "What does he look like?"

Wals missed the joke. "He's another one who has a trail of women following him all the time. He doesn't warm to it as much as Lance does. Or, I should say, did, until he married Kimberly. They have a son Peter and another baby on the way."

"Okay, I get it. Lance is married!"

"Don't you want to know what Kimberly looks like?"

Okay, he didn't miss her joke. "Now you're just being petty, Wals." An airy wave cut off his rebuttal. "Let's get back to this clue. It obviously points to the Carousel of Progress, which used to be at Disneyland."

"And the World's Fair back in 1964. It was actually created for the Fair and Walt arranged for it to be brought it back for Tomorrowland. Also, Lincoln, Small World, the dinosaurs."

Her mind on the Carousel of Progress, she ignored the trivia. "There's a washing machine in every scene, but a hand-cranked one is only in the first act. Right in view of the audience."

"Only part of the time. Then it rotates for a different scene to play." Having seen it so many times, Wals knew the show almost as well as Rose did. "But, your point is part of the problem. How to get to it unseen."

Rose quit talking to stare at Wals, measuring his character. When he began to squirm, she let up on the intensity. "Sorry. This is just so bizarre. You obviously can't just jump up on stage with that screwdriver and go at the washing machine."

He did have a solution, but wanted her to be the one to voice it. It was her attraction, after all. Her job. Her reputation.

Rose turned away and gazed in the direction of the Liberty Tree and the hanging lanterns. "I could get in so much trouble." Her words were quiet, mumbled, as if she didn't realize she spoke them out loud. "But what other option do we have?" She focused back on Wals. "You know what has to be done, don't you."

It wasn't a question and Wals understood that. "You need to get me behind the curtain and let me work on the washing machine without anyone seeing me."

"Is it worth it?"

It was a fair question; one he wasn't surprised to hear. It was one of the things Wals had been pondering the three days he'd been in Florida. When he finally answered, his words were deliberate as he thought it through. "Yes, I think so. For me. Walt never did anything by halves. If he put some sort of treasure hunt in place, it must have meant something to him. Whatever the reason, I really think I need to see this through. And I need your help." He paused. There was one more, equally important, question that needed to be asked. "Is it worth it to you?"

Her eyes narrowed. "Is that why you chose me? Just because you needed my help?"

"Chose you?" The question stumped Wals, causing him to think back. "No, I didn't have any thought of anyone in particular helping me at all." The serious expression on his face was suddenly broken by a skewed grin. "Besides, you approached me first. I was trying to stay invisible."

"Oh, that's right. I did, didn't I. Okay, that's fair." She looked away again. The Hall of Presidents had just let out and a stream of guests began to flow past them. She noticed Wals slip the clue back into his pocket. The screwdriver was still buried in there somewhere. With a grab at his hand, she pulled Wals to his feet and tucked her arm through his. "Let's get back to Tomorrowland."

Surprised by the sudden movement, he pointed over his shoulder. "But the Country Bears are right there. I wanted to…"

"We'll do that another time. It's getting late. The timing is perfect."

There was a conspiratorial aura about her. His wariness shot to the next level. "Perfect timing for what?"

"Dinner."

Wals glanced at her to see if she was serious. "Dinner? I'm not hungry."

"But most of the guests are." She gripped his arm tighter and leaned closer. "And the Carousel will be almost empty."

Wals ignored how her whisper tickled his ear as her meaning became evident. "Ah, you are the devious one, aren't you?"

"I might be devious, but you're the one who's going to have to work on the washing machine. And quickly, too."

Wals' mouth suddenly went dry.

It was going to happen.

One minute Wals was standing next to Rose in an empty theater section trying to look nonchalant. The next minute he had been pulled through a hidden door and found himself in the middle of the curved sets, behind the scenes. It happened so fast he wasn't sure he knew exactly where they had gone through.

He could hear Father talking on the other side of the set. From the whirl of sounds, it must have been the third act. Suddenly there was a grinding noise. He jumped when the curtained area next to him rotated so it would face the audience. The lights were still fading on the scene just completed.

Rose silently tugged on his arm and pointed across the dimly lit, round room. He followed her and knew he was now behind the first act—the one he needed to get into. Rose leaned in to whisper in his ear again. "The audience isn't in this one yet, but they will enter as soon as that one finishes. I hope Anne did what I asked her to do."

Wals felt a trickle of panic run down his spine. "You hope?"

"Shh. There are a few other cast members around somewhere. They might hear you. Yeah, I hope Anne is with me on this. She has an odd sense of humor sometimes."

"Should we wait?" The movement of her short hair brushed his face as she shook her head. He could smell strawberries.

Not knowing why he moved in to lean closer, she continued.

"Too risky to try again. Then there's Rob."

"Colossus? What would he do?"

"Your voice is getting higher. Calm down. Well, he wouldn't do anything to me..."

"That doesn't help."

The next sound they heard was the mechanical vibration of the theater seats moving so the audience could face the next act.

"Do you have the screwdriver handy?"

Wals held up the small gold tool. "I'm ready."

Rose was doing a count in her head. "All right. It should be empty now. Go, Wals. Work fast." She pulled aside a dark curtain that shielded any light in the back from disrupting the show.

Scrambling up on stage, Wals was first struck by how creepy it was to see the audio-animatronic people frozen in position. A few feet away, Mother stood silently, poised with an iron in hand, a pleasant smile on her face. Ignoring the little girl who held the crank of the round washing machine, Wals felt all over the wooden barrel. Not even sure what he was supposed to find, Wals moved to the metal bucket under the machine when he heard an ominous click. The set he was in the middle of was just about to spin into place for the show. Before he could react, the force threw him to the ground as Father started talking about the first robin of spring.

Crawling on his knees, Wals searched the back panel to find where it was Rose had let him through. There was a screen door behind Mother, but it was bolted shut. Just when he found a loose piece of the backdrop, the lights came on all around him and Mother began to talk about how laundry only took five hours now. The little girl next to him began to pull on the crank and the metal wheel on the washing machine started to whirl.

Peeking around the edge of the wooden box the little girl stood on, Wals could see about twenty people out in the audience. Not knowing what else to do, he immediately froze and tried to become part of the scene. His head stiffly turned as he looked from the mother to the little girl and back again, afraid to even breathe. Finally, after an interminable length of time, the lights faded and the set swung back around.

Wals collapsed onto his back, his heart pounding in his chest. He could hear Rose softly hissing for him, but he was too shaken to answer.

His wits finally gathered, he let her know he was fine.

"Get it done faster."

"Yes, dear."

His breathing finally normal, Wals went back to the washing machine, figuring he now had about ten minutes to examine it. Since the screwdriver had a small head, the screws would have to be small. The top of the machine had no openings other than where the vertical metal rod went up and down for the show. The only screws he found were holding on the faceplate that proclaimed the machine was a Pullman. Above the brass plate, etched deep into the wood, were the initials **W E D**. Running his fingers over them, not realizing their significance, Wals gave them an uninterested, "Hmm," and concentrated on the brass. "This must be it." Knowing he would be right in front, closest to the audience, he gritted his teeth and started on the small brass screws.

"Oh, shoot!" Wals hit the floor behind the little girl again as the set swung around to the front one more time. "I thought I had ten minutes!" He vaguely wondered if the audience would notice the nameplate hung by only one screw as it slowly swung side to side. This time he kept his face to the floor and didn't move until the set swung back out of sight.

Not even waiting for any word from Rose, he rushed to the washing machine and stuck his hand into the hole he had created. His fingers first found the metal rod and he moved on. When he felt the smooth, cool plastic, he grasped it and tugged. It was too long to come out of the small opening, so he had to tilt it sideways and gently pull. Once it was on the carpeted floor, he returned the faceplate to its proper place and secured the screws. Capsule in hand, he crawled to the back and whispered for Rose. "Get me out of here!"

It was only a second before the edge of the backdrop raised and he scooted through, holding the capsule aloft like a trophy. "Got it!"

Ignoring his triumph, Rose was seething. "Oh, that Anne! I'll pay her back later. She ran a second group through when it was supposed to be an empty theater."

Adrenaline still pumping through him, Wals didn't care. He would have run in a circle if there had been enough room in the crowded space. "What now? I assume we have to get out of here."

The anger ebbed. Wals hadn't cause it. "We need to get that thing out of sight. What did you bring to put it in?" She shouldn't have been surprised when his face went blank.

"Bring? Uh, I didn't think that far ahead."

The eye roll he received wasn't the first of the day. "Men." Hands on her hips, she looked around the dim work area. There were maintenance items for working on the sets when minor problems happened. Custodial also had a few things stored. Finding a black plastic liner, she handed it to Wals. "Here. This should work if you don't drag it around like a trash bag."

"I'll do my best."

Exhausted, Wals suggested dinner at the Contemporary Resort. He was staying there and didn't stop to consider where her car might be parked or how far she might have to go afterward to get to it.

Rose, on the other hand, had considered that small problem. Once they left the Park and she got to the Hotel, her car would be approximately two miles away on the other side of the Magic Kingdom. Yet, after a brief pause, she accepted his invitation. The desire to see what was inside the capsule had her intrigued. Another reason was the thought of getting to know Wals better and the possibility of visiting him in California and continuing this odd quest.

Under the Main Street Train station, past the floral Mickey, they exited the turnstiles and headed for the Monorail Station. One of the ferryboats from the Wilderness Lodge was coming in to the landing dock, awash with white twinkle lights.

"I suppose you're going to tell me your ferryboats are prettier than that."

Wals wondered if she was reviving their earlier game. "No. No ferryboats. Across from our entry is another Park, Disney's California Adventure. We don't have a lagoon." He felt her hand slip into his as they walked. Not knowing how she felt about him, he had hesitated to initiate any physical contact and was pleased by her gesture. It felt different from the times she had put her arm through his during the day, somehow more personal. "There is something else you can help me with."

"My, you seem to have a lot of problems to solve."

He enjoyed the sound of her low chuckle. "No, nothing major

like breaking into an attraction. I've been trying to find the five-legged goat."

That was unexpected. "The one in Mary Blair's mosaic? Why?"

Wals had to shrug. "I don't know. It just interests me. I know she added it to the mural to show that not everything has to be perfect. But, there are a lot of murals with a lot of goats in the Grand Canyon Concourse of the Hotel."

"I'll show you."

In companionable silence, they trudged up the ramp to the Monorail Station and waited for the next train. When Monorail Purple whispered into the station, its doors automatically opened to allow guests to exit and enter.

In the next car, hidden by the influx of guests, an irritated Rob quietly took a seat.

After having a drink at the curved, under-lit bar, Wals and Rose were taken to their linen-covered window table overlooking the Magic Kingdom. The warm yellows and creams of the California Grill on the fifteenth floor were muted and elegant. The modern light fixtures overhead were ready to dim when the Park began the nightly fireworks show.

While Rose enjoyed her pork tenderloin with polenta and wild mushrooms, Wals dug into his scallops and duck confit. "Wow, these are good. Are you sure you don't want one?" His extended fork was lowered as he looked out of the window. "I will give you this, Rose, we don't have a view for dinner like this back home."

Cinderella Castle, Space Mountain, and Big Thunder were all beautifully lit now that darkness had fallen—and clearly seen from their vantage point.

The music for the fireworks show was piped into the restaurant as the colorful bursts lit up the sky over the Castle and Space Mountain. The 'oohs' and 'aahs' inside the Grill probably matched the ones being heard down on Main Street and in Fantasyland.

Taking another bite of their shared S'mores Crème brûlée dessert, Wals smiled over at his companion. "You know, I think this is the most enjoyable fireworks show I've ever seen." Both reaching for the last bite, their forks clanged in mid-air. "You go ahead, Rose."

"No, it's all right. You take it."

Reaching into his pants pocket, Wals fingered through the various items searching for a coin. "Well, we're going to have to settle this fairly with a coin toss. More civilized than Rock, Paper, Scissors." A slight scraping noise from the table reached his ears. Looking up, he let out a surprised, "Hey!"

Rose had snagged the last bite of the creamy concoction while his attention was diverted. Eyes closed, she let out an appreciative murmur before returning to their discussion of the fireworks. "You did seem to enjoy the display."

The pilfered dessert forgotten, he reached across the table to squeeze her fingers. "I think it has something to do with the company."

Suddenly shy, a soft blush began at her neckline. Touched by his simple comment, her eyes lowered to the tabletop. "Thank you. I think so, too."

After paying the bill, Wals led her to the elevator for a trip to the main concourse. "Why don't we find a quiet place down here to open the capsule? I think we've waited long enough."

Noticing and appreciating that he didn't suggest going up to his room, she relaxed the sudden knot of anxiety in her shoulders. When irritation flitting across his face, her sigh of relief was covered by, "What's wrong, Wals?"

Hands on hips, he was looking up one side and down the other of the huge lobby and walkways. Up a couple of floors, another Monorail had pulled into the station and disgorged a mass of guests. People were entering and exiting the many doors of the Hotel. Excited children were chasing each other in a make-shift game of Tag. "There's people everywhere!"

"Yeah, what was Walt thinking making his Parks so popular?"

He had to laugh. "Okay, I get it. We wouldn't exactly have jobs if no one came, would we?"

Rose led him to a quiet, shrub-surrounded nook away from the gift shop and the elevators. "This should work. Oh, you want me to open it?" Surprised, she took the gray plastic from his outstretched hands and stared at it. "But you've been waiting for moment this for weeks."

He settled back in the comfortable chair. "You earned it with your help. Go ahead." He watched as the endcap easily slid off in her hands. "How'd you do that so fast? I almost needed vise grips on the first one."

"I may be small, but I'm strong."

"I'll keep that in mind." Leaning forward, his heartrate sped up when something round and shiny fell into her open palm. "What in the world is that?"

It was brightly polished, gold in color, with small white crystals on the cover that spelled out **W E D**. When Rose pushed a protruding button, the top popped open. "Well, I didn't expect that. It's a compass."

"Why?"

She turned it over to the back, then to the front again. "No clue."

"Speaking of clues, is there anything else inside?"

"Oh, that might be good to check. I'm new at this treasure hunt thing, you know." Rose had to reach in with her fingertips to retrieve the one piece of paper curled around the inside of the canister. After silently reading it, feeling waves of curiosity from Wals rush over her, she handed it to him. "Well, I understand the words."

He immediately recognized the paper as being the same type that had been ripped out of some small notebook. His curiosity turned into confusion. "Well, this is different."

The clue read:

33° 48' 45.5652" N

117° 55' 21.2448" W

Don't get wet.

Rose handed him the compass. "There you go. Figure it out."

"Do I look like a Boy Scout?" At her cocked grin, he had to add, "Well, I'm not. I've never used a compass." The compass and the clue dropped into his lap as he thought. "This is going to take some research. I have a computer at home, but not here, of course."

Her excited look fell. "Oh. I thought we'd be able to work on it together."

Gathering the small pile of things, he moved over to the sofa where she sat. "I thought so, too. But, I don't know how to figure this out. Why don't you copy the numbers and work from here and I'll work from California? You know I'll be calling you all the time." When she didn't shoot him down, a silly grin settled on his lips.

"Then, when you do come out to visit, we'll see where Walt is sending us. Together."

"I'd like that. But, I can't get any vacation time for another two or three months."

"Oh." Wals had hoped she would somehow be able to jump on the plane with him tomorrow afternoon. "Well, I'll just have to contain my enthusiasm and wait for you." His arm around her shoulder, she leaned into the warmth of his body. "It won't be easy."

"Won't be easy to wait for the clue or...for me?"

"Yes."

"Charmer. Okay, it's a date then. I'll see you in the spring. But," as she half-heartedly pulled away and stood, "I have to get home. Some of us minions have to work tomorrow."

"Work? I thought we could go over to the Animal Kingdom together for a couple of hours."

"Sorry, Wals. I can't." As he stood with her, she stood on her tippy toes to give him a quick kiss. "Thanks for a most interesting day."

"Let me walk you to your..." Wals stopped short. "Oh. Your car isn't just outside the Hotel, is it?" At her slow shake, he scratched his head. "Where exactly is it?"

She gave a vague wave toward the north. "Just over there. A bit. I'm fine. I'll just hop on the Monorail." She could see he didn't like the arrangement. "Really, Wals, I'm good. It isn't that far with the Utilidor under the Park. I'll catch a ride in one of the golf carts. Don't worry. I'm fine. Really."

Giving her one last hug, Wals reluctantly headed for the elevators. It didn't feel right for him to leave her like that, but she insisted again and again.

Once Wals was inside the elevator, Rose ducked into the gift shop. As she looked over the displays, she could feel someone standing right behind her. A small, pleased smile spread over her face. "I thought we settled this, Wals."

The voice that answered wasn't Wals. "So, he just left you to find your way back to your car alone? What a gentleman."

"Rob." She turned with a sigh. "How long have you been here?" Wondering if he had seen the capsule, she became wary. It was something she didn't want to share with anyone but Wals.

Even though Wals hadn't said anything, she assumed there was some secrecy attached to the treasure hunt.

"The whole time. I did relax a little when I saw he didn't drag you up to his room."

"See? He is a gentleman. What are you doing here?"

"I followed you." At her irritated look, he held up his hands. "Hey, you just met the guy. How was I to know he was harmless? You are alright, aren't you?"

She put a hand on his arm. He was looking out for her and it was appreciated, deep down, hidden under all the irritation. "Yes, I'm all right, Rob. Let me just buy this and you can walk me to my car. Any of your friends have a security cart handy? That might save us some time."

"Don't worry. I'll take care of you. Like I've always done."

CHAPTER 5

Fullerton, California

"**O**h, I forgot your bag in the car. I'll be right back."

"No, wait! You just rang the bell. Wals, don't leave me..." Rose found herself alone on the front entryway—the word porch sounded too small—of an unexpectedly large three-story mansion. Wals had told her she was invited to stay with Lance and Kimberly for the week she was visiting, but apparently he had left out a few details. Like the fact that the Brentwoods must be incredibly wealthy.

Her hiss was cut short when the oak front door clicked and swung open. *Please be Kimberly. Please be Kimberly.* "Uh, hi. You must be Lance."

"I must." Since Wals' 300ZX was parked near the garage, and thus out of sight, Lance didn't know exactly who this red-faced person was. Coming to the quick conclusion it must be Wals' mysterious friend, he tried to ease her obvious embarrassment. "I'm sorry. I was expecting an order of meat."

"I'm beginning to feel like one."

A delighted laugh came from Lance's lips. She could tell why he had the reputation he did. "You must be Wals' friend. Come on in. Kimberly will be delighted you're finally here." Without another word, he pulled her into the house and slammed the door behind her.

"But, Wals..."

"He's a big boy. He knows where you are. What he didn't tell me was your name."

49

"He didn't?" She held back from rolling her eyes. The natural shyness that had been her bane since grade school had melted with Lance's friendly, easy manner. "Men... I'm Rose..."

Suddenly amused, Lance cut her off. "Rose. Really?" He caught himself when her arms folded over her chest. "I mean, it's nice to meet you, Rose. Rose..."

She had heard his mumble and impatiently tapped her foot on the mosaic tile floor. "Yeah. Rose Hyacinth Tyler."

"I could go so many places with that," he muttered to himself. Sticking out his hand, he grabbed hers for a hearty shake. "Nice to meet you. I'm Lance Percy Brentwood."

Her expression immediately thawed. "You said Percy about the same way I say Hyacinth."

"Yeah, family tradition. And I've stuck both my sons with it. Peter is five and little Michael is two months. Both are too young to be traumatized by the stigma yet."

Once again on friendly terms, he turned to guide her through the massive house. "The kitchen is in the back." He waved a hand toward an arched entry on the left. "Formal receiving room, for some reason. Over there's my office. Even though he didn't find the time to tell us your name, I assume Wals did manage to mention the party we're throwing tomorrow."

"What? We've been planning this trip for three months!"

Lance seemed taken aback. "Really? He just asked us yesterday if we had room for you."

"Yesterday. Friday."

The disbelief in her voice was obvious. "Maybe he thought you'd come to your senses and stay in Florida." *Okay, that didn't help.* "What I meant was that Wals is one of our best friends. He sometimes gets distracted, but he's loyal, helpful, obedient..."

"You sound like you're describing a puppy." Still not sure if she should be upset at Wals or not, Rose had to work to keep her lips from twitching into a smile.

"He's a good boy. Yes, he is. What a good boy."

Trying not to picture her new boyfriend as a happy, tongue-lolling, brown haired puppy, Rose attempted to get the conversation back on its previous track. "Speaking of Wals..." She gestured back toward the front door but her eye caught something in the family room just off to their right. "Hey, is that a Mr. Toad ride car?"

Rose had been trying to be a polite guest and not to gape at the furnishings. The house was a mixture of elegant antiques, modern eclectic, and a splash of Disney thrown in for good measure. The odd collection of styles shouldn't have worked, but was oddly comforting and inviting.

Still walking, Lance hadn't realized she had stopped in her tracks as he continued to chat about their annual Security Guard and Princess Party. "You'd better wear knee pads if you plan on playing croquet... Where are you? Oh, go take a look."

Not needing to be told twice, Rose slid over the tufted black leather seat to grab the round steering wheel. "This is so cool!" The delighted look on her face turned suspicious. "Isn't your Toad still running? How'd you get this?"

"Ah, that's right. You work at Walt Disney World. So, how do you like humid Florida?"

Well, he deflected that question nicely. "Florida is lovely, especially in the spring like this."

As he led Rose from the room, he noticed she kept looking upward. "You can't beat Southern California for spring weather... What are you looking for, if I might ask?"

"A Dumbo elephant or a Rocket Jet hanging from the rafters."

"Haven't figured out how to secure them without damaging the textured tin ceiling. But, I'm working on it. And, here we are. Kimberly, honey, this is Wals' friend. Rose."

Rose became the color of her namesake when the beautiful blonde's green eyes widened and shot back to her husband.

"Rose Tyler," Lance helpfully added, biting the inside of his cheek to keep from smiling. *Doctor Who* was one of their favorite shows.

Kimberly ignored Lance as she rushed over to give Rose a welcome hug, something made slightly more difficult by the hand whisk she had forgotten to put down. "I am so happy to meet you! Hope you had a good flight. I hate the red-eye, but you do get a full day..." Realizing she was rambling to overcome the surprise of her guest's name, she stepped back. Not sure if she should let Rose know cookie batter was stuck to the back her blouse, she vaguely gestured up at the ceiling as she continued to talk. Batter flew off the whisk and landed in a clump on the granite countertop. "Now, we have a cozy guestroom here in the house, or you're welcome to use the apartment over the garage if you'd rather have more privacy."

Before Rose could answer, a smaller version of Lance burst into the kitchen. "Mom, are the cookies done yet?"

Proud Papa put a hand on the boy's head. "And this is our son, Peter. Pete, say hello to Rose."

"Wíyuškiŋyaŋ waŋčhíŋyaŋke."

.The smile on her face froze. Not sure if the poor child had a speech impediment, she didn't know how to respond.

Lance nudged Peter's back. "In English. Though, Uncle Wolf would be proud of you."

At the mention of Uncle Wolf, Peter's face broke out in a huge grin. "Pleased to meet you." Determining the longed-for cookies were nowhere near done, he lost interest in the adults and wandered out back.

"Lakota Sioux," Lance told her by way of explanation.

Her expression remained a polite blank. "Okay. Why?"

"Did Wals mention Wolf?" At her slow nod, Kimberly turned back to the cookie batter and started scooping small balls onto a baking sheet. "Well, Wolf is Lakota Sioux. He's been teaching Peter the language since he was born."

"Peter called him Uncle Wolf?" There was no way either of them had Native American blood running through their veins.

"Honorary title."

As they continued to chat and get acquainted, the steady ringing of the doorbell became an irritating drone. When the chimes finally stopped, they could hear muted pounding on the solid wood door.

"Wonder if that's the caterer." Lance gave the women a wink and slowly headed back to the front door where Wals had been locked out all this time.

Wanting something to do and feeling completely at home in the massive kitchen, Rose helped with a second tray of cookies and slid them into the oven.

"So, you've come to help Wals with the next leg of his Hidden Mickey treasure hunt."

"Oh, that's right. Lance gave Wals that canister. I forgot that you'd know about it." She wondered why Kimberly looked secretly pleased as if a fond memory suddenly struck her.

"Yes, we know all about it. It's exciting! Wals has had a hard time waiting so long for you to come and help." Kimberly put down her dishcloth and indicated the doorway. "Let's get you upstairs so you can freshen up and rest before lunch, if you like. You might want to change your blouse..." She pulled Rose in for an impromptu hug. "I'm so glad you're here! I think we're going to be great friends."

Rose was touched by the warmth of the Brentwoods. There were none of the airs she expected when she had seen the mansion. Open. Honest. Funny. Loving. Yes, this was going to be a lovely week.

"**Y**es? Who is it?" Lance stuck his face out the crack he had made with the door.

Wals almost shoved the door open, only stopping when he realized it would have probably broken Lance's nose. The frown he wore morphed into a wicked grin. It wasn't out of probability just yet. "Knock it off, Lance. Let me in. I've been standing out here pounding for hours."

"Oh, hi, Wals. I was expecting the caterers."

An eye roll was the only reply Lance received as Wals rolled two suitcases inside. "Where's Rose? She'd probably like a change of clothes."

"More than you realize." Lance folded his arms and leaned against the door frame as he stared at his friend. "Rose? Really, Wals? Rose?"

What could Wals do but shrug? "Hey, I didn't name her. Whatever you do, don't make a big deal out of it. I'm having enough trouble dealing with it."

"Too late."

Wals clearly heard Lance's mumble. "What do you mean? You didn't make her self-conscious again, did you?"

"Again, huh?" Lance started up the curving staircase. "She's up here."

Left at the bottom with both suitcases, Wals now regretted not shoving the door into that smug face. "Can't we use the elevator?"

Once the guys were ejected from the guest room, Kimberly helped Rose unpack. The room was in lovely shades of soft blue, the queen-sized bed covered with an old-fashioned quilt. The wooden headboard was engraved with a Castle, fireworks shooting out from the spires. Rose was shown a switch that started the fiber-optic show.

"Disneyland Hotel," was all the explanation Lance had given before being sent to the kitchen to check on baby Michael and the cookies.

"The guys will probably eat more than they save for the party tomorrow."

"So, Kimberly, tell me about the other Rose."

Kimberly's hand stilled as she transferred some clothes to the dresser. "What did Wals tell you?"

"Not much."

Level amber eyes challenged Kimberly. She smoothed the tops under her fingertips and turned to sit on the bed. Clearing her throat didn't earn her much time. "Well, Wals probably told you he had been quite taken with her." At the brief nod, she sighed with a shrug. "It was a relationship that just wouldn't have worked out and Wals was devastated."

"Why couldn't it have worked? Opposition from family?"

Yes, King Stephan was quite indignant, I was told. "Yes, you could say that. Rose had been promised to..." She almost said Prince. "Phillip. He...he had been gone for a long time and when he came back, all their feelings for each other returned."

"An arranged marriage? I didn't think that was done in this day and age."

Kimberly swallowed. The smile on her face was kind. "Well, like Wals doubtless told you, it happened a long time ago." *A long, long, long time ago in a beautiful white fairy castle.* "He had a difficult time after she went back to Phillip. We tried to do our best to keep his mind off things."

"Is that when he was put on Casey Jr.?"

A sheepish look came and went over Kimberly's face. "That was Lance's idea. But, we were so glad when he told us that he had met someone at Walt Disney World. Wals is a great guy. And you seem like a lovely woman who's spunky enough to keep him on his toes."

"Spunky. I haven't been called that in years."

"I'll leave you to finish with your clothes. We'll have lunch in about an hour." Kimberly paused at the door. "You and Wals will have fun with the treasure hunt. That's how Lance and I got to know each other. Oh, the party tomorrow starts around noonish. People come and go as their shifts allow and then they usually come back to make an evening of it. Be prepared. It's an all-day thing."

Rose just nodded that she had heard, her mind on the half-story she had been told. Hopefully Wals would trust her enough to tell her the whole story some day. "Just not today," she sighed as she zipped the suitcases closed and stowed them in the spacious walk-in closet.

Dressed for the day in white shorts and a pale pink polo shirt, Rose handed the grateful Kimberly a plate of eggs and bacon. "I heard Michael crying last night and thought you could use a hand today."

"Oh, this is so nice. Thank you! Smells heavenly." Kimberly sank into one of the kitchen chairs and dug in. "I could get used to this! Lance does a lot of the cooking, but usually has an early shift at the Park." When Rose sat across from her, coffee cup in hand, Kimberly added, "It's going to be nice having an adult to talk to again. I haven't taken the baby out yet."

"I thought Lance was on leave with you."

Whatever Kimberly was about to say was cut off by Lance swooping into the room with a delighted Peter on his shoulders. The ambulance noise Lance was making drowned out any conversation. "Woo woo. Woo woo. Hey, is that bacon?" He gave Kimberly a quick kiss on the lips. "You're wonderful, after that bad night you had."

"Actually it was Rose who fixed breakfast."

Lance circled over to their guest and gave her a quick kiss on her cheek. "I can already tell you're too good for Wals. Come on, Pete. We need to get the golf course set up. Woo woo. Woo woo." Bacon in hand, they burst out the back door and into the backyard.

Kimberly took a long sip of her coffee. "Like I said, it's nice to have some adult conversation again."

Somewhat stunned by the flurry of activity, Rose pointed at the open back door. "What did he mean by golf course?"

Another sip. "Like I said…"

"**S**o much for being invisible." Rose had been pulled from her relatively quiet corner of the yard and found herself on a small knoll. At the edge of the massive backyard, beyond the gazebo, about twenty men and women were lined up. A golf club had been shoved into her hand and a bright yellow golf ball was at her feet. She thought the club was a sand wedge.

"Okay, Tink, you're on our team."

Rose discovered the woman who looked a lot like Belle was talking to her. "My name is Rose."

She was waved off. "Sure. You know what to do, right?" Belle was wielding a crochet mallet.

"No!"

One of her new teammates chuckled. "Welcome to the club. Just go for it. See that flag?" Tim pointed to something about a thousand yards away.

"That orange spot in the neighbor's yard? At the bottom of the hill? On the other side of the fence?" The tinge of panic in her voice went unnoticed.

"Yeah." Tim bent down to set his orange golf ball on the grass. "That's the first hole. The pool is the water hazard."

"As it should be," she muttered. Even from that distance she could see a large, fresh hole with a flag stuck in it dug next to the pool. "Don't they mind?"

"Oh, they aren't home." His voice raised. "Everyone ready? This is a Par Eight, people. The next hole is around the corner a street over. And no do-overs, Dennis. Clubs Ho!"

Rose saw everyone raise their assorted golf clubs, mallets, yard rakes, and one, lone sledge hammer into the air. She did likewise with her wedge. "Oh, this is going to be bad..."

"Ready? Set? FORE!"

With a roar, the twenty cast members swung and then, as one, all raced down the hill.

Three hours later, a sweaty Rose dropped into a yard chair. Within minutes Wals came over to her shady spot, his hair dripping wet. "Where've you been, Rose? I lost track of you at the third hole. Couldn't get my ball over the river."

"You were playing? Really? I never saw you. If I remember

right, that was a Par Fifteen."

"I was already up to twenty strokes." He handed her his iced tea. "You looked like you were having fun."

"It's too bad you quit. Downtown… Fullerton, is it?.. was interesting." She had to laugh. "There's one thing all cast members have in common. We all know how to direct traffic."

"Sorry I missed that. When I dropped out, I came back to the pool."

Rose looked over at the solid mass of humanity and swan-shaped floats. "Is there any water left in there?"

"Uh, good question. You hungry?"

"Starved."

He held out his hand to help her to her feet, ignoring the whistles and helpful comments from a couple of security guards walking by.

"Is that a basketball hoop in their hands? And yard darts?"

Wals shrugged. "I think so. I know Lance hasn't installed a hoop yet. Peter's too young." He tugged her arm. "Come on. I don't think it'll to be safe here in a minute or two."

That earned a laugh. "I don't think it's safe anywhere around here! I keep looking for Peter but haven't seen him."

"Oh, the kids are having a blast. They know to keep away from the archery range."

When her mouth fell open, he grinned. "Just kidding. That was last year. Not a good idea. See those holes in the top of the gazebo? When one of the arrows just missed the PeopleMover car, Lance put a stop to it."

"Well, we wouldn't want a PeopleMover car to get hurt."

"This is my third party. It's chaos, but it's controlled chaos. No one has gotten more than a sprained shoulder from volleyball or a couple of cuts and bruises from croquet."

At the grill, Rose found herself being scrutinized by a pair of sharp, sapphire blue eyes. The shyness that had vanished the day before suddenly returned. Backing up a step, she ran into a block of Wals. "Um…"

"Rose, this is Wolf, fellow cast member. One of the security team. And barbeque master. Keeps the angry mob at bay. Both here and at Disneyland." Wals wondered why his humor wasn't being appreciated.

The sapphire eyes blinked and the intense gaze was gone. Wolf reached up to push a stray strand of blue/black, silver-tipped hair off of his forehead. He appeared oblivious to the throng of women who had carefully arranged themselves around the barbeque station. A warm smile transformed him from intimidating to incredibly handsome. "Nice to meet you. Wals taking good care of you?"

She had to swallow before she could answer. "Yes, he is. He mentioned you when I met him in Florida."

Wolf turned back to the steaks sizzling on the grill. "All good, I hope." He tested two of the steaks with his finger. "Here, take these two and some corn. Then, you might want to stand back."

Rose wondered why Wals literally jumped to accept the plates, shoved one into her hands, and then pushed her all the way back to the PeopleMover car. Then she heard Wolf.

"Steaks are ready!"

"Oh. My. Word. Is he all right? I can't even see the grill anymore."

Wals, busy with his garlic bread, looked up. "What? Oh, that. Yeah, well, it's Wolf. That's why Lance keeps him in charge of the grill. Lives could be lost in that shark frenzy."

"Wow, this ribeye is good. Where'd you get the bread? I didn't get any."

Wals looked at the half-eaten slice and offered it to her. "I have no idea. Maybe Wolf has a hidden stash."

She took one bite and stood. "I'll be right back. And don't touch my steak! I'm going to check what's in the house. You want anything else?"

"Whatever you bring back is fine. Just keep a safe distance from the grill."

In the kitchen, she found Kimberly feeding Michael a bottle. "Rose! I haven't seen you all day. Having fun?"

"Ooh, eclairs! Yes, I'm having a blast. I didn't know what to expect but this is...something."

Kimberly had to laugh. "Yeah, I don't know how to describe it, either. Changes every year. You eat yet? I heard Wolf announce the steaks were ready. Is he still alive?"

"Last I saw. I think he was trying to get everyone into a straight line."

"Well, if anyone can do it, Wolf can."

Rose pointed down a hallway. "There's no need to go upstairs for a bathroom, right?"

Michael had been shifted to Kimberly's shoulder for a burp by the time she returned. With her thumb, Rose indicated the day room over her shoulder. "Did you see that pile of presents in there? Looks like a baby shower on steroids."

"What?" Kimberly shoved the contented baby into Rose's arms and rushed from the room. In a minute, she was back clutching a knitted baby sweater, tears in her eyes. "Oh, those guys. I had no idea." After wiping the tears with the burp pad, she sniffed. "I've been on leave for months and months. There usually isn't a shower for a second baby." She examined the careful stiches of the small, blue sweater. "Did you see that six-pack of beer with the big blue bow? The card said to give it to Michael in twenty-one years! I'll have to thank everyone before they go. Gosh, what a great group."

Lance, face dripping, came into the kitchen and stopped when he saw Rose with the baby. "Well, that was fast."

Kimberly retrieved Michael and shooed him away. "Play nice, sweetheart."

Lance stuck his head inside the opened fridge. "I'm starved. What do we have to eat in here? Ooh, potato salad. Wasn't that supposed to go outside?"

"I'll take some of that." Rose stood and handed him two plates. At his amused look, she rolled her eyes. "One of them is for Wals."

"Wals can take care of himself. Want some cheesecake? There's caramel, raspberry, and chocolate swirl."

"Gosh, I'll have to play another round of golf to work off all this food."

That impressed Lance. "You played golf already? On your first day? Nice. You'll do."

"Thanks." Sarcasm dripped. "I'm glad you think so."

Lance sat next to his wife once Rose had gone back outside loaded with potato salad and cheesecake. "I like her."

"Maybe you shouldn't push so many buttons until she and Wals get to know each other better."

Kimberly's advice was airily waved away. "This one can handle it." Once he finished his second slice of raspberry cheesecake, he stood from his chair to go back out into the fray. "And, they already know each other well enough."

"**G**osh, what day is this? Wednesday or Thursday?"

"Still Monday, Sweetheart."

A blurry-eyed Lance glanced from his wife to their guest. "Can't possibly be Monday. And what are you doing up so early, Rose? I thought you'd want to sleep in after that... that... whatever that was yesterday."

"It's noon, Lance." Rose bent over the plate of leftovers in front of her. "I got up early to help clean up the backyard." Her head slowly shook back and forth. "I couldn't believe it was spotless! Not one paper plate. Not one napkin. Not even a hole in the grass from the golf game. Quite impressive."

"It's like that every year. We do learn how to keep things clean at Disney." Kimberly gave a contented sigh. "I love it."

"That, or they're afraid we won't have another party next year." The whole container of leftover deviled eggs was in front of Lance. "How did I miss these yesterday?"

"The parties I've been to back home have been a little more... unrestrained, I guess. Too much drinking for my taste." Reaching for one of the eggs, Lance playfully slapped her hand away.

"Mine. Sunday is pretty busy at the Park. With everyone going back and forth to work all day, they know not to push that boundary."

Kimberly managed to snag one of the eggs before Lance could eat them all. "What time is Wals coming? I'm sure you're excited to get to work on your clue."

"I thought he'd be here already." Rose glanced at her wristwatch. "Maybe he slept in."

"Or stuck in traffic."

Lance snorted in agreement. "Daily occurrence."

"How far away does he live?"

"About twenty miles. Should be less than an hour."

"An hour? For only twenty miles?" Rose wasn't sure she liked the California freeway system.

Lance could only shrug. They were used to it. "We're just over four miles away from Disneyland. Some days that could take half an hour."

When the doorbell chimed, Rose jumped to her feet, her heart suddenly pounding. At the amused expressions surrounding her, a blush stole up her neck. "I wonder if that's Wals."

"Why don't you grab your purse and meet him outside." Kimberly stole a glance at her husband. "Might be quicker for you two to get going." *And safer.*

Disappointed that his fun was taken away, Lance waved. "You two kids have fun."

"Kids, Lance?" Kimberly chose a caramel-covered crepe from the tray. "They're the same age as we are."

"Yeah, I know. Wals has some catching up to do."

Standing from the table, Kimberly licked some caramel off her fingers. "He's working on it. I need to go up and check on Peter. It's too quiet. You keep an eye on Michael."

Lance glanced over at the bassinet. "Why? Is he trying to escape again?"

"You never know."

CHAPTER 6

Disneyland

"We're going to play tourist today." Driving his car down Harbor Boulevard, Wals had to keep his eyes on the road. Traffic was thick. "This is odd for a Monday. The Park shouldn't be this busy. Ah, I think I see the problem." The left lane was blocked by a stalled Volkswagen.

Head swiveling in every direction to take in the sights, Rose wasn't sure what he meant. "Tourist?"

"Instead of parking in the cast member lot, I thought we'd use the parking structure on Disneyland Drive and go in through the main gate." He took a moment to glance over. "I'd like you to get the full experience."

"Whatever you say. I'm in your hands."

"Ah, here we go." Turning right off Harbor, Wals navigated the confusing lights on Ball Road, and swept over to the ramp that led to the parking structure. "This used to be a KOA campground back in the day. Over there were strawberry fields, and a Disney-themed miniature golf course that sounded like a lot of fun."

Rose had to laugh. "We used to be a swamp."

"Don't the Utilidors keep everything above swamp-level?"

"That, too. I thought you had transportation tunnels."

Slowly winding through the structure, Wals didn't immediately answer. Excited children, eager to start their day, didn't pay attention to oncoming traffic. "Only a couple, but they're mainly used to get stuff into the shops."

Once Wals found a parking space on the third level, they used the escalator to get down to the trams. The blue and white transports zipped under Disneyland Drive and over to a dedicated tree-lined path leading to the Park. Wals pointed to an overpass ahead of them. "That's Downtown Disney. Used to be part of the parking lot and the bus entry to the Disneyland Hotel." The tram swooped around a tight corner and pulled to a stop. "This is part of Downtown Disney. That's the Grand Californian Hotel over there. Nice place. I'll take you over at some point to show you. Maybe we can have dinner at the Napa Rose."

Joining the other guests who were walking to the left, they could smell some enticing aromas from small kiosks lining the wide path. Wals' stomach began to growl. With a longing glance at the bakery, he picked up the dropped thread of conversation. "We could have parked somewhere else and gone in on the Monorail, but I wanted you to see the Esplanade and the entry to Disney's California Adventure."

"Ah, you do have Security bag check. I wondered where it was."

There was no need to get in line for an entry ticket since Wals used his cast member identification to sign in himself and Rose. The turnstile chirped as they passed through. "And, here's our floral Mickey."

Spring was definitely in bloom at the Park. Mickey's smiling face was filled with white anemones and surrounded by a profusion of pink and white tulips. A small sparrow hopped around the surrounding grassy area, uncaring of the hundreds of people walking by or stopping to take pictures.

A familiar whistle sounded as the *E P Ripley* pulled into the station, its green engine bright in the sun and red wheels squealing to a stop. A whoosh of steam escaped as guests eagerly exited the Main Street Station.

"It's so small."

"What!?" Wals had expected a delighted expression of pleasure. She looked disappointed.

Rose hadn't intended for that to slip out. She knew Wals was proud of his Park and wanted to show it off to her—just as she had done in Florida. A conciliatory smile was offered. "I mean, the station is a bit smaller than the one in Florida."

He didn't quite believe her, but wasn't going to let it ruin their fun. Disneyland had a certain charm that he thought the newer, larger Walt Disney World didn't. He was positive he would win her over by the end of the day.

She slipped her arm through his and leaned closer. "Do you have the compass?"

As they went under the train tracks, the vista opened onto Main Street. The Omnibus was parked in front of the station steps, loading. A streetcar waited on the other side of the street. The black Belgium horse stamped his foot, eager to get moving. In front of the white and gold Opera House, a long line of guests patiently waited to visit with Mickey Mouse.

Her question was forgotten as she looked over the Town Square and adjacent shops. A feeling of familiarity, *home,* swept through her. "Oh, this is so cute! It's been so long since I've been here, I couldn't remember exactly what it looked like. There's your Emporium and City Hall." Using the two-finger point, she indicated the Fire Station. "Isn't that where Walt's apartment is? Can we go there?"

Wals made a face. "Well, we used to be able to do tours, but someone messed it up during a race a couple of years back. Not sure exactly what happened, but its closed now. I once asked Lance about it, but he seemed, I don't know, evasive for some reason."

"Oh, that's too bad." Her disappointment was easily dismissed by the thoughts of what was in store for them. Her face glowed. "Are we going to head to Frontierland now?"

"My old stomping grounds. Oh, the compass. I forgot to tell you." Surrounded by people coming and going in all directions, he hoped he wouldn't be overheard. "I showed it to Lance and Kimberly the other night, along with the clue, since they asked about it. Remember how heavy it felt when it came out of the canister?"

She gave a brief nod, wondering why he seemed so excited about an old compass. "I thought it was some kind of gold-colored metal. But it isn't. It's solid gold! And those little crystals that spell out his initials? They're diamonds."

Now she understood. "Wow, what a nice gift to leave. So, I take it you didn't bring it with you."

"Ha, no! You know what's funny? When I packed to come home from Florida, I just tossed it into my suitcase like any cheap souvenir. Now it's in my safety-deposit box."

Wanting to see it again, to touch it, Rose felt a little letdown. Talking regularly for three months, solving the clue they had found together, she felt as though their relationship had progressed. It didn't feel like *Wals'* treasure hunt. It felt like *their* treasure hunt. *Was everything they found going to be locked away by Wals?* Glancing up at his open, cheerful face, a small frown came and disappeared over hers. *Maybe he's just being careful*, she chided herself. *This is new for both of us.*

Unaware of the internal conflict that he had inadvertently caused, Wals continued to lead her through the throng of guests. "You hungry? We could eat at the Carnation Café back there. Oh, I know! How about dinner at the Blue Bayou? I think you'll love that."

Her mind snapped back to the present. "Hungry? No, for breakfast we stuffed ourselves on leftovers from the party. Gosh, Lance can put away a lot of food!" At first she couldn't understand his crestfallen look. "Hey, we thought you'd be there early. I'm sorry. Can we get something fast to hold you over to dinner? What's the Blue Bayou?"

Always good-natured, Wals pointed to a corndog cart. "I'll just get a dog, then. Oh, I'll need to secure a reservation at the restaurant for a water table. You want a soda?"

"Yes, that would be great." As Wals waited in the short line, Rose took the opportunity to look around Central Plaza, the hub of the Park. Like the spokes of a wheels, the entries to each land radiated out from this central point. "This is all so cool," as she gazed at the bronze Walt and Mickey holding court in the middle. It felt familiar, but so different. If she had been standing in the same place in her Park, there would have been a wide waterway off to the right. Its grassy banks held huge topiaries of swans and a sea serpent as they led the eye to the arched entrance to Tomorrowland. The elegant, blue-tipped spires of Cinderella Castle rising 183 feet into the air commanded the view. A smile tugged at her lips. "We have a restaurant in ours." Not wanting Wals to possibly hear her, she whispered to herself as she gazed at the smaller Sleeping Beauty Castle. Red pennants lazily blew in the slight breeze as a white swan swam out of sight beneath the bridge.

A lovely grotto on the side of the Castle caught her eye as she looked toward the towering Matterhorn Mountain. After a red fire engine slowly putted by, Rose felt herself smiling at all the beautiful trees, flowers, and shrubs that filled in every available space. "Okay, Wals, I'll admit it. You're right. This is lovely."

"I'm right about what? Here's your soda." He wondered why an appealing flush spread slowly across her cheeks.

"Just talking to myself. The hanging pots of flowers are beautiful."

One point for the home team. "We're going to take a detour into New Orleans Square."

The detour took them through the Adventureland entry. "I like your waiting area for the Tiki Room. Is there a show before you go in?"

Two shots sounded from the Jungle Cruise as they passed the line of strollers out front. "We can get a FastPass for Indy after we see what we can find in Frontierland." Finished with his impromptu lunch, Wals dropped the stick and papers in an always-handy trashcan. "Tarzan's Treehouse, Indy, Pirates," he pointed out as they went along, ending at the pedestrian bridge that crossed over the queue to Pirates. "Okay, I will admit that your Pirates has a great entry and queue."

One point for the home team, Rose secretly smiled to herself.

Turning left, they entered the crush of people who were either exiting Pirates, wandering through the quaint streets of New Orleans Square, or in line for one of the restaurants. Wals stopped in front of an ornate double entry. The cast members working the Blue Bayou wore turn-of-the-century costumes. "Dawn, am I glad to see you. Didn't think the Park would be so busy today."

The cute brunette grinned from ear to ear. She had been trying to catch Wals' eye for some time now. From his friendly greeting, she thought she had finally succeeded. "Hey, Wals. Glad to see you, too. How can I make *your* day more magical?"

He had no idea why Dawn was batting her eyes at him. "Um, any chance I can get a water table for dinner around seven tonight?"

Dawn didn't even check the reservation chart. "For you? Anything."

A red flag was trying to wave itself in front of his face. "Great." He wasn't even sure why he took a step backward. When she entered his name and then handed him a reservation card, he had to give it back. "Oh, I'm sorry. You forgot to make the reservation for two." Wals reached over and set his hand on Rose's shoulder.

"Oh." The card was snatched back and the 'one' was angrily rubbed out.

Wals wasn't used to seeing such a messy reservation card. The 'two' could barely be seen in the middle of all the black smudging. When she looked up, Dawn's eyes were no longer flirty. The expression 'daggers' came to his mind. "Thanks?"

"Hmpph. Hope you have a magical dinner."

Rose pressed her lips together to keep from smiling. She knew 'magical' could be exchanged with 'hope you choke'.

Wals led her through the winding walkway and past the train station. "That was weird."

Not sure if or what she should say, Rose kept quiet. Wals would figure it out. Eventually. She just hoped there would be a water table waiting for them when they returned at seven.

They crossed through the tree-filled Magnolia Park and went past the entry to the Haunted Mansion. Splash Mountain had a screaming group in the log that was plunging down the steep hill. Rose pointed back over her right shoulder. "What was that ship, Wals?"

"That's the *Columbia*. She usually comes out on busy days." He chuckled. "As you can see, there isn't any covering for anyone standing on deck. During the summer, it can get pretty hot. It was called the Floating Skillet at one time. There's a nice museum on the lower deck. Set up just like it would've been when it sailed around the world. The *Mark Twain* is running today." When the familiar steam whistle sounded, he added, "And she's just over on the other side of the Island right now, heading for the dock."

As they headed into Critter Country, Rose had a question. "I never asked you this before. How long did it take you to figure out the clue?"

"The longitude and latitude thing?" At her nod, he made a face. "Longer than it probably should have. I tried to figure it out with a gridded map of the world." He glanced at Rose, expecting her to give him a look indicating he was stupid. "Ha, you did the same thing! I can see it all over your face."

"Yeah, I thought that was what we were supposed to do. Then I found it was sort of like geocaching. Once I found that map of the whole world—probably the same one you used—it was easy to figure out it pointed to Southern California with the 33° latitude and the 117° longitude." She warmed up to the topic, showing how much effort she had put into it. "I hadn't realized the 48' and the 45.5652" in the clue weren't feet or inches. They indicated minutes and seconds. Since each degree, like the 33°, was sixty-nine miles wide, it would have been really difficult to pinpoint where we needed to go. Those additional numbers made it the exact location."

Wals nodded. It was just as he had found. "We didn't even need the compass at all. I guess Walt added it to show it meant navigating of some kind. So, where do you think we're going?"

"Well, the website I used just pointed to the River in Frontierland. It's somewhere before the big bend in the River."

"Oh, I must have used a different map. Mine showed exactly where we needed to go. My favorite spot." His hand swept out to indicate a ramp and a dock.

"The Canoes! I didn't guess that." She eagerly ran down the ramp only to be stopped by a rope barrier. "They aren't running today. Then we'll certainly be able to follow Walt's instructions on not getting wet."

Having been off work for a few days, Wals hadn't realized the ride was closed. "Rats, I wanted to take you on a tour of our River."

Not caring at that moment, her eyes were wide and excited. "Okay, show me the next capsule."

His mouth fell open and then snapped shut. "Uh, I don't know where it is."

Her arms folded over her chest. "But this is your ride. You worked here for years."

"And I never once saw any capsule. I was just as surprised as you are when I discovered the location." Hands on his hips, he had to look at his dock and the two canoes tied up in a different light. *Where could something be hidden for forty years*?

"Well, I was hoping you could tell me. And, yes, that was out loud."

Ignoring her amusement, his fingers tapped on his lips. "Well, Walt said not to get wet, so I am *hoping* we don't have to look under the dock."

"Have the canoes always been here? Sometimes rides move."

"Boy, wouldn't that be difficult if it had moved. No, they've always been here, thank goodness. The Land they're in has changed three times, though. Bonus points if you can name them."

"Hey, this is your Park. No bonus for me."

"Fine. Be that way." He let out a mock heavy sigh. "Indian Village, Bear Country, and now Critter Country."

"Feel better?"

"Yes, thanks." His laugh died on his lips as he happened to glance over his shoulder. It became apparent that they were attracting some unwanted attention. The nearby Hungry Bear Restaurant was busy with guests at lunch and some people stopped at the ropes hoping the Canoes were running. This was a problem, however, that he had anticipated. "Rose, that jacket you have tied around your waist? Put it on and hold this clipboard."

"It's kind of warm. Why? Where'd you get that?"

"The clipboard came from the console over there. We record the trips and any problems we might've had. The jacket is to cover your cute pink top." He cast a glance up at the restaurant. "And, I'm trying to make you look more like a manager."

"Oh, I get it. A Suit."

"Yeah. Hopefully no questions or anyone reporting that two guests are poking around a closed ride." Once she looked as professional as she could be wearing shorts, he turned back to examining the dock. He pointed at a couple of boxes built into the dock. "Can't be in there. The one near the fence uses to be a phone and I know the others are empty." His grin turned sheepish. "We used to hide beer in there for some after-hours canoe races."

Rose was studying the tall light poles, pretending to make notes on the clipboard. "I don't see anything up on the light fixtures. What's under those tarps?"

"Just paddles."

While he walked the length of the dock, testing each board with his foot, Rose kept staring at the paddle bins. "They're kind of deep."

"They have to be. The adult paddles are pretty long."

Walking closer, she stood next to the tallest one to measure it with her eyes. Peeking under the tarp, she called over to him. "These paddles aren't that big."

Humoring her, he came to her side. "It's just because you're what? Four-foot six? Seven?"

She wasn't amused. "I'm five-foot-four, I'll have you know. I'm petite."

"Yes, you are," as Wals gave her a fond hug. Remembering they were still being watched from the second floor of the Hungry Bear, he stepped back. The tarp was pulled completely off the bin. "See? Just paddles."

"Then why are those four in the back sitting taller than the ones in the front?"

"Because... Hmm, good question." He ran a hand through his hair. "I've worked here for years and never noticed that. And, I've seen those initials carved into the wood and never thought a thing about it."

"That **W.E.D**.? Did you see it last time at the Carousel?"

Wals nodded slowly as he stared at what was becoming a common sight at the clue locations. "Maybe I need to start paying more attention to what's around me."

Since Wals seemed distracted, Rose started to pull the paddles out of the bin, and made another meaningless notation on her clipboard. Without looking at him, she murmured, "Do you have a flashlight in your backpack?"

"No, didn't think I'd need one. There's a spotlight, though, in the control box."

Once most of the paddles were out, Wals shone the light into the slightly damp wooden bin as he leaned far inside. The smell of the River water was trapped inside. "Nope, there's nothing... Wait, a minute. There's something like a small box down here. It's built away from the walls." There was a grunt. "It also nailed down." A hand reached back. "Hand me something to pry it with."

An object was pressed into his palm. "A pen, Rose?"

"Hey, it's all I can find. I didn't think I'd need a crowbar..."

"Hold my feet. I need to lean into this thing."

"Yeah, that won't be noticeable."

"I heard that." His voice was muffled by the wood. "You could be in here, you know."

"I'm a manager. I wouldn't do that."

A low chuckle echoed around inside the bin. "Hope you didn't want this pen back... Okay, I pulled off the extra wood... Got it! Here, grab it and get it out of sight."

Her motion to seize the capsule and get it out of sight inside the backpack was one, fluid movement. Any attention still on them would be centered on Wals' struggle to get out of the bin and put the paddles back.

Once the tarp was secured in place, Wals found his heart was pounding against his ribs. "Let's get out of here in case someone put in a call."

Rose removed her jacket as Wals returned the clipboard to its hook.

Just as they reentered Frontierland, Wolf and another security guard were jogging toward the canoe dock. Seeing Wals was about to say hello, Wolf kept his eyes forward and subtly motioned for him to keep moving.

Seeing Wolf's gesture, Rose tugged on the lagging Wals. "Somebody must have ratted us out. Where's a good place to get lost?"

Mouth dry, Wals diverted their course and ducked into the open gate of the Haunted Mansion.

Once they blended into the queue, Rose relaxed. "Oh, good! I wanted to go in here."

It wasn't until they were in the secure confines of the shrinking room, surrounded by other guests, that Wals let out a huff of air. "Man, this doesn't get easier, does it?"

Rose was practically jumping up and down on her toes. "This is so exciting, Wals! I love it. Wonder where we get to go next."

The doors parted and a dark, spooky passageway beckoned. Lightning flashed behind crimson velvet drapes and the portraits on the wall morphed into skeletons and cats. "Now we get into our own private Doombuggy and I can try to get my heart back in my chest."

Pressed closely together in the crush of people slowly edging forward, Rose happily clung to Wals' arm, her eyes taking in all the details of the Mansion.

CHAPTER 7

Flashback — Disneyland — 1960

"Grandpa, can we ride that?"

Walt and three of his grandchildren were on their way to the northern edge of Frontierland. A new section had been added to the Mine Train and they had the honor of cutting the ribbon to officially open it to the public.

Walt looked around to see what was being pointed out. "You want to ride the mules?" At their eager nods, a fond look came over his face. "Sure, that's one of my favorite rides! Just as soon as we finish smiling for the camera. All right, Sweetheart?"

The four-year-old had been smiling for the camera all day. Grandpa had invited his family and over seven hundred members of the press for the all-day event. They had already driven down Main Street in Walt's favorite horseless carriage. Hundreds of people had lined the street waving and calling out to them. One quick trip on Peter Pan for a break and now they were headed to the Mine Train and the new Nature's Wonderland attraction. A heavy, resigned sigh came from the small body dressed in white. "Okay."

The popular Mine Train was still closed to the public, but Engine #3 was fired up and waiting for the family and press members. After a quick trip to the cab to ring the bell, the procession settled into the bright yellow cars. As the train left Rainbow Ridge and entered the first tunnel, Walt grinned to himself, the youngest settled into his lap. *They aren't used to it like I am*. The train immediately came to a gentle stop in front of the new Beaver Valley with its realistic beaver dam and floating denizens.

Exiting the train, the girls gave a delighted gasp when they neared the water. Two beavers held a brightly colored, twisted ribbon that stretched between them.

"See, Sweethearts? They're waiting just for you." Walt kneeled behind the youngest as the three children were handed rubber hatchets. "Remember, only the ribbon, not the beavers." He glanced up at the entourage who had followed them off the train, their cameras poised. "You all ready?" At their nod, he wisely stepped back. "Careful now. Watch your sister…"

The hatchets immediately bounced off the ribbon and threatened to do more bodily harm than was wise. Tired of the uncooperative ribbon, the youngest turned to whacking handy leaves and twigs.

"Okay, I think we have enough pictures. Here, let me help." Walt came back down to their level as he pulled a small knife out of his pocket.

"What's that, Grandpa?"

Older than the two girls, Walt had figured his grandson would be drawn to the sharp object. "Here you go. I have another one."

The boy pushed his red cowboy hat off of his forehead. "Look! It has Davy Crockett on it!"

Walt flipped out the longer of the two blades on the second pocketknife. "Help me here with the ribbon while the girls watch."

The steel blades made quick work of the ribbon—much better than the rubber hatchets from the Trading Post.

Before the girls could start splashing in the water, they were ushered back to the train to complete the journey through Nature's Wonderland. Walt used the time to explain how this knife had been the prototype of one they were selling in the Frontierland shop near the Shootin' Arcade. Once the train exited the Rainbow Cavern, they were back at Rainbow Ridge. All the mule trains were out on the trail, so the youngsters' wandering attention was drawn to movement on the nearby River.

"I want to ride the canoes!"

"Yes, canoes, canoes, canoes!"

I guess we're done talking about knives and hatchets. Walt watched the canoe that had diverted their interest float out of sight around the corner of Tom Sawyer Island. "Are you sure? You'll have to help paddle."

All three bounced up and down. "We know! I'll help you, Grandpa."

Always ready for a ride, Walt dismissed the Press and assured his family that he had it handled. "I've got this. You all can either go back the apartment or go ride something."

The children were led around the River to the canoe dock in the Indian Village. Once they were outfitted with flotation rings around their waists and handed three short paddles, the children eagerly climbed into the waiting canoe. Walt allowed a few more guests to join them to help the native guides with the paddling.

The canoe floated out into the open water of the River as the front guide instructed the guests on how to paddle. They soon joined a canoe that had started ahead of them, but was having trouble getting everyone on the same page.

In the middle of the canoe was a girl about ten years old. Bored by the inactivity, she was delighted when the new canoe drifted next to them. "Hey! Want to race?"

Walt looked behind him and saw eager looks on the faces of the other guests. With a laugh he turned back to their challenger. "You're on!"

At Walt's word, the canoes lunged forward as most of the paddles dug in. There were a lot of shrieks, taunting, and more water in the canoes than the guides would have liked.

A drenched Walt and his canoe won the race. Soaked but jubilant, his grandchildren jumped up and down on the dock. "That was so much fun! Can we do it again?"

Collecting their child-sized paddles, Walt dropped them into the smaller of the two bins. As he went to return his, a strange look came over his face. The question was momentarily forgotten as he peered into the dark bin that held the adult-sized paddles.

Concerned by the abrupt silence, one of the guides edged closer. "You all right, Boss?"

As if testing the depth of the storage bin, Walt moved his oar up and down before he finally dropped it. Then, hands on the sides of the wood, he shook it a little to test its stability. He reached back inside to move the oars around before measuring the width of the opening with his forearm. Realizing he had been asked another question, he mumbled, "What?" Looking up, Walt could see all the people in line intently watching him, and more than a few cameras pointed in his direction. Flashing his trademark smile, he waved away their curiosity. "Uhm, yes, Wolf, it's very well made. Don't have to worry about this ever falling apart." He gathered the children around him to further divert the attention and waved good-bye to the crowd. "Come on, kids, let's go see Grandma in our apartment. I think we all need to dry off."

"Aww. What about the mules? You said we could ride the mules."

His brain, always working forward, made it possible to instantly ward off the impending crisis. "Oh, we'll come back to them later when we're dry." *And I'll come back to the canoe dock later when it's empty.*

Disneyland—2009

"**A**ll right, Wals. I'll give you another one. I like your Haunted Mansion." Rose glanced over at her companion as they traveled up the ramp at the end of the ride. Hand in hand, she moved closer and lowered her voice. "Do you think the guards are gone by now? Wolf wouldn't be waiting for us, would he? He did wave us off."

His mind still on the capsule they had just found, Wals was confused. "Wolf? Oh. No, I don't think so. He probably turned in a lack of evidence or something like that. The only indicator we left behind was the ruined pen hanging from the clipboard."

"Yeah, you really made a mess of that."

He let out an unbelieving snort as they emerged into the sunlight, the ghostly voice inside urging them to 'Hurry back.' "Me? You're the one who handed it to me." When they headed toward Frontierland, he let go of her hand so he could put an arm around her slender shoulders. "You look like you're enjoying this mayhem way too much."

Rose ran the word around her mouth. "Mayhem. Yeah, I like that. We all need a little mayhem in our lives. I wonder what we'll have to get into next." Her arm snaked around his waist. "When can we open the container?"

"I do believe you'd be jumping up and down right about now if I wasn't holding onto your shoulders." Glancing at her upturned, smiling face, a warm glow suddenly traveled through Wals, one he hadn't felt in a long time. Happiness. That's what it was. No wonder he didn't recognize the feeling. He felt happy as he lifted his face to the cloudless blue sky. Eyes closed, a red glow from the sun soon spread across his vision. The moment of bliss abruptly ended when there was a sharp poke into his ribs. "Sorry, not ticklish." *Except for my feet and I'm not telling you that.*

"Well?"

"Well what?" He resisted the overpowering impulse to poke her back.

"Are you trying to tell me that you aren't even the least bit curious about what we found?" She jumped in front to face him as she walked backward, keeping pace.

You look adorable. "Of course I am. But, we need to find a secluded spot so we can open it in private." A silly grin spread over his face. Eagerness oozed out of her every pore. "The Park is so busy today, I'm not sure where that'd be."

"Backstage? You haven't taken me there yet."

"Might have to be. Let me see." They stopped at the railing around the River to look around. The *Mark Twain* was just beyond, loading another group of guests. The pilot, casually leaning out of his wheelhouse window, watched the goings-on three levels below. Wals took stock of their surroundings. "Okay, Big Thunder Trail—too open and too busy. Third deck of the *Mark Twain*—too many people in line. End table at the River Belle Terrace—none available. Golden Horseshoe—show going on. Back to Adventureland? No, nothing there."

As Wals continued to ponder, Rose did her own assessment. "What about that?"

"What? Where are you pointing? The Stage Door Café? No, that's just a window-service restaurant."

"No. Those two huge, wooden fort doors with a big sign that says Cast Members Only."

"Oh, that. See those windows over to the right? Above the tables and chairs?"

Rose followed his finger. "Yes."

"Those are the dressing rooms for the performers in the Golden Horseshoe. There's also a break area that the Jungle Cruise skippers like to use. Access to the back of the restaurants, too."

Rose tugged on his arm. "Let's go check it out. Sounds like it could be private enough."

"Which part of skippers, performers, and restaurants sounds private to you?"

Her reply was a bright laugh as she towed him toward the tall gate. "Come on. We can at least check it out to see."

Her enthusiasm was infectious as he returned her grin. "Fine. But I'm not sharing you with the skippers."

"You're so cute."

Wals let out a long, fake sigh. "Yeah. Cute. That's just what I've been shooting for."

The backstage area, snuggled between Adventureland and Frontierland, was an enclosed, rectangular island. Congested with stairs leading to the dressing rooms and offices, tables and umbrellas for the break area, trash compactor and lockers for Custodial, and an out-of-place truck that would be loaded and removed after the Park closed, it didn't have much free space. Many of the doors leading into the backs of shops and kitchens were open to let in any breeze that might come into the area. The backstage doors that led into the Golden Horseshoe were closed while the Billy Hill show was in full swing. Two skippers lounged at a far table. After Rose received a long, appreciative look-over and Wals an uninterested glance, they returned to their lunch.

"What's that wonderful smell?"

Wals gave a tentative sniff. Eyeing the trash compactor, he wasn't sure if she was being serious or sarcastic. "Smells like the Bengal Barbecue. Great chicken or beef skewers. Maybe we can have lunch there tomorrow."

"It's making my stomach growl. I'm glad there's only a couple hours until dinner. Hope we get a table."

Wals wasn't sure about her last mumble and checked his pocket for the dinner reservation. "We'll have a table. Don't you remember I made a reservation with Dawn?"

"Yeah, I remember." *No clue*.

"Okay..." There seemed to be an underlying meaning to her words, but he had no idea what. Before he could ask, Wals noticed the two skippers got up from their table to drop their trash into a nearby can. He knew they would exit near the Bengal Barbecue in Adventureland and head back to the dock. "Seems we have the place to ourselves right now. Judging by the noise from the Horse-shoe, I'd say the show is about half-way." He led Rose to a shady spot and held out a chair. "Let's get down to business."

Eager, Rose leaned forward as Wals set the backpack onto the table and pulled out the canister. It had been stained dark brown to blend in with the wooden paddle bins. "Wow. I'm surprised you could even see it down there. That's pretty smart of Walt to think of that. Well, if it was Walt, that is."

Wals gripped the endcap and started to tug. "I'm almost positive it was Walt. The handwriting is so distinctive."

"Why are you grunting?"

"It must be stuck from the paint." He glanced over at the back door of the River Belle Terrace. "Let me see if Diane is working. Maybe I can borrow a knife."

Rose gave the cap an experimental pull while he was gone. "Hope it doesn't come it off. Wals' ego would be crushed." A smile stole across her lips when her mind drifted to the muscles bunched under his shirt.

Back in a minute with a knife, Wals wondered why a soft, adorable pink covered her cheeks. "You too warm? Thought you'd be used to the heat after Florida's humidity."

The pink darkened. "No, I'm fine. I see you got your knife." Anything to divert the attention.

After one more glance at her warm glow, he turned back to hack away at the capsule. "Oops. Hope Diane doesn't expect her knife back."

"Wow, I didn't know they could bend that far back and not break."

"Hey, there it goes!" The endcap popped off and rolled across the table. "Snag that, Rose!"

"Got it. Well, what's in there?"

"My, you are an eager little thing, aren't you?"

"I'll let that 'little' crack pass, and yes, I am. What is that?"

Wals had tilted the container and two things fell into his open hand. "Looks like a pocketknife. Hey, that's Davy Crockett. What's this?"

Wals handed Rose a short length of rolled-up off-white cloth with something red sticking up from it. "It's some kind of headband with two feathers."

"Really? Let me see." Wals examined the intricate embroidery on the headband. "You know, I think this is one of the bands the native guides who steered the canoes had to wear back in the day. See? That's what this stitching is. Their costumes were more elaborate than ours are today. Cool. This makes a great addition to my costume collection."

Rose noticed he again mentioned 'his' collection and bit back a tinge of disappointment. Trying to keep her voice neutral, she asked, "What year would it be? Would it be from Walt's time?"

The headband dropped into his lap as he thought back. "Let's see. The Indian Village had the Indian War Canoes. Did you know that they didn't load like ours today? They had individual docks that jutted out from the queue area to load vertically. The canoes had to be drug out from their docks before they could get going. I think that lasted until around 1971. Everything else was basically the same as we know it. Bear Country opened in 1972 and the canoes then became part of that land." He gave a wide grin. "So, yeah, this and the Davy Crockett knife would definitely be from Walt's time." He handed her the knife. "Do you remember the Davy Crockett craze that hit the world in the Fifties and Sixties?"

"I'm not that old, but, yes, I do remember hearing about it." She flipped out one of the blades and examined the housing. "This looks odd, though. There isn't the usual trademark stamp or any indication of who made it. I thought the oldest items had a WDP on them."

He held up a hand when she tried to return it to him. "No, you hang on to that. You might need to protect me from some horrible enemy."

The two-inch blade winked in the sun as she moved it back and forth. "Yeah, this'll definitely scare off any horrible enemy. Well, I'll do some research on it later to see what I can find. Thank you!"

Wals was busy pounding the capsule onto the tabletop. "There's something else in here, but I can't reach it."

"Hey, be careful you don't break anything else. Let me see it. My hands are smaller than yours."

Wals watched as her slender fingers reached inside the container. "Can you reach it?"

"Got it. It looks like the same paper as the clue in Florida. You want me to read it?" At his nod, Rose looked over the hand-printed message. "This is odd. It's written like a poem, but it doesn't make sense."

**Up above the World You
fly Like A Tea-Tray
in the Sky.
Enjoy the view from the window**.

They were both quiet as the words hung between them. Wals broke the silence first. "I have no idea what that means. Rats, I was hoping we'd just be able to go to the next spot and find the next clue. You?"

Her head slowly shook back and forth as she re-read the puzzle. "Is it a ride? Is it a building? It mentions the world, flying, and a window."

"And a tea-tray, whatever that is. Well, I think we're done here." Wals stood and began to gather the items to get them out of sight in the backpack. The bent dinner knife was left on the table. With a grin, he put on the headband, making sure the red feathers were centered in the back.

"You look dashing."

Now it was his turn to blush. "I, uh, used to get a hat of some kind every time we came to the Park when I was a kid. This reminds me of that time in my life."

The disappointment Rose had felt melted away. Let him remember his family and the happy times they shared—even if it meant him keeping the hat and everything they might find. With a gentle hand she straightened the band across his forehead. "It fits like it was made for you."

"Yeah, it feels pretty good." Reaching into his shirt pocket, he pulled out a couple of tickets and held them up. "It's almost time for our FastPasses to Indy. Let's head that way and we'll work on the clue tonight at Lance's. I'm sure he'll let us use his computer."

Hand in hand, they exited through the cast member door to the left of the Bengal Barbecue. That put them across from the entry to Indiana Jones.

Before they could go three paces, an irritated Wolf stepped in front of them. "You really need to keep a lower profile, Wals. We got a lot of calls about someone hacking up the canoe dock."

"Hey, it was inside the canoe bin." Wals' eyes narrowed. "As you well know." He noticed Wolf kept glancing up at his new hat. "Like my new old headband? Walt put it inside the capsule."

Wolf didn't return his grin. "Ah, so that's where it went. I knew I shouldn't have trusted him with my stuff."

Wals' eyes went wide at the implication. He, of course, knew Wolf had worked with Walt, but he always seemed to forget how long ago that really was.

Rose, on the other hand, had no knowledge about Wolf or his special ability. She didn't know whether to be dubious or amused. "Your stuff? Who is 'him'? You couldn't possibly mean..."

The men had forgotten Rose was new to their group and the Hidden Mickey searches. After a quick glance, they both broke out with a hearty, if fake, laugh to cover it for now. Wolf would leave it up to Wals to tell her if he thought it necessary.

"Oh, Wolf is always kidding around. You know what a joker he can be." Wals knew he was starting to ramble and grabbed her hand. "Come on. We don't want to miss our FastPass time. You're going to love Indy. Wait until you see the queue. Wolf? You coming?"

"No."

After Wolf returned to his security detail, Rose let herself be distracted by the highly-detailed queue of Indy. Wals continued to rattle on about how far they had to walk, where the Jungle Cruise river got diverted, when they went under the surrounding berm, and more of the hidden details inside the Temple of the Forbidden Eye. She quietly filed away another question that would be answered at some point in the future.

"**A**re you having a good time? Are you glad you came to California?"

Much to her surprise, Rose actually was seated at a river-side table in the Blue Bayou. She would have bet any amount of money they would be turned away at the door. After watching another boat of guests slowly glide by in the dark water of the Pirate flume, she gave a contented sigh. This was a special place for a romantic meal. There was a full moon in the misty sky above them, the muted sounds of frogs croaking, fireflies winking in and out, a distant banjo slowly plucking out a tune, all mixed with the quiet conversations and clink of silverware around them. She took Wals' offered hand next to the dim, flickering light in the middle of the table. "Yeah, I am. To both questions." She looked up at the Chinese lanterns strung over the tables. "This is such a great place. Thanks for bringing me here."

I'd take you anywhere in the world for a smile like that. "I thought you'd enjoy it. It's one of my favorite dinner spots. Wait until you taste the food."

"We haven't ridden Pirates yet. It'll be fun now to see the restaurant from that perspective."

"We can do that next, if you want. I wasn't sure how late you wanted to stay, or if you wanted to get back to Lance's to work on the clue."

She tugged on his hand to bring him closer. When he leaned in expecting her to whisper something about the clue, she lightly kissed his lips. "I don't care about the clue right now. I'm enjoying this time with you."

Wals was going to take a second kiss, but was interrupted by an "Ahem."

Andy, the waiter, stood just back from their chairs, his arms laden with plates and bowls. "And who had the Filet?"

The darkness of the ambience covered Rose's embarrassment. She didn't mind the kiss. She just didn't like being caught. "That would be mine."

Wals took another sip of his Mint Julep as a steaming bowl of Jambalaya was placed in front of him. He'd find another opportunity to finish what had been interrupted.

"I have something for you." Rose took the last, savory bite of her Filet Mignon and pushed the plate to the side of the table. "Man, that was good."

Wals looked intrigued. "For me? When did you have time to go shopping?"

"I brought it with me." She dug through her purse. "Where is that silly thing? Oh, on the bottom, of course. Wrapped it myself."

Wals took the small, plastic Disney bag, the same one in which every souvenir from the Parks is dropped. "And you did a wonderful job. What is it?"

"Well, it wouldn't be a surprise if I told you. Open it."

"I like the tape sealing it shut. Nice touch. You have that knife handy?"

"Use your teeth."

He laughed at her suggestion. "Maybe next time. Hey! It's

the five-legged goat from the mural. Ha! Perfect. Thank you."
Wals took the blue and white pin and attached it to the front of his
shirt. "How does it look?"

She glanced from the headband he was still wearing to the pin.
"Somehow it all works. Could be the next, big fashion statement."

"That's me. Always a trendsetter." He tugged on her hand and
claimed the second kiss. "Thank you, honey. This means a lot."

"Ahem."

With a small chuckle, Wals pulled away. Andy had their bill.
"Great timing, dude."

With an apologetic shrug, Andy accepted Wals' credit card and
vanished to the back.

"I am going to get a full kiss before the night is done."

Rose indicated the boat gliding past the restaurant. "Let's go
ride Pirates. We can kiss the entire length of the restaurant. Andy
can't get to us there."

"I like how you think, Miss Tyler. Let's see if we can keep it
going down the waterfalls."

"You're on, Mr. Davis. Wait a minute… What waterfalls?"

CHAPTER 8

Fullerton

It was nearing midnight when Wals and Rose headed back to the Brentwood mansion. After riding Pirates, they had headed to the Frontierland River to watch the show *Fantasmic!* Still not wanting the day to end, they joined the masses on Main Street for the fireworks show over Sleeping Beauty Castle. Then, it only made sense to go on all the dark rides in the deserted Fantasyland as parents with sleepy children headed home. A comparison of the Tomorrowland in California to Florida's led to a challenge on Buzz Lightyear's Astro Blasters. When Rose beat Wals by a whopping twenty thousand points, that naturally led to a rematch.

Tired but jubilant, they now stood close together on the Brentwood's front porch, the inevitable parting delayed by neither wanting to say the first good-night.

"You think Lance and Kimberly are still awake?"

Wals glanced upward. "If they are, we're probably centered on their security camera."

A shy giggle escaped her lips. "Then let's give them something to record."

The kiss was deep and long. Contended and reassured, Wals pulled her in for a hug. "I guess you should go in. Dad's probably worried." Her chuckle vibrated against his chest. *Oh, if only your name wasn't Rose.* "What time should I come tomorrow? We can get the research done in the morning and, hopefully, go into the Park by noon for the next clue." The air around them altered and

Wals felt her body stiffen in his arms. "What's wrong?"

Rose slowly pulled away from his warm embrace. Not wanting to meet his eyes, she started to fumble through her purse for the housekey Kimberly had given her. "Nothing. Nothing's wrong. I'm just tired, and, uh, need to get some sleep."

Confused by the change in her voice and body language, Wals tried to peer into her face, but she kept her head down. "You sure?"

Rose could only nod. Turning away, she had difficulty getting the key into the lock. "Bye," she whispered as she slipped inside the house. The door shut with a quiet click.

"Night." Wals stared at the closed door as a wave of panic erased the warm glow that had filled his heart. His fist raised to knock, his movement stilled when the deadbolt slid into place. Not sure what had just happened, he figured they would sort it out in the morning. It had been a long, exciting day and he still had a thirty-minute drive home to Huntington Beach. "See you tomorrow."

"**W**hat do you mean she's gone!?" Open-mouthed, Wals stood in the Brentwood's hallway. "Where'd she go?"

"Apparently back to Florida." Leaning against the doorframe of his office, Lance studied his flummoxed friend.

Kimberly was positioned right behind Lance. A frown covering her face, she moved forward to slap an object into Wals' hand. "She handed me this right before she got into the airport shuttle and said to give it back to you."

It was the Davy Crockett pocketknife. "I don't understand. Airport? She went home!?"

Lance didn't look as judgmental as his wife. He took a step back and gestured for Wals to come into his office. "Have a seat. You look like you're going to drop."

"Did she say anything, like *why* she was leaving? We were supposed to work on the clue today."

Kimberly's expression hadn't cleared. "Can you think of something you might have said?"

"Said? We just kissed good-night and I mentioned we were probably on your security camera." If possible, Kimberly's frown deepened. "That's all! We were making plans for tomorrow… today."

"Are you sure?"

Lance sat back to let his wife handle it. She's the one who had sat up with the sobbing Rose for two hours last night.

Wals stared at the blonde. "Yes, I'm sure. We had a great day together. Everything went really well." One side of his mouth turned up in a brief grin. "Well, other than Wolf chewing us out for being spotted on the canoe dock, but that was more funny than upsetting."

Kimberly's green eyes bore through him in reply to his attempt at humor. "You can't think of anything you might have said on the porch last night?"

Wals began to get flustered. "Since you seem to know, why don't you just tell me?"

"Does this sound familiar? 'If only your name wasn't Rose.' Do you remember saying that?"

"I didn't say that..." Wals' mouth abruptly closed as his hand smacked over his eyes. "Oh, gosh. I did it again. I...I didn't mean to say that out loud. I was just thinking it. It didn't mean anything."

Kimberly's voice was almost a whisper. "Well, it meant something to Rose." Pacing the room, her words became louder. "How could you even think something like that? It's not her fault her name is Rose. And, besides, what difference does it make? They are two completely different women. And this one really liked you, Wals. She was...she was devastated."

"I didn't mean anything by that." Wals looked back and forth at the two Brentwoods trying to garner either some support or understanding. "When did she leave? Do I have time to reach her at the airport?"

From all his flying back and forth across the country during his own Hidden Mickey quests, Lance was quite familiar with sudden trips to the airport. He knew exactly how long it would take to get from Fullerton to the Los Angeles International Airport. "Not with the traffic this time of day. Her flight leaves at ten."

All heads swiveled to the clock on the wall. As if on cue, the chime struck once for nine-thirty.

With that option evaporated, Wals turned on Kimberly. "Why didn't you call me last night, Kimberly? I could have come back and fixed this."

An accusing finger pointed at his chest. "Hey, don't put this off on me." Her rigid stance began to relax. He looked absolutely miserable. "I was going to call you, but she made me promise not to."

Wals pulled out his phone. "I'll text her. That'll clear it up. Maybe she'll miss the flight and come back."

"Dude." Lance shook his head while he strode over to Wals' position on the couch. A hand covered the face of the phone. "Put that away. You need to do this in person."

"You already said I can't make it to the airport in time..." Wals glared up at Lance. "Move your hand."

"Dude."

The phone fell into Wals' lap as he let out a heavy sigh. "I know. I know. I have to go to Florida. If she'll see me."

"Flowers would be nice."

Wals looked over at Kimberly. At least she didn't look like she still wanted to kill him. That was a bonus. "Roses?"

"Big red ones. A *lot* of big red ones."

"I was thinking yellow."

Lance let out an amused snort. "Yellow? Really? You want to be in the Friend Zone with Rose?"

"Okay, now I'm confused." Wals pinched the bridge of his nose. A headache was starting to throb. "What does the color yellow have to do with anything? Roses are roses."

"Isn't that the attitude that got you into trouble in the first place?" At Wals' irritated frown, Lance waved him off. "Sorry. All colors have a special meaning. White means purity or innocence. Yellow means either friendship or jealousy, depending on who you ask. Pink stands for elegance or grace. Dark pink means gratitude. And red means love." Lance threw a loving look at his wife. "I learned all this early on. Had a good teacher."

"Okay, okay. Now I'm really getting a headache." Wals ran a hand over his face. "I don't even know where to send them. Since she was coming to California, I never needed her address. Should I take them into the Magic Kingdom when I see her?"

"That should be interesting. If you tell the main gate you came to get your big feet out of your mouth, I'm sure they'd allow it."

Wals stared at Lance's passive face. He couldn't tell is he was kidding or not. Probably not. Still, it was the only option he had at this point. "Fine. A dozen..." He saw Kimberly slowly shake her head. "Two dozen long-stemmed red roses." A small ray of hope shot through Wals. This had to work. It just had to. "Can I use your computer to check flight times? Looks like I need to make a reservation. And find a florist in Orlando willing to deliver to the Contemporary Hotel."

"First smart thing you've said all morning."

"I heard that, Lance."

"Good."

"How can there be a weather system this time of the year? It's spring, for crying out loud. I can't get a flight until Thursday."

"It's Florida. Just be glad it isn't a hurricane." Now that tempers had calmed and Kimberly was off taking care of baby Michael, Lance was leaned back in his office chair, feet up on his massive desk. "You know what you're going to say?"

Wals shrugged. "No. But I'm assuming a lot of groveling will be in order."

There was a snicker. "You can be sure of that. While you're here, did you want to work on the clue? From what you said, you found something." Lance was trying to play it cool, but he was burning with curiosity and the craving to dig in and help. His Hidden Mickey quests had changed his life. It was difficult to give them up.

Unaware of Lance's true interest, Wals stared at the pocketknife Rose had returned. "Yeah, we did get a couple of things. This was part of the find. Rose was supposed to research it and find out why it doesn't have any marks on it."

"Then give it back to her on Thursday."

"Good idea. I see married life has taught you a thing or two."

"A wise man would have learned them before marriage. But, yes." Lance heaved himself to his feet. "If you want to use the computer again, have at it."

There was a long moment of silence as Wals stared at the machine. "Thanks, but, no. I'd rather wait for Rose to help me. It doesn't seem right to do it without her."

A pleased smile spread over Lance's face as he headed for the kitchen. "You're learning."

Florida

Wals was never one to fidget, but he found that flight to Orlando was one of the longest five hours of his life. Rose had never answered or returned his many calls or texts during the three days she had returned home. He wasn't even sure she knew he was coming. And, more importantly, he wasn't sure of the reception he would receive.

Then there was another aspect of this return trip to Florida that bothered him: Even though his name had never come up during Rose's California visit, Wals figured he would have to face-off with The Hulk... No, he had to stop that. Rose didn't like it. What was his real name? Mordred? Bob? Rod? Rob, that was it.

Wals snorted, and then had to turn away from the inquisitive look from the passenger in the seat next to him. "This is going to be fun."

Trying to ignore the wistful sighs of the women and the smug chuckles of the men, Wals attempted to hide his fragrant bouquet as best he could. But twenty-four long stemmed red roses were always ready to say, "Hello! I'm here!"

The woman at the main gate had insisted on pulling the flowers close to her face to inhale the heady aroma. "Who's the lucky woman?"

Walking down Main Street was the next trial. "Mommy! Mommy, look at all the flowers! Can I have one?" Even young girls appreciated the beauty of the crimson petals.

"Dude, you're making us all look bad." Wals received an angry stare as a 20-year-old pulled away his doe-eyed girlfriend.

Wals' mumbled, red-faced apology was unheard as he stomped toward the entrance to Tomorrowland. "Sheesh, can it get any worse?"

The moist paper towels that encircled the base of the stems had begun to seep. The clear pink cellophane wrapper that held the flowers was slowly unwrapping, and the heart-laden bow started to droop.

"What do you mean she doesn't work here any longer!?" Unbelieving, Wals stared at his former nemesis, Anne.

Unmindful of the daggers in his eyes, she leaned forward to examine the roses. "Nice. Can I have one?"

"No. These are for Rose."

"Who isn't here. My, whatever did you do? Must've been something really stupid to merit all these lovely flowers."

His frown deepened. "You look like you're enjoying this way too much." Standing near the entrance to the Carousel of Progress, Wals tried to move the flowers into the shade. He wondered how much longer they'd last in the humid heat of the day. "Can you at least tell me if she still works in the Magic Kingdom? Or do I have to visit every ride to find her?"

Anne held out a hand. "Magic comes with a price, dearie."

Biting back a less-than-magical word, Wals pulled one of the roses out of the bouquet. Before he handed it to Anne, he held it out of reach of her eager grasp. "You promise to tell me where she is."

"Yes, yes, yes. Gimme."

Wals would have thought she'd been awarded Cast Member of the Year by the expression on her face. *Maybe she never gets flowers from anyone*, he thought, stilling his irritated response. Perhaps Rose wouldn't realize one was missing... "Well? Where is she? Over in Buzz Lightyear?"

Eyes closed, Anne was inhaling the perfume of the rose. "No. She transferred to another Park."

"And?" He could see a malicious gleam come into her eyes. "No, you don't get another one. You promised."

"Fine. Just because you're a nice guy." When Wals' eyebrows shot up, she held the rose out like a sword. "Don't ask. She transferred to Animal Kingdom."

His shoulders sagged. "Now I have to go through everything all over again to get into that Park. Great."

"Hey, you're the one who did this."

"I know." There was nothing more to gain by staying in the Magic Kingdom. "So, what part of that Park is she in? It's not exactly a small place."

Anne paused long enough to make him think she wouldn't cooperate. But, she knew how Rose had felt when she returned from California. She was impressed that the guy showed up at all. The roses were a smart bonus. "She's supposed to be working at the Dinosaur ride." She could see a blank look tinged with panic come over his face. "You don't know where that is?" Anne stepped back to a small kiosk near the entry and pulled out an Animal Kingdom map. Opening the colorful folds, she pointed to the lower right side. "This is DinoLand U.S.A. The ride is at the bottom corner of the Land."

Grateful, Wals accepted the brochure. Another rose was pulled from the bunch. "You've been very helpful. Thanks."

The brown eyes that stared into his soul narrowed. "I might tease her now and then, but Rose is a good friend. Don't mess this up again."

With a contrite nod, Wals turned away and began the trek to the Transportation Center and a bus that would take him to the entrance of Animal Kingdom.

Once Wals had rounded the corner near Stitch's Great Escape, Anne went to the hidden telephone just inside the entrance to Scene One of the Carousel. She punched in a special code. "He's back and headed to Animal Kingdom."

CHAPTER 9

Walt Disney World—Animal Kingdom

Departing from the Transportation Center, Wals had a nine-mile bus ride to try and figure out what to say to Rose. As the bus roared down World Drive and turned onto Osceola Parkway, he didn't even see the entrances to the Hollywood Studios and Blizzard Beach. All he could think about was Rose, how she had made him feel, how much he cared for her, and how badly he had blown it.

Exiting the bus at the lush, welcoming entrance to Animal Kingdom, he took a moment to still his wildly-beating heart. A glance down at the roses didn't help. The effects of the Florida sun were becoming more evident. *Maybe water would help.*

"There's a fountain over there, but you could probably get something cooler in the restaurant."

I did it again. "Uhm, thanks. That's a good idea." Smiling at the helpful guest, Wals headed into the cool, tropical jungle of the Rainforest Cafe. A huge walk-through fish tank separated the gift shop from the dining section. Calypso music formed the backdrop as jungle creatures looked down from their leafy perches. Wals was staring up at a leopard when he was approached by Staci, one of the hostesses.

"Ahhh, those are so pretty! Can I get you a table to let your adventure begin?"

An elephant trumpeted somewhere inside the jungle. "Oh, hi. No, I was hoping you could help me. I could *really* use some cool water. My roses are drying out."

His hand was grabbed so Staci could stick her face into the

93

bouquet. "They smell so good." Recalling his request and her position, she pulled back, smiled, and became practical. "All righty, let's see what we need." Trying not to disturb the wilting flowers, she poked around inside the cellophane. "Yeah, they're pretty dry. Would you like me to take them back stage and soak the paper? I can also rewrap them, too, if you want. They look pretty beat up."

Wals let out a breath he didn't know he had been holding. "That sounds wonderful. Thank you."

She pointed over at the bar situated under a huge mushroom. "Why don't you wait over there. It won't take long."

Sitting on a stool shaped like the lower half of a giraffe, Wals ordered a cola. As he waited, all the lights suddenly dimmed. Lightning began to flash and thunder pealed throughout the restaurant. The tropical storm quickly ended, and the excited animal squeals from inside quieted. "Maybe we can come back here for dinner."

Wals used the condensation on the outside of his frosty glass to make a hidden mickey on the bar top. Taking another sip, he smiled to himself. "Well, at least I'm planning on a good outcome for all of this."

Staci came back with the roses. The cellophane wrapper was cool to the touch and the flowers did look perkier. *Was there one more missing*? Grateful for the help, Wals didn't care. He took out a stem to give to Staci. His suspicion was confirmed when she sheepishly held up a hand to refuse it.

"No, no, that's all right. I'm just glad I could help. Hope they do the trick for you."

"So do I." Wals took a deep breath. His heart began to pound again. "So do I."

Once Wals showed his pass and the entry gate chirped, he followed the crowd around the welcoming Oasis. A flock of pink flamingos waded in shallow water while an anteater waddled into the shade of the vegetation. A short bridge took the guests over the Discovery River and onto Discovery Island that held the magnificent Tree of Life.

"Don't let the giraffes see those flowers!"

"Hope you aren't taking those into the aviary."

"Hey, which gift shop sold those? I need to get one for my girl."

Long inured to all the comments, Wals gave only a small smile of acknowledgement to each. After a quick glance at the towering Expedition Everest and a small regret that he couldn't stop to enjoy the view, Wals turned right and crossed another bridge to head into DinoLand U.S.A. Off to the left was a tall dinosaur skeleton and kids happily digging in the sand of the Boneyard to find their own fossils.

Two tall, square pillars marked the entrance to the Dinosaur attraction. The attached poster naming the ride showed a fiery meteor storm raining down on an angry T-Rex. "Hope that isn't prophetic of the reception I'm about to receive," Wals mumbled as he strode forward. Thick trees lined the path as tall skeletons peered out from their protection. Aladar, the huge Saltasaurus, stared at him as he approached the entry doors. A sign that read 'The Friendliest Fossils in America' seemed at odds with the meteors crashing through the marquee.

Rose wasn't the cast member welcoming guests inside. "Should've known it wouldn't be that easy."

"I'm sorry?" Rhea smiled at the roses, unsure of what the embarrassed guest had meant. "Would you like to come inside? Our next expedition is about to begin."

Knowing the description of the ride and that the track was the same layout as the Indiana Jones ride back home, Wals shook his head. "I don't think the flowers would survive the trip. I'm...I'm looking for Rose. Rose Tyler? I was told she was working here today."

A light of recognition, an 'Aha' moment, flickered over Rhea's face. Her cast member smile froze in place.

Great, Wals sighed to himself. *Here we go again.*

"Oh, Rose. Yes, she's here."

There was a long delay as Rhea welcomed more guests inside the popular ride. The prolonged, pointed silence extended even when there was no one approaching the entrance.

"Rose?" When he received no answer to his reminder, Wals resignedly held out one of the blooms. He had to force himself to not roll his eyes. "Could you please call her for me?"

Using the rose, Rhea gestured to the side of the entry. "Wait over there." Moments after she disappeared inside, another cast member, Silas, came out to take her place. Wals was given a penetrating glare.

Gosh, she didn't even ask for my name. Does everyone here

know what happened? He ignored Silas and looked around as if interested in the design of the building.

It seemed like hours, but was more like five minutes before Rose slowly emerged from the entry. Wals' face broke out in a wide, relieved smile as he went to greet her. "Rose! Uh, these are for you."

Rose looked down at the flowers that were thrust into her arms. They were beautiful, but there were explanations to be heard before she would acknowledge that fact. "Wals. I wasn't expecting you."

The cool reception threw him off. "I repeatedly called and texted you. You never responded."

Rose took one of the roses out of the bunch and handed it to a woman entering the ride.

"What are you doing? Those are for you." Wals could only stare when another flower was given to someone else.

"I'm on a break. Do you want to take a walk? Or we could just sit here."

Not sure what was going on, Wals ran his fingers through his hair. Now that his hands were empty of the diminishing bouquet, he wasn't sure what to do with them. He doubted Rose would hold hands with him as they walked. "Uhm, do you want to walk around the Tree of Life? I haven't seen it yet."

"Sightseeing? Ah." Rose handed off another rose to a passing guest.

"No, I just thought it looked like a nice spot to talk. If you know of another place, I'll go there."

The next rose was pushed back into the remaining stems. "All right. There are some quiet spots over there."

Rose led the way over the Discovery River and past the entry to It's Tough to be a Bug. The tantalizing smells from the Flame Tree Barbecue floated in the air. Now past noon, Wals' stomach growled. "Would you like some lunch? I missed breakfast when I went over the Magic Kingdom to look for you."

"I don't work there any longer. How'd you know where I was?"

"Anne told me. It took a rose for her to tell me."

The first smile of the day passed quickly over Rose's lips. "Sounds like Anne."

"Would have been nice to know you changed locations."

The smile vanished. She gave a stem to a little girl walking by with her family.

His mouth clamped shut, Wals was starting to see a pattern. If she didn't like his answer, she gave away one of his roses. His $180 investment was quickly disappearing. "Sorry, Rose. I tried to contact you. I know you've been mad at me." Her hand hovered near the bouquet. "Kimberly told me what you heard...what I said." He ran a hand through his messy hair again. One more pass and it would be standing straight up. "I didn't mean to say that out loud. You know I have a bad habit of saying something out loud what I was thinking."

Another rose vanished into the crowd. Trying to control her emotions, she was breathing hard, her lips pressed closely together.

Wals stepped closer and put a hand on Rose's shoulder. It was the first time he attempted to touch her. When a rose wasn't handed off, he let out a relieved sigh. That was a good sign, wasn't it? "Rose, you know I care for you. I...I didn't mean what I said. It just came out. It didn't mean anything. You can't help what your name is." A growl escaped his lips when she handed a rose to a good-looking man standing by the railing. "That's not what I meant!" At this rate, she would soon be holding an empty cellophane wrapper and a heart-covered ribbon. "Can we please go over to the shade? I'm starting to sweat and the roses are starting to droop again."

They found an intricately carved wooden bench by a running stream. The area gave off the impression of lush coolness even in the heat of the day. Wals was also thankful to see that it was a little-used path which meant less possibility of losing more roses. By his guess, there were only about fifteen left. "Maybe I need to start over." At her blank look, he continued. "Rose, I'm so sorry I said something that hurt you. I've only known you a short time, but I care for you. A lot. I don't care that your name is Rose. I never compared you to the other Rose. I...I was devastated when I learned you had left. I was going to rush to the airport, but there wasn't time. I knew I had to fix this in person. I just had to see you." He paused when her hand hovered over the flowers. "I had to tell you I'm sorry. I can't lose you." He froze when she broke off one of the flower heads. "I..."

"Shh." She leaned forward to put the stem into one of the buttonholes on his shirt. "I forgive you."

A look of relief flooded his face. "Gosh, couldn't you have told me that earlier?"

The happy smile vanished when she tossed a rose over the nearby fence. A porcupine wandered over to sniff the new treat.

Wals watched as the flower was slowly eaten. "Sorry. You aren't supposed to be feeding the animals, are you?"

His attempt at humor to diffuse the situation didn't work. Another flower flew over the fence and landed in the lagoon. "You're right. I should know better."

"At least it's floating." He turned back to Rose to put a sweaty hand on her arm. "What can I say to make it up to you? I can't lose you. You mean too much to me."

"Then kiss me."

"Really?" Not wanting to take the chance of blowing it again, Wals immediately scooted over on the bench to take her in his arms. "This day just got better."

Just as their lips were about to meet, they were startled to hear, "Rose, is this guy bothering you?"

The look of irritation on Wals' face turned into anger. "Lurch? What are you doing here?"

"Lurch?" Rose seemed to want to smile, but held out a rose to the security guard instead. "Hi, Rob. How long have you been here?"

Wals had jumped to his feet. "Yes, *Rob*. How long have you been here, and why?"

The two men stood toe-to-toe. Wals, five inches shorter, had unknowingly formed a fist. Rose knew she had to do something fast. Setting the roses down on the bench, she managed to wedge herself in-between the glowering opponents. "Rob, back off. Wals, knock it off. He's my brother, Wals. My over-protective, extremely bad-timing brother."

Wals' expression immediately cleared. "Brother? How could Colossus...I'm sorry, Rob," as another rose flew into the water, "be your brother? He's, like six-foot-fourteen, and you're...Hey, there won't be any more roses if you keep doing that! I was just going to say petite."

"Oh." Rose managed to look contrite. "Sorry." She looked over at the three roses floating away in the Discovery lagoon. "I think they're goners."

All three looked at the floating flowers and the tension was broken.

Rob spoke first. "Are you all right, Rose?" He ignored the irritated stance Wals resumed.

Rose put a hand on the security guard's chest. "Yes, I'm fine. Wals managed to clear up the misunderstanding. And look! He brought me a dozen roses."

"Two dozen."

Rob ignored Wals' mumble. "As long as you're sure. I won't let you get hurt like that again." This time he stared right at Wals.

Before Rose could say anything else, Wals knew he had to speak up for himself. "And I will never hurt her again like that. I was stupid. Unthinking." He turned to Rose to put his hands on her arms. "I will probably do or say something stupid again, but I promise I'll never do it on purpose."

Her smile was all the answer he needed.

Turning back to the hovering Rob, Wals stuck out his hand. "I'm Wals. Wals Davis. And I'm going to date your sister. Whether you like it or not."

Rob shook the offered hand. They both resisted the manly urge to see who could squeeze the hardest. "Rob. Rob Tyler. And, if you hurt her again, I will come after you."

"Not going to happen. Here, have another rose. Everyone else in the park has gotten one."

With an amused snort, Rob declined Rose's offer to join them for the rest of the day. He had to get back to his assignment in Epcot. Plus, he knew he had made his point.

Wals had held back his bad knee-jerk reaction when he heard Rose's invitation. Glad to be back on friendly terms, he would have agreed to anything she suggested. He extended his hand to her. "Do you need to get back to Dinosaur?"

Lacing her arm through Wals, she stepped closer. "Nope. I have the day off."

"Really? That's great. I thought you just said that to Rob to irritate me."

"Oh, I did," as she snuggled against his side. Her overwhelming sense of relief that Wals was back and had apologized made her so happy that she wanted to break and run. Her grip was a little tight to prevent that from happening. "But I knew he had to work today. I pulled a few favors when I heard some guy was here with a huge bunch of roses."

"You knew it was me?"

"I hoped it was you. Who else would bring flowers to Walt Disney World?"

"Glad to hear I'm unique."

She smiled up at him. "That you are."

They had wandered over the lagoon and into the African section. Wals was glad when Rose suggested the Kilimanjaro Safari. He had wanted to suggest it, but remembered her reaction when he mentioned the Tree of Life. He was here for her, not the animals. Now he was getting a bonus.

As their open-air Jeep-like vehicle bumped and rumbled over the dirt paths, Rose had a question for him. "What did you find with the clue? Where did you go next?"

Concerned only with Rose, their Hidden Mickey adventure had been shoved to the back of his mind. He hadn't done a thing with it since she left. "I never tried to figure it out. I...I wanted to wait for you to help me solve it." Her warm smile told him he had said the right thing. "It didn't seem right to do it alone any longer."

"Aww. Then you didn't go to the Skyway Chalet?"

His mouth fell open. "You solved it? When did you do that?"

"Oh, look! The lion pride is out! Hmm, pretty quickly after I got home. I figured you'd go ahead with it and I was curious to see what I could find."

Wals recalled the strange words of the clue. "So, what does the tea-tray in the sky mean? The Skyway buckets never looked like that."

"Aww, baby rhino. You aren't even looking at the animals."

"I'd rather look at you."

She scooted closer on the bench. "Charmer. That quote came from the original *Alice in Wonderland* book. I think it was the dormouse." Rose warmed up to the subject as she recalled all her research. "I first thought it must be the Tea Cup ride since the dormouse is in the pot in the middle, but that's on our ride. Not the one in Disneyland. Then there's the Alice in Wonderland ride. But, the tea party scene was added years later." She lowered her voice before she continued. "If Walt did leave the clue, that scene wouldn't have been there."

"I'm impressed."

"Not done yet. So, I did a search of the actual words and how they were written on the clue. And there they were."

In the ensuing silence, Wals realized she was waiting for him to ask. "Okay, where were they?"

"They are painted on the outside of your Skyway Chalet. Exactly like Walt wrote them on the clue."

Wals look flummoxed. "Really? I rode the Skyway for years and never saw anything painted on the outside of the building. Now that the ride is closed, I'm not sure what we're supposed to do. The empty building is still there, but it's in pretty poor shape." He could feel her shrug.

"Maybe you need to check it out."

"Maybe *we* need to check it out." The Jeep lurched and they bumped foreheads. "Ouch. Maybe you shouldn't be sitting in my lap."

"I'm not in your lap! I could be... Quit changing the subject, Wals. Did you mean it?"

"Mean what?"

Another rose flew off the side of their transport.

"Hey, we've been talking about a hundred different things. What are you referring to?"

Her smile turned shy. "That *we* should check it out."

Wals placed a finger under her chin. "With all my heart. I'd kiss you right now, but I don't want to lose a tooth."

The Jeep took a momentary pause to allow the viewing of a baby elephant. Rose used the still moment to kiss Wals.

"When can you come back to California? I don't want to finish the search without you." *Or finish the rest of my life without you.*

With a sharp jerk, their transport continued its journey. "Can you give me a couple of days to make arrangements for another vacation?"

"I'll wait." *I'll wait forever.*

By the look on her face, he wasn't sure if that last part had been silent.

But, by the look on her face, Wals didn't care.

Chapter 10

Disneyland

Once Rose had been happily ensconced in the Brentwood's house and she and Kimberly had gone over every moment of the 'Rose Debacle,' as it came to be called, Wals realized it was in his best interests to get her back to Disneyland as quickly as possible. He wasn't sure he could take one more high-pitched scream of laughter at his expense. The backing and support he had expected to get from his good buddy Lance had, of course, never materialized.

The women who had worked the Casey Jr. Circus Train with Wals spotted him when Rose paused at the entry to admire the blooming flowers that covered the arches. "Hey, Wals! We need a fill-in engineer! Give us a hand. It should only take a year or so." They kept imploring him when he made no move to approach the gate.

Rose couldn't understand why he hung back. "Aww, they really miss you, Wals."

"Yeah, they miss torturing me." He put a broad, fake smile on his face as he waved good-bye. "Never going to happen again, ladies. Ever."

"Bye, Wals! See you soon." The brightly-colored circus train pulled into the station and the women had to get back to work.

"They seemed nice."

He shot an amused glance at Rose's face. "What part of torture sounded nice to you?"

She hugged his arm. "Aw, I'm sure you looked really cute

wearing the lederhosen. Do you still have them?"

"And the day just gets better and better."

Hiding a secret smile, Rose knew when to quit. "Is this it?" A white and brown building could barely be seen peeking through the dense trees above them. A series of wide, flat steps led upward and curved out of sight.

Memories shot through Wals as his mind's eye saw beyond the untrimmed trees and roped-off entry. "I loved riding the Skyway. It gave such a unique view of the Park. I was here in 1994 on the last day of operation to get in one last ride."

"We had a Skyway, too, you know."

"Yours didn't go through the Matterhorn."

Rose started to laugh. "That is true."

"Did you know we had two different gondola designs over the years?"

"No, I didn't know that. Why did they change?"

"I'm not sure." Wals scratched his head. "There must've been some good reason."

Flashback—Disneyland—1964

Walt sat quietly in the back of the Skyway Chalet. Few people were riding. It was a cold day. Rain threatened, but had never materialized. The information he had been given indicated a low ridership on his beloved Skyway, and he wanted to see for himself.

In his dark corner, he had been unobserved. On this dismal day, he wasn't surprised there were few guests. He wouldn't have been too anxious to venture out to be exposed to the elements, either.

Other than the ticket-taker below the stairs, there was only one cast member to man the Chalet. The buckets came in at their steady pace and this young man worked tirelessly to swing the metal gondolas over to the next wire that would return them to Tomorrowland. As he sat, Walt watched this cast member. He couldn't detect any irritation or despondency that the ride was still running with no riders. He even thought he heard a low, whistled tune as the cast member steadily worked. Walt guessed that the young man was probably nineteen, twenty at the most.

Having seen enough, Walt stood from his chair. The young

man was startled to see anyone there, let alone his boss. Not sure what to say, he motioned at the empty gondola that would arrive in a few moments. "Would you like to take a ride, Mr. Disney?"

Walt looked at the incoming cab and nodded. "Yes, I would. And, call me Walt. But, I'd also like to ask you a question."

There was a silent pause and an audible gulp. "Uh, sure, Mr... Walt."

Walt had already checked the young man's nametag. "Andy, why do you think the Skyway isn't getting the riders it used to?"

Eyes wide, Andy realized he was expected to give an answer. "From what I've seen, Walt, people don't like the design of the gondolas." Nervous, he swallowed, but then noticed that his boss didn't seem offended by his statement. Emboldened, he continued. "The entry into the cab isn't right. I've seen a lot of people hit their heads when trying to get inside. It should be taller."

The round, blue gondola came squeaking into the Chalet. Andy expertly caught it and flipped open the door for Walt.

Nodding, Walt thanked Andy for his help, turned, and instantly whacked his forehead on the low entry doorway.

Later that year, the new Skyway gondolas were rectangular with room for four people, and had a taller entry and roof.

Disneyland—Current Day

Looking over the surrounding area, Rose couldn't help but notice the ice cream cart and souvenir kiosks blocking the stairway up to the Chalet. Her voice lowered as she leaned closer to Wals. "So, how are we going to get up there unnoticed? We have Casey Jr. right there, restrooms across the way, and, from the looks of those fort gates, an entry to Frontierland. It's pretty busy."

"That it is. That's why I brought these." Wals pulled off his backpack and unzipped a small pouch. He handed Rose a cast member nametag. "Here you go, Amy. You may call me Fred."

"You don't look like a Fred." When she took a clipboard from his pack, Rose instantly understood what Wals had planned. Just like at the canoe dock, they might get further if they looked like cast members. "At least I didn't wear shorts today."

"A tragedy we can rectify later in the day." Resisting a glance at her shapely legs, he watched the flow of the crowd. "Let's wait until there's more people around. If the guys working here get too busy, they might not notice us heading up the stairs."

It didn't take long. Once the Casey Jr. had unloaded and a large group all dressed in the same bright yellow T-shirts swarmed the kiosks, they knew they had their chance.

Wals made a show of pointing upward to Rose as if explaining the building and the route the gondolas would have taken. Rose nodded, made diligent notes on her clipboard, and then asked a question. Wals shook his head while she argued her point. Then, with deliberate steps, Wals went to the rope barrier and unclipped it. Once Rose stepped through, he reattached the clip as they walked steadily upward, not daring to look back. Once the walkway curved out of sight, they sprinted up the rest of the way to collapse, hearts pounding, against the faded entry.

"Oh, my word. It feels like my heart is coming out of my chest. This is so much fun!"

Amused by her conflicting emotions, Wals wiped a line of sweat off his forehead. "Well, we're not in the clear yet. We still don't know if anyone called Security. Let's just find whatever was left behind and get out of here."

Rose peered into the dark interior of the abandoned building. All of the ride's mechanisms were long gone. The huge wheel that had carried the gondolas from one side to the other, the steel cables, even the control panel the ride operators had used were gone. All that remained were the low wooden walls that had kept the waiting riders safely away from the swinging cabs, mounds of dead leaves, and a few folding tables. "It's so empty. Do you think Walt's clue might still be here?"

"It has to be." Wals ran a hand through his hair as he let out a pent-up breath. "It has to be."

"You noticed the clue painted on the outside of the building when we came up, right?"

Wals gave a light laugh. "I was so worried about being spotted I didn't even look."

Secure behind the heavy cover of branches, they took a step outside to look upward. Designed to look a Swiss chalet, the lintels had been painted a dark brown. The gold trim that accented the front façade was still bright, as were the colorful sun and moon of the clock above the two doors. And, above the carved scrollwork of the three open windows, was Walt's clue.

"How in the world did I never see that? I never noticed all the flowers and curlicues painted below the windows, either. I rode this for years. Hmmph, didn't even realize how it matched the design of the Bobsled's entry and queue."

Rose could only shrug. "We need to get to work, Fred. Walt told us to enjoy the view from the window. Which window? There's some on each side."

Hands on his hips, Wals looked from one side to the other. "Not sure. I have noticed with the other clues that there was an engraved **W E D** somewhere near the hidden clue. Maybe we should look for that and then try to find the next clue."

"Hope you have a couple of flashlights in that backpack. Everything in here is dark brown."

He started to dig through his backpack. "I did try to plan for a couple of things. I knew it would be dark. Here."

Grinning, Rose shone the light into his face. "Yep, it works."

"Great. Now all I can see is a big, yellow spot."

"Aw, you'll do fine. You know, since Walt used the quote on the outside of the building, I think we should start with the windows under it."

"Lead on, Sherlock."

Right away, Rose got to work on the window closest to the entry door. Wals took the opening next to the drop-off point of the gondolas. He gave a smug, unseen wave to the train far below as it wound its way through Storybook Land.

Working methodically, they used their lights and their fingers to try and find either the next clue or any tell-tale markings to show the way. Rose had already moved to the second window when Wals called her over.

"Rose! Come see this."

Scooting over, she pointed at her nametag. "Amy. What'd you find?"

"I think this is the place. See? It looks like Walt's initials are carved under this windowsill."

Rose ran her fingertips over the deep **W E D**. "I think you're right. This must be the window. Did you find anything down here?"

"No, just the initials." Wals ran his beam of light up the sides of the carved window. "Nothing. It might be up on top." He looked around for a moment. "Help me pull one of those tables closer. I can stand on it."

Careful not to scrape the table over the cement floor, it was soon positioned under the window. Wals could now run his hands across the top, a steady rain of dust motes sparkling in the filtered sunlight like pixie dust. "Here. This beam seems to be a little wider than the others. It's about ten or twelve inches long and nailed to the top of the window beam. If you can hand me that screwdriver in my pack, maybe I'll be able to pry it loose."

"How did you get a screwdriver past security?"

His mind on the possibility that this was their answer, Wals gave a dismissive shrug. "I know Laura. She didn't even go through my pack. Did you find it yet?"

"Oh, here it is. Wait, you brought a corkscrew and a can opener, too? What exactly did you expect to find? Champagne and a tin of caviar?"

"Hey, I tried to prepare for any emergency, though that would be nice. Hand it up here."

"Yes, Boss. Is it working?"

A steady shower of brown paint chips was Wals' only answer.

Mumbling, Rose took a step back to shake the paint out of her hair. "I guess that means yes. Need any help?"

"Nope. Got it. Hold the table steady so I can jump down."

Rose looked down at the piece of wood placed in her hands. "Gosh, are you sure you didn't just carve out part of the Chalet?"

"No, no, this has to be it. Everything else up there was smooth. This was the only piece that looked like it was out of place." Wals wiped his dusty hands off on his pants, leaving behind twin streaks of dust.

"Interesting. This is lighter than it looks. It's painted brown like the rest of the wall and window." Fascinated, Rose turned it over to show him. "Except for the back. See? This isn't painted. I think this is an opening. Hand me the screwdriver."

"Yes, Boss."

A faint smile crossed her lips as she gently pried at the slight gap. It took a little more pressure for a hidden latch to flip out. A bronze piece of metal immediately fell out of the hollow interior and clanged onto the hard floor. "Oh, no! Grab it, Wals. Did it break?"

"Hey! It's a Conductor badge from the early days of the Disneyland Railroad. See the design? It isn't used any longer. Wow, these are impossible to find." Eyes wide with excitement, he looked over at the ingenious hiding place. "Is there another clue inside?"

"There's something else rolled up in here. It's bright orange."

Tightly curled up for decades, the material didn't want to lay flat. The collector in Wals instantly recognized it. "That used to fly over the Main Street Train Station. It was the official flag of Disneyland. See how old Mickey is? There aren't many of these left. Nice."

As Wals examined the flag, Rose unrolled the piece of paper that had been hidden within the folds of the flag. A frown came over her face that dampened her enthusiasm. "I don't understand this at all. What does this have to do with Disney?"

Tearing his eyes away from the important historical finds, Wals turned his attention to his partner. "What? What does it say?"

"King George V had trouble with his boilers."

At Wals' blank look, Rose nodded. "Yeah, that's what I thought, too. What in the world does an English king have to do with Walt? I don't know much about the British monarchy, but I know he was somehow related to the reigning queen."

An amused snort suddenly came from Wals as a thought hit him. "Hope that doesn't mean we have to go to Buckingham Palace to search the boiler room for Walt's initials. I don't see that going over very well."

Laughing, Rose started to stuff the discovered items into Wals' backpack. After a confirming nod from Wals, she left behind the hollowed-out beam. "Yeah, your screwdriver and corkscrew would be hard to explain to the Palace guards. I think we're going to have to start doing a lot of research. There has to be a logical explanation. Let's try to get out of here without causing too much fuss. We're not out of the woods yet."

Clipboard back in hand, Wals and Rose descended the concrete steps, apparently in the same argument mode as when they started. It didn't go as smoothly as they had hoped. The two cast members at the kiosks were still busy with customers. However, a guest wearing two full pin lanyards, customized mouse ears, and a Mickey fanny pack stopped them.

"Please tell me the Skyway is going to reopen! Oh, this is so exciting!"

Going into cast member mode, Wals pulled his surprised look into a smile. "Well, hello there. Enjoying your magical day?" He ignored the amused chuckle from Rose behind him.

"Yes, yes, but, tell me the truth. When will it open again? I saw you taking notes. Got a picture, too." The man helpfully held up his elaborate camera. "I run a fan site. Best one on the Internet. Let me give you my card and we can do a full interview. Can I be the first rider?"

Wals cast a leery eye at the telephoto lens on the camera and wondered what exactly he had gotten a picture of. "Well, now, let's not jump to any conclusions. We were just assessing the situation. Rose and I…"

"Amy."

"Amy and I were just looking over the old building for, uh, OSHA requirements…" Wals realized he was starting to babble. "So, I can neither confirm or deny the possibility, uhm, of the Skyway being reopened."

When the camera lifted toward his face, Wals immediately stuck out his hand to the guest. Forced to lower the camera, the guest slowly shook the offered hand, disappointment evident on his face. "So, no scoop?"

"Not right now. But, you can always check back at City Hall for an update."

Realizing he wasn't going to get what he wanted, the guest stepped back with a defeated grunt. "Okay, thanks." With one last, longing look upward at the Chalet, he turned and trudged back into Fantasyland.

A sigh of relief came over Rose and Wals. Turning, they melted into the crowd on the trail behind Big Thunder. After removing the nametags, they simply became two tourists.

Two tourists whose minds were churning to find some connection between the Greatest Storyteller who ever lived and one of the former kings of England.

CHAPTER 11

Flashback—London—1951

"It's right up here, Lillian. 112 High Holborn." Walt's eyes were shining when they reached the large plate-glass window of the Bassett-Lowke Ltd. Shop. He pointed at the words printed above the displays that could be seen through the glass. "See? Model Railroads. Ships. Architecture."

"Oh, so we're getting a ship for the backyard diorama you plowed through my garden? Or are we redecorating the front of the house?"

Reluctantly tearing his gaze from the shiny, colorful, beckoning trains, he could see she was teasing. "Ha, that's a good one, Lil!" His hand went to his chin as if seriously pondering one of her suggestions. "Hmm, though, you know, I might find some ships for my little park."

Used to his distractions, her hand patted his arm that was linked through hers. "Your 'little park' gets bigger and bigger each time you describe it. Now you're going to put in a fleet of model ships?"

"Yes, yes." Eager, not really hearing what she had said, he tugged his wife to the entry door. "I wanted to get here early enough to have time to see everything. Let's go in."

"Yes, let's."

Walt stood in the doorway a moment to take in the well-built, elegant shop before him. In one section, there were counter-to-ceiling, dark wood display cases packed with artfully displayed locomotives and cars. A different, separate section had the boats on

111

display, tanks of water available for testing the prospective pur-
chases. After giving the boats a quick, uninterested glance, his full
attention returned to the sections of track set up for running the locomotives. He took a deep breath to inhale the familiar, heady fragrance of steam, oil, and '*train*.'

"This is going to be wonderful."

Hearing his whisper, Lillian fondly smiled as she pulled a book
from her purse and went to find a comfortable chair. It would not
only be wonderful, it would also be lengthy.

The owner himself came out to help his distinguished customer. After meticulously going through many of the trains that were
on sale, going back and forth on what he actually wanted, Walt decided on the *King George V* locomotive with its sleek, barrel-shaped
engine. Walt made the purchase with the agreement that he would
return later that afternoon to finalize everything and arrange for
shipping it back to the States.

Remembering Lillian had come with him, Walt went to collect
her. "The British Museum Station of the Central London Railway is
just a minute's walk from here. Let's go check that out before lunch
and then we can come back."

Shortly after Walt and Lillian left, another American entered the
shop. This man had come for two purposes. The first resolve was
to buy that same engine he had heard was for sale. And, the second reason, he heard rumors floating around that Walt Disney was
also interested in that locomotive and he wanted to meet Walt.

The shop owner relayed the information that the *King George
V* was sold, but the deal wouldn't be finalized until that afternoon.
Could he possibly return in case the other person changed his
mind?

Returning to Bassett-Lowke Ltd., Walt and Lillian were
promptly greeted by another American who had been patiently waiting for their arrival. Always eager to talk to a fellow train enthusiast,
Walt engaged the man in what turned out to be a lengthy conversation. When asked what he did for a living, Harper told Walt he
was an artist. With a tip of his hat as he was leaving, Walt said to
Harper, "Come talk to me when you get to California."

Harper never did get to buy that *King George V*, but he did become one of Walt's leading designers for the Disney movies. Some
of his many conceptual ideas for Disneyland included Main Street

and the Jungle Cruise.

After a relaxing cruise across the Atlantic and back home to California, Walt returned to find the crate containing the locomotive he had purchased had already been delivered to his house on Carolwood. It had traveled on the same ship as Walt and Lillian, but, unlike its new owner, it had to ride in the cargo hold of the ship for fifteen days, resulting in major salt water damage.

"It's ruined." Dejected, Walt stared at what had been his prize purchase on that holiday in Europe. He pulled on the lever on the front of the barrel engine to open the access door and survey the corrosion inside. The flash of a camera bulb startled him.

"What are you going to do now, Walt?" the photographer asked as he popped out the burning hot, spent bulb.

With a sigh, the engine door was softly shut. "I'm not sure. Think I'll send it to the Studio and work on it there. More resources, you know." With a hand on the back of his neck that ached from a polo injury, Walt looked around his work barn at the back of his house. "I need to get to the Studio anyway. Lots of exciting things happening with my little park. So, are you coming with me?"

Shortly after, the train was relocated to the Studio. There it sat—unrepaired and unused since 1951.

Fullerton—2009

Rose was excited. "We get to go to the Studio. I've always wanted to tour it."

"It's a train." Engrossed in reading the information on the Internet, Wals repeated himself, still unable to believe what their research had revealed. "How come we never heard about this one?"

"If there's an article about it, someone apparently knew enough to write it." Lance was surreptitiously watching Rose on the other side of his office. For too long she had been staring at a black-and-white photo on the wall. Wals' announcement had distracted her, he was glad to see. Hoping to keep the distraction going, Lance walked over behind Wals, still seated at his desk and oblivious to what else was going on in the room.

Thinking the movement behind him was Rose, Wals reached

back with a hand to stroke her arm. It was rather hairier than he had anticipated. "What?"

Lance gave him a wide grin. "I love you, too."

"I didn't… I thought you were Rose."

"I get that a lot."

"Boys." Kimberly had come in with baby Michael. When she, too, saw Rose by the framed picture, she threw a concerned glance at her husband. The slight shake of his head stalled any comment she might have made. Always quick on her feet, her question led in a different direction. "So, what did you find, Wals? Anything important?"

Wals tore his embarrassed, irritated look from Lance's amused face. "I think we need to go to the Studio to look for this forgotten train. But, since it isn't open to the general public, I'm not exactly sure how to accomplish that."

"Surely you know someone who can help." Leaving the fascinating picture, Rose had come to the desk, not knowing why Wals was red-faced. "Anything wrong?"

"No." With one last glare at Lance, Wals indicated the computer screen. "I do know a few people who work at the Studio, but I don't know how to get into any warehouse, or the Archives, or wherever else it might be stored. The backlot and Archives aren't usually part of the tours."

Lance knew he could easily arrange for Wals and Rose to get onto the Studio lot, but he wasn't certain that would be the answer to their problem. "Do you mind if I take a look at the story? Something doesn't add up."

Wals gladly scooted back to give Lance access. "Anything would be a big help right about now.   But it's pretty clear to me that the train went to the Studio."

"Yeah, in 1951," Lance murmured as he started to scroll. "A lot can happen in all that time."

"What are you thinking, Lance?"

He glanced up at his wife who had handed the baby to an eager Rose. Biting back a comment that would definitely have made Wals uncomfortable, he refocused on the clue search. "We know the train did indeed go to the Studio, but when Walt suddenly died in 1966, a lot of things changed and were rearranged. His office, for example, eventually went on display at Disneyland. A fact

I well know since Adam and I had to search both for it and through it."

Rose's eyes lit up. "You had a clue to search through Walt's office? Wow, that must have been exciting."

"Specifically, his desk." Lance recalled that part of their Hidden Mickey quest with a smile. "We ended up behind those glass windows inside the Opera House going through the desk. Thanks to a helpful security guard, we had about fifteen minutes alone in here. I still felt like a monkey on display at the zoo."

"So you think the train might also have been moved somewhere else?"

Lance could only shrug. "I'm running on assumptions here. While this train was important to Walt, you'll notice it's scale was completely wrong for his backyard set-up. It never would have been able to run on his tracks. It also didn't have any significance for Disneyland and the trains running there. The design is too different."

"You don't think the Studio would have kept it?"

"Again, speculation," Lance admitted. He clicked on his computer screen and scrolled to a different article. With a motion to Wals, he pointed at the screen to his new finding. "I think it ended up in Walt's Barn."

"The barn he had in his backyard? But the article said Walt himself sent it from there to the Studio." Rose looked baffled. "And I thought Wals told me that house was torn down years ago."

"Yes, Rose, you're correct. You're thinking of the right barn, but in the wrong place."

Excitement building, Wals fairly shoved Lance out of his chair to read the next article. "I've heard something about this place, but I've never been there." He turned to Rose with a huge grin on his face. "Want to take a road trip to Zoo Drive in Griffith Park?"

"Okay, I'm even more confused. Now we're going to the zoo? I love animals, but I'd rather work on the clue."

Putting his hands behind his head, Wals leaned back in Lance's comfortable chair. "Trust me."

Her eyes narrowed with skepticism at his smug expression. "Okay."

"Wow, that oozed confidence."

"Maybe you should get her some more roses…"

Wals shot Lance an irritated glare when the women burst out laughing. "A little less help from you would be great."

"Just saying."

Trying to stop her giggles, Rose leaned over Wals to see what he had been reading. "Oh! They really did move Walt's barn."

Lance filled some of the missing information. "After Walt died and the house was going to be sold, his daughter arranged to have the barn and a lot of the track moved to Griffith Park to preserve it. She was quite generous with other donations to the site, too."

"Ah, now I get it. But there is one problem that I can see."

"What's that, Rose?"

"It is only open on Sunday from eleven to three. We'll have to wait until the weekend unless you plan on breaking in." She had said it with a laugh, but noticed the others weren't chuckling at her humor. They actually seemed to be considering that as a viable option. "Guys, I was just kidding."

Knowing a little about what Lance and his partner Adam had gone through, Wals was a bit slow on his answer. "No, no, you're right. We'd never do that."

Lance looked sheepish. Kimberly looked vastly amused. And Wals didn't meet her gaze.

"Wals?"

He could hear the challenge in Rose's tone. "I said we'd never do that."

"Listen, helping you get back stage at the Carousel of Progress and looking into the paddle bins at the empty Canoe Dock were one thing... Well, okay, two things... But this is totally different. I'm not at all comfortable with what you're planning."

Wals could see now wasn't the time to kid around any longer. He came to put an arm around her shoulder. "Honey, I was just kidding. I'd never do something like that." Out of the corner of his eye he could see Lance silently whistling to himself while looking away. "Let's just go to the Barn on Sunday and check it out. We'll have four hours to figure out what to do with the train. There might be someone there who'd be able to help us. Maybe Lance and Kimberly can come along, in case we need a diversion or some-thing."

A warm, fuzzy feeling stole over Rose when she heard the en-dearment. They were still new at being a couple and had been tiptoeing around affectionate nicknames. But, not about to let that sidetrack her, Rose took a moment to stare into his eyes to make sure he was telling her the truth. Her hackles settled down. "All right. I believe you. This is all exciting and fun, but I don't want to do anything possibly illegal. Right?"

Again, Wals was a little slow on his reply. "Right. Nothing illegal. Right, Lance?"

With the memory of Adam and him breaking into the darkened warehouse of Disney memorabilia in San Francisco still vividly in mind, Lance's expression became a pleasant mask. "Absolutely. Who would do something like that? Gosh, Wals, I can't believe you would even consider it."

Wals' mouth fell open. "I didn't..."

Kimberly had been quietly feeding Michael on the sofa and now was gently patting his back. When a rather loud, wet burp sounded, Lance interrupted, a proud smile covering his face. "That's my boy!"

Sensing that the unnecessary conflict had been broken, Kimberly turned back to Rose. "So, what would you like to do for two days? There's so much to see in Southern California."

Wals suggested the beach at the same time Lance suggested Knott's Berry Farm.

Kimberly and Rose both said, "Shopping!"

Lance looked over at Wals. "You're going shopping."

"Yeah, I can see that. Hmm, maybe I should go back to work for a couple of days to make sure I have more vacation time."

Lance waved his objection away. "Naw, you're good. You have at least two weeks off."

Wals knew better than to question how Lance would know that bit of information about his work schedule. He still wasn't sure how it all worked, but, being around Lance and Wolf for as long as he had, he knew to take their word at it. After he had gone back in time with Wolf and spent so many years on Tom Sawyer Island, he knew other forces were at work than what he fully comprehended. He hoped someday to ask Wolf for a more satisfactory explanation than he had been given, but the chance had not yet arisen. Wals also knew that, unless Wolf wanted to give him a straight answer, he would never learn the whole truth anyway. Having a time-traveling, security guard wolf for a friend could be challenging, to say the least.

His attention on his son, Lance glanced back at Wals when he heard a resigned chuckle. He was now waved away.

"Never mind. You wouldn't tell me, either."

"Fine. Enjoy shopping. So, are you going to the Citadel or to the South Coast Plaza?"

"Well, from what I can hear your wife telling my girlfriend, probably both."

"More than likely."

On Sunday, the four friends, baby Michael, and an excited Peter, were all strapped into the Brentwood's black Cadillac Escalade, heading north on Interstate 5. It was only a thirty-five-mile drive, but Wals seemed to be having a difficult time in the third-row seat.

"Oh, my word. I've lost the feeling in both my legs! Whose idea was it to put us way back here? Are we there yet?"

Lance adjusted the volume of the classical music playing throughout the car. "What? Sorry, can't hear you way back there, buddy. Enjoying the smooth ride?"

"Why can't I change places with Peter? He has more leg room. He's just the right size for this…this luggage space."

Rose put a calming hand on his arm, since it was right there crammed into her side. "Now, Wals. Peter needs to be behind his mom, next to the baby's car seat. We're fine for the trip. It can't be that far. Can it?"

Despite her efforts, he could still hear the desperation in her voice. "It should be just under an hour. Unless we hit traffic. But, thankfully, it's been smooth sailing so far."

"Wow, Dad! Look at that. All the cars are stopped. Traffic jam! Traffic jam!"

Wals groaned. "Leave it to a five-year-old to be happy about a traffic jam." He thought he could hear Lance chuckling from his comfortable driver's seat. It was confirmed when Kimberly gave him a playful whack on his arm. Amused, Lance's eyes glanced up into his rear-view mirror to stare straight at Wals.

"I knew I should have driven my Z. Who needs their help, anyway?"

"Aww, quit grumbling. You could tell me how much you like my new top and shorts that you've never so much as mentioned."

Eyes wide, Wals caught the subtle warning. Not sure if he was in trouble, he struggled to put an arm around her shoulder. Once that herculean feat was accomplished, he tugged her closer, if that was possible. "You look adorable. That shirt really, uh, brings out the color of your eyes." *There, that ought to be good.*

"My pink eyes? Why, thank you." Rose appreciated the situation enough to chuckle and nestle into his side.

Wals tilted her chin and gave her a kiss. "You do look adorable. Pink eyes or not."

Lance noticed their embrace and resisted the urge to brake harder than necessary. At their close proximity, they might have cracked their skulls. Instead, he reached across to hold Kimberly's hand while he navigated the dense traffic. Knowing her husband, she mouthed, "Good choice."

Walt's Barn was located on the northern edge of Griffith Park. Bordering the 134 Freeway, it was barely two miles from the Disney Studio. Activating the power seat in the second row, Lance held out a hand to assist Rose from her cramped seat. Wals had to fend for himself.

"How about if I drive home, buddy? You can relax in the back."

Lance lifted Peter to his shoulders with a laugh. "I'm six-foot-two. No way in..."

"Lance." Kimberly's warning stopped whatever he was about to say. "Why don't we let Peter run ahead with Wals and Rose. I wanted to ask you something."

Rose held out her hand for the happy Peter. "Come on, little one. I see a cool-looking train over there!"

Once alone, Michael comfortably secured in his stroller, Kimberly continued. "I just wanted to say that I don't think Peter should see whatever it is we'll need to do to find the next clue."

"Why ever not? He's only five."

"Yes, but he's very sharp. He's already seen Uncle Wolf go into that... whirlwind, or whatever you want to call that terrifying thing he does when he goes back in time." She had to pause as a shudder went through her. Her voice lowered even though there was no one around to hear. "He's young and impressionable. I just don't want him to get any ideas about breaking into places or things to find something hidden from Walt."

Lance gave her a supportive hug. "I agree. Maybe you can take him for a ride on Walt's train while we do whatever. He gets enough crazy ideas without us helping him along."

Now reassured that their son would have no involvement in this, or hopefully, any future Hidden Mickey quest, his parents hurried to rejoin Wals, Rose, and Peter.

CHAPTER 12

Walt's Barn—Griffith Park

Lance and Kimberly were about to push the stroller over the third set of narrow-gauge tracks when the warning lights began to flash and the two crossing arms dropped to bar their path.

"Aww, isn't that cute? It's set up just like a real train. Should we just go around it?"

Lance was ready to continue across the tracks when they heard a steam whistle and the unmistakable sound of an approaching train. "I thought they weren't open yet."

Before Kimberly could respond, the whistle sounded again and they heard a familiar, happy yell. "That sounded like Peter."

A green engine pulling the five passenger cars rumbled by, Rose, with Peter held tightly in Wals' arms, waved and smiled from their straddled perches.

"Hi, Mom! I'm riding Walt's train!" Peter let out another whoop that could have doubled for a Lakota war cry, thanks to Uncle Wolf's language lessons. Wals cringed, as most of the yell was aimed straight into his right ear.

Kimberly's lips pulled into a pout as the train rounded a bend to the left and was out of sight. Peter's round trip would take fifteen minutes. "I wanted to ride the train, too. Hey, was that train named the *Dingle Belle*?"

The warning lights dimmed and the crossing arms raised to their upright positions. "Yeah, me, too. Leave it to Peter to find a way to ride before anything is open." Lance suddenly smiled. "Carolyn must be here already. That would explain a lot. I wasn't looking at the engineer. It might have been Scott."

Sharp green eyes appraised her well-liked husband. "Carolyn, is it? I don't remember hearing that name before. Someone I should know about?"

"You'll love her."

They hadn't taken four steps when they heard a high-pitched, happy shriek and a body hurtled into Lance's arms. "Oh, my word! It is you! Lance, you old charmer! We've missed you, buddy."

Lance untangled himself from the five-foot-nothing dynamo who was alternately trying to hug him, see the baby, and shake hands with Kimberly. "You remember my wife, Kimberly? And this is Michael. You already met Peter, I see."

Carolyn stood back from the baby stroller, her blue eyes sparkling. "Oh, I knew that boy was yours the minute I laid eyes on him. Looks like just you, only shorter."

"Well, you would know short, Cary."

Kimberly was appalled. "Lance! That's rude."

Doubled-over laughing, Carolyn wasn't the least bit annoyed. "Oh, that's a good one, String Bean!" She turned to Kimberly, a huge smile threatening to take over her entire face. "Don't you worry, Kimmy. Me and Lance go way back. I had to keep this tall drink of water in line at the Park." With a saucy wink, she tried to poke Kimberly in the ribs with her elbow, but only managed to hit her hip. "You know how he is."

"That I do."

"Hey, I'm right here." Lance couldn't pull off an affronted look. With a fond chuckle, he turned to his wife. "Carolyn here was in charge of the new hires for Security. She may be little but she's mean. We were sorry when she left. Hasn't been the same, Cary."

"Yeah, I miss all you big lugs, too, Lance. Especially Wolf. Why didn't he come with you? But, it was time to leave the Park. You know, sometimes you gotta do what you gotta do."

Lance indicated the park-like setting around them. "This is a good fit for you. Not as strenuous and still a Disney connection."

"Yeah, I don't have to throw a hundred-and-eighty-pound guy over my shoulder here. Well," she paused for effect and then grinned, "not usually." Enjoying the stunned look on the beautiful blonde's face, she turned and waved for them to follow. "Come on and see the sights. Scott'll probably take the train on a bonus trip, so they'll be gone for another fifteen minutes. Then you can tell me what you're looking for."

That earned a raised eyebrow from Kimberly. Lance had to shrug. "I've never been able to put anything past her. She can sniff out a clue in a field of garlic."

Once Rose and Wals, with Peter clamoring for another ride, were back, Carolyn showed them around the red barn that used to be in Walt Disney's back yard on Carolwood Drive. They had about twenty minutes before the gates opened to the public already lined up outside the metal gate.

The barn itself was shaped like any barn found in the Midwest, Walt's old stomping grounds. Dark brick red, trimmed in white, it had an extension reaching out in front with white shuttered windows. A white, multi-holed bird house with a horse and buggy for its weathervane perched on the shingled roof. Along one side of the barn was a covered walkway. Out in front of the double swinging door entry was a train-shaped mailbox.

Inside were a multitude of glass and wood cases that held Walt's personal treasures and all types of train memorabilia dating back decades. Inside the extension was Walt's original electronic switches that had run his railroad. His small bathroom stall had been converted to a broom closet, but his shaving items were in a small plastic box attached outside. One table held a replica of the blue-barreled *C. K. Holliday* train. On the floor was a dynamite canister that used to sit by the Disneyland Railroad. There were pieces of track from Walt's back yard scattered here and there. Pictures and tickets and signage covered all the walls and hung from the ceiling. On one wall was a front panel from the first Monorail. There was even an orange Disneyland flag fluttering overhead just like the one Wals was gifted with his last clue. While the railroad artifacts and the personal links to Walt were fascinating, Wals and Rose kept drifting back to the *King George V* engine set on tracks in the middle of the room.

After a quick glance at the clock, Carolyn came over to the two stragglers. "So, this is where you think you need to look?" At their tight-lipped expression, she gave Wals a light whack on his arm. "You don't need to worry about me, Willis. I've got more secrets in me than the Pentagon. Lance wouldn't have called me if he didn't trust me."

Rose and Wals exchanged a wordless question and came to a silent agreement. "All right. Yes, the clue we got from Walt said this train had a problem with its boiler. We weren't sure if we had to search the whole train and the cars, or just the engine. Or the cab." He ran a hand through his hair. "Or the underside. We just don't know where to look."

Carolyn glanced at the open entry doors. "I don't see any of the docents yet. We'll have to be quick. If we're caught touching the train, there'll be... Well, let's just say that it won't go well for any of us, and I don't want to lose my job."

Wals looked surprised. "You're not one of the tour guides?"

"Naw, I'm here for the trains. Scott and I double as engineers and conductors."

They could hear the pride in her voice. Not everyone qualified to drive the trains. "Well, where would you suggest looking first? Where would be a good place to hide a clue?"

"Are we talking a piece of paper, which could be anywhere?"

After peering into the cab of the dark green engine and seeing no obvious hiding place, Wals had to admit, "We're never sure."

"Well, that doesn't really narrow it down, now does it?"

Wals liked her blunt, straight-forward nature. "No. It's what we've had to face each step of the way. But, Walt always seemed to give us a hint."

"This time he specifically mentioned the boiler. Maybe we could peek inside there?" Rose had been carefully feeling along the attached coal car, but couldn't find anything like a lever or switch to open some secret panel.

Their cohort did one more glimpse at both the clock and the doors. "I'm really not supposed to do this." She shot a glare at Wals. "But, if I don't, I'm sure you'd find a way to open it yourself."

What could he do but shrug?

"Okay, here goes." Carolyn turned the lever on the front of the boiler. The resulted metallic screech had all of them looking back at the door. "Dang, should have used some WD-40 on that. There."

"It's empty."

"Of course, it's empty. Just corrosion, rust, and engine parts. Did you think a piece of paper would have lasted very long in there?"

Wals felt like he was back in grade school getting a lecture.

"Well, we weren't sure what we'd find. Before, the clue's always been sealed inside a plastic container."

Carolyn's eyes went wide. She held her hands out about fifteen inches. "About this long? Gray?"

Rose bit her lower lip and nodded.

"Well, gosh, why didn't you say so before? Of course, it isn't in there. It would have been grabbed years ago."

"You know where the canister is?" Wals wasn't sure if she was messing with him or not. Lance and Kimberly had taken the crying Michael and bored Peter out to look at the lawn. They were probably over exploring the yellow Disneyland Combine car.

"Of course, I know where it is, William." Carolyn went to slap him on the arm again, but he wisely backed out of her reach. "Gosh, I wouldn't be much of a caretaker of the trains if I let just anyone take what they wanted out of the trains, now would I?"

Not sure how to answer that, Rose led her back to their problem. "I think that's the capsule we need to continue our quest. From Walt." She needed Carolyn to understand the importance of their Hidden Mickey search. "We won't be able to continue without the clue that might be inside that container. Would you be willing to give it to us?"

Without an answer, leaving to them to follow or not, Carolyn turned and barreled out the double doors and turned right. Going under the overhang, she led them to a wooden storage box tucked near the back corner. Painted the same brick red, it blended into the sides of the barn. Pulling out of her jumpsuit pocket a massive set of keys, she put a finger on her chin. "Hmm, haven't opened this in a long while. Wonder which key it is."

The sound of a lot of voices chatting on the front lawn could be clearly heard. Knowing their time was limited, a sense of urgency overcame Wals and Rose.

"Rose, go talk to Lance and make sure we're left alone back here. We don't know how long it will take her to find the right key. He's pretty good with diversions if we need one."

"All right. Be right back."

"Found it, Wayne!" Carolyn opened the storage bin and flung back the lid. The self-satisfied grin turned into a frown when she looked back over her shoulder. "Where'd the girl go?"

"She went to cause a diversion in case we needed one."

"Hmph, why'd she do that? I've got it covered." After a moment of pushing aside assorted garden tools and dusty tarps, Carolyn pulled out a familiar-looking piece of plastic. "Odd, it's longer than I remembered. So, Wesley, you think this is it?"

"Yes! Gosh, I could kiss you, Carolyn. We appreciate you keeping it safe for us."

The usual bluster was gone. Carolyn turned as red as the barn. "No need to get all worked up. I knew something was special about that canister when I found it wedged into the boiler. Did you see that photo of Walt with the engine opened?" At Wals' nod, she continued. "Well, that's where it was hidden. Not in the front part I opened for you. I moved it the very first day. I'm just glad the right owners found it. Now, let's cut this mushy stuff and go see Scott. I owe you a train ride, Wilford."

Despite her protests, Wals pulled her in for a hug. "I mean it. Thank you."

"Carolyn, what are you doing back there with one of the guests? They aren't supposed to be near the storage sheds."

Wals heard a snort under her breath. "Docents. I guess we're open for business." Pulling herself to her full height, she said louder, "Yes, Julie, I know that. Thought I saw a rat, yeah, a rat. Had to check it out."

"A rat! Then you need to call pest control."

"Calm down, Julie. Turned out to be a small cat. Harmless." She waved a vague hand toward the back fence where a different engine pulling the flatcars full of guests was just then passing on its way to the mine tunnel. "It went over there. Let's go, Wally. Thanks for your help in chasing it off." She ignored the docent as they hurried over to where Lance and the others waited.

"Hey, what's he carrying? Isn't that part of the display?" Julie, suddenly suspicious, started after them.

After hearing the conversation, Lance suddenly stepped in front of Wals to grab the canister. "You have a display of dirty diapers? Wow, that's odd. I must've missed it inside." He made a motion as if he would open the endcap that was aimed at Julie. "Want to see inside? I can guarantee it won't be pretty."

"No, no! That's fine. My mistake." Hands out in front of her, Julie backed away from the gray container as if it was a bomb about to go off. "Enjoy your day."

"Slick one, Slick. You always could talk your way out of anything." Carolyn slapped her old friend on the behind. "You'd better get that thing out of sight so the rest of them'll forget all about it."

"Good idea. Since they think it's diaper-related, let's just slide it under the stroller for now. Wow, this is bigger than most of the canisters. Oh, and something moved around inside when I waved it at that Julie gal. Hope it holds what you need, Wals."

A bead of sweat was wiped from Wals' forehead. "Yeah, me, too, Lance. I thought we were going to have to hand it over to that woman."

Carolyn harrumphed. "She would've had to go through me first."

Carolyn's husband, Scott, came around the building that housed one of the original Disneyland railroad cars. Taking a break from the trains, he plopped an engineer's cap on Peter's head. "Who's ready for another train ride?"

"Me! Me! Me!" Peter jumped up and down, a hand gripping his new, striped headwear.

Lance shot an amused look over at Scott. "You do know you aren't getting that back, right?"

"Oh." The look on Scott's face fell. "Um, sure, no problem. I have another one in the car."

"You mean *my* cap in the car?"

Scott looked at his wife and a big grin replaced his frown. "Yeah, that would be the other one."

With a laugh, the friends headed over to loading station and joined a large group of tourists also eager to ride. With a whoosh of steam, they were soon traveling over the trestles, through the Disney tunnel, and past a small wooden town and surrounding scenery.

Fullerton

"**W**ow, would you look at that?" Lance let out a low whistle as Wals kept pulling items out of the large canister.

With Michael and Peter both worn out from the exciting excursion and down for a nap, the adults were huddled around the kitchen table.

When something heavy and solid thunked onto the table, Kimberly leaned over to examine it. "What in the world? It looks like a lump of coal."

"Ooh, somebody's been naughty."

Wals tried to ignore Lance. "Must've been Rose. I've been nice."

"Hey!"

"Just sayin', honey."

"Don't honey me! Can I see that, Kimberly?"

"Sure." Kimberly examined her spotless fingertips. "That's odd. If it was coal, wouldn't it have stained my fingers and everything else in there?"

The rough-shaped object was turned over and over as Rose scrutinized it. "I don't know much about coal, but I think it's is too heavy for coal. Lance?"

Lance accepted it. The first thing he did was test the dull finish with his fingernail. "Nope. Not coal. Something slightly better, I'd guess."

Wals looked up from a heavily engraved piece of paper that had been rolled inside. Breathing heavily, his eyes were wide. "What'd you say?"

Lance's gaze narrowed as he watched Wals hand off the ivory sheet to Rose. "I merely said it wasn't coal. What's that?" Using the rock, he indicated the paper. By Rose's expression, which now mirrored Wals', it must have some importance.

"Um, Walt left us something."

"Yes, that's what all of this is. And?" Wordlessly, Rose handed him the certificate. Lance, in turn, casually handed the black rock to Wals. "Here, check this out. I think it might be gold. And, judging from how it felt in my hand, I'd guess maybe fifteen to twenty ounces. Probably closer to twenty."

Wals almost dropped the nugget. "What'd you say?"

Lance didn't look up from the document. "Hmm? Nothing. I just think it's gold, that's all."

Wals turned it over and over in his hands until he came to the spot where Lance had rubbed off the flat, matte paint. His voice had become shaky. "Kimberly, do you by chance have any paint remover?"

"Er, no, not that I know of. How about nail polish remover?"

She didn't wait for his reply and hurried out of the kitchen.

Rose didn't know who to watch, Lance with the certificate, or Wals with the large, possibly, gold nugget. "Lance? Is that what I think it is?"

"If you think it looks like a Disney Stock Certificate dated November 12th, 1957, then, yes, it is." He rechecked one of the lines of elaborate print. "Correction—a Disney Common Stock Certificate."

"Is that date relevant? The way you said it made it sound like it was."

Having once studied to be a lawyer, Lance examined the gold-edged, grandiose writing with a specific eye. "Yes, it was. That was the date Disney Common Stock first hit the Stock Exchange. At $13.88 a share, if I recall correctly. And, this certificate is for fifty shares." He leaned back, eyes closed as he began some mental calculations. "Let's see, fifty-two years, compounded interest, of course, dividends rolled back in, multiply that by… Hmm, not bad, Wals." He handed the stock certificate back to the stunned Wals.

"What…what do you mean not bad?"

"Well, I could be off a bit, but I think that's worth, in today's recessed market, somewhere between $600,00 to $700,000." Ignoring the open-mouthed stares, he indicated the black rock in Wals' hand. "Now, if that is a gold nugget, large nuggets are worth maybe three times spot, so, at today's rate of approximately $335 an ounce, times three, and then times twenty for the weight, it might be worth around $20,000." Hands back behind his head, he smugly smiled at their astonished looks.

Kimberly rushed in with a plastic bottle of polish remover and some cotton balls. "What'd I miss? Anything good?"

"Uncle Walt left them a tidy windfall. There were a lot of papers in there, Wals. Anything else?"

Unable to think, Wals shoved the remaining papers over to where Lance sat. "You look. I don't know if I could comprehend anything else."

"Ooh." Eager to comply, Lance handed one of the folded sheets to his wife. "Here, you check this one." Indicating the other piece of paper still in his hand, Lance remarked, "I think this might be the next clue." After a quick scan, he held it out to Rose. "Nice. Here, Rose. You look like you need to do something with your hands."

"Hands? Yes, thanks." The flushed look on her face receded. Lips dry, her eyes darted over the familiar piece of paper. It looked like it had been ripped out of the same small book as all their other clues. "You're right. It's a clue. My word, there's more to come. How much more…"

"What does it say, Rose?" Kimberly's gentle voice brought Rose back to the present.

"It says, '**Ask for my silhouette. Say "Walt sent me.**"' I think I know where that is, if you have one here at Disneyland." She looked relieved that she was back on familiar ground with a clue in hand. All that money, all that would mean for Wals. And her? How did she fit in at this point? She didn't know what to think of that just yet.

"You're referring to the Silhouette Studio?" At Rose's nod, Kimberly smiled over at Lance. Also thanks to Walt, they had a secret apartment above that very shop. "Yes, it sounds like that's the place to go next."

Lance had unrolled a large sheet of drafting paper. A small sheet held within had fallen to the tabletop. "This is interesting. Goes right along with where we were today."

Wals still seemed unable to talk. Kimberly answered for the pair. "What do you mean?"

Lance flipped around the drafting paper. "This is the schematics to Walt's backyard train layout on Carolwood. He drew it. And, he added a note, which just fell onto the floor." Setting down the drawing, he retrieved the fallen message. "Shall I read it, or do you want to do the honors, Wals?"

He was given the go-ahead with a vague wave.

"All right, if you so insist. It says, obviously referring to the blackened nugget you're still grasping, and I quote, 'You might think this lump of coal could fuel my trains. But, instead, I think you'll find that it can really fuel your dreams! Walt.' He always was generous." Lance reached over to take Kimberly's hand while he continued speaking to Rose and Wals. "Did you know he had this house built for Kimberly's dad who was his behind-the-scenes right-hand man?"

"Wals?" Kimberly waited until he looked up at her. "Do you have a safe deposit box at the bank?"

At the sound of something practical, Wals came around. "Box? Oh, yes, I do. All the papers from my parent's trust are still in there." He ran a finger over the gold curlicues on the certificate. "Yeah, that's a good idea. They need to be put away until Rose and I can deal with them. Did you find another clue?" He couldn't understand why everyone snickered.

Rose put a hand on his shoulder. "Yes, we did. We need to go to the Silhouette Studio. Do you know where that is?"

"You figured it out that quickly? I'm impressed."

"Yeah, I'm highly intelligent, you know. Are you all right?"

He ran a shaky hand over his face. "I will be. Just a lot to take in all at once. Wow." He shook his head as if to clear it, a frown on his face as he looked over at Lance. "What do you have there?"

"Oh, Wals! You're a basket."

He didn't know why Rose collapsed against him laughing. But, having her in his arms, he didn't care.

CHAPTER 13

Disneyland

Arm in arm, happy to be in each other's company, Wals and Rose slowly strolled up Main Street, taking in the sights and sounds of the busy street. A warm, sunny, spring day, Main Street was full of eager guests heading to their own special destinations. Bright petunias hung from the vintage street lamps, their pink and white blooms spilling over the sides of moss-filled baskets. As Wals and Rose crossed the Center Street intersection, the sounds of ragtime piano drifted down from Refreshment Corner across from the Hub.

"This never gets old, does it?"

Wals didn't even have to ask what she meant. He knew. No matter how long he worked at the Park, no matter how many times he visited as a guest with friends, it never became stale. As well as he knew the Park, he could close his eyes, walk down any path, and know exactly where he was and what he would see when he opened his eyes. But, it didn't matter. It was still fresh and exciting. Whenever the seasons would change, the crowds would change, subtle decorations would change, and perhaps something new was added. The Park would announce new parades, new flowers and plants would be updated to match, new shows would fill the theaters, new cast members would add to the mix, and there might be something he somehow missed seeing in all those years. Even his preferred Rivers of America in Frontierland would regularly change. The trees got taller and fuller as they matured. Some fell due to age or thinning. New scenes were added along the banks. Major changes were made to the Island when new theming was publicized. But none of that mattered to Wals. It all still felt familiar, comfortable, and even reassuring, somehow.

He inhaled the scent of vanilla being piped from the Candy Kitchen. "Nope."

"Even though I haven't worked at the Magic Kingdom as long as you've worked here, I still get a thrill walking down our Main Street. Our *bigger* Main Street."

Wals didn't take her bait. *Ours has more charm.* "Let's sit up here for a minute and strategize."

Almost to Central Plaza, there was one empty building next to the Silhouette Shop. It had the only porch on Main Street. A popular spot for relaxing or people-watching, it boasted one of the best views of the parades. Lacy curtains covered the windows, blocking the view of the interior. The wooden chairs on the porch were occupied, but the bench in the corner behind the white railing was available.

Rose first tried to peer behind the curtains. "What's in here?"

Wals had to think. "I believe it is just lockers now. Haven't been in there. Did you know this shop used to be called the Wizard of Bras?"

"Surely that's not what they sold."

"Yep. And you could also buy a piano in Town Square."

The idea made Rose chuckle. "Well, I certainly hope whoever bought one didn't have to lug it around with them all day."

"Yeah. That store didn't last too long. I can't imagine some Mom saying, 'You know, I think we need a grand piano for the front room. Let's go to Disneyland and buy one.'"

The horse-drawn streetcar clanged its bell as the Belgium horse slowly clopped along the tracks in the street. Rose returned the wave of a happy child. "So, what's our plan, Boss?"

"You know, in all the years I've been coming here, I've never been inside the Silhouette Studio."

"Hmm, I can't say I've seen ours, either. Sounds like it may be a great souvenir."

"We could have ours done while we're here."

His suggestion brought Rose's natural shyness to the surface. "One for each of us?"

An arm already around her shoulders, he tugged her a little closer. "I was thinking as a couple."

"I'd like that." A soft, appealing blush stole up her cheeks.

"Then, it's a date." When her lips curled into an amused smile, he added, "Well, you know what I mean." Clearing his throat, he got back to the matter of the treasure hunt and lowered his voice. "I think we should first check out the shop, have our silhouette made, and then try out the password on the cast member at the cash register. We know what to say. We just don't know what to do after we say it."

"If we draw a blank, do we have to go back to square one and rethink this?"

Wals had to nod. "It seems pretty straight forward, but, it has been a long time since Walt placed the clue. I'm just glad the shop is still there in the same place."

"Well, let's give it a whirl."

The Silhouette Studio had opened on Main Street in January of 1956. One of the only places in Disneyland encouraged to look messy, tiny scraps of paper littered the floor. Continuing Main Street's theme of turn of the century, the walls were covered with beige-on-pink textured wallpaper and a lush carpet of dark maroon highlighted with gold flowers covered the floor. Wooden frames held a large beveled mirror and examples of the work of the artists. The large plate glass window out front with its cheery display of silhouettes and flowers was separated from the interior of the shop by a low brass rod covered with a short, dark green drape. To the side stood a dark mahogany, old-fashioned dresser holding an album of designs. In the back, just past the cash register's nook, they could see a large passage into the other shops.

"These are so cute!" Rose took a moment to look over the oval-framed cuttings on the wall. As many as there were, she didn't see any that looked like Walt Disney. Mickey Mouse was there, but not his boss.

While she looked around, Wals made arrangements to have their portrait done. Calling Rose over, Francine asked her to sit in the wooden chair that faced the front window. "You're first."

As she sat, not sure of what she was supposed to do, she began to fiddle with smoothing down her top and deciding where to drop her purse. "How long does this take?"

"You're done." Francine never got tired of the expression of disbelief that came over her customer's faces. "You're next." She motioned for Wals to take the chair.

Amazed, Rose slowly stood from the chair. "But, I was only here for a minute."

Francine held up her silhouette. "I was already done, but you were fiddling with your top."

Wals took his place and held still for the twenty-five seconds it took for his portrait.

Rose's head shook slowly back and forth as she watched her speed and efficiency as Wals' profile emerged from the paper. "That's amazing. Thank you."

"My pleasure. Now, if you would like it framed, please see Diane."

While Diane, a younger cast member, worked on centering their portraits, Wals thought it was as good a time as any. "Can I get Walt's silhouette?"

Not looking up, Diane figured he must have talking to his girl-friend. As she attached the backing, Wals repeated himself. Surprised, she realized he was speaking to her. "I'm sorry. I thought you were talking to someone else. Who do you mean?"

His heart fell once he recognized the blank expression on her face. She wasn't the one. "I…I meant Walt Disney. Walt sent me."

Baffled, Diane looked over to Francine for help. Her cast member training kept her pleasant smile plastered on her face, but she had no idea what this man was talking about. Her relief was evident when Francine got out of her chair, rather hurriedly, she noticed, and joined them in the back of the shop.

"I didn't mean to listen in, but it is a rather small shop." Eyes wide, eager, Francine looked back and forth from Wals to Rose. "What was it you asked?"

A glimmer of hope spread through Wals. This older woman tightly clutched her scissors to her chest as she stared at him, almost breathless as she waited for his response. "I asked for Walt's silhouette."

That wasn't what she needed to hear. Her shoulders visibly sagged with disappointment. "I'm afraid we don't sell his likeness."

Not yet wanting to give up, he had to try again. "Walt sent me."

The change was immediate. A smile transformed Francine's face into delight. She nodded once, made a move to leave, and then realized she was still holding her scissors. Turning, she handed them to a still-confused Diane. "Would you please put these back at my station? I need to get something from the back."

Diane looked over at the two steps it would take to return the item. "All right..."

Francine didn't waste any time to explain her odd request or what had just happened. She hurried out of sight to their storeroom.

Wals and Rose exchanged a look of possible victory while they waited. Diane took the opportunity to ring up their sale and wrap their silhouette. Francine still wasn't back when she was done. Not sure if she should make small talk or pretend to work on something so she wouldn't have to, Diane opted to dust the pictures on the wall. The two guests didn't seem to notice. When a family came into the shop, Diane rushed over to help them make a selection.

Her face flushed, Francine burst back into the shop. Knuckles white, her hands gripped a small, dusty package. When she realized there were other customers in the shop, her lips clamped shut and she made a subtle motion for Wals to wait a moment.

"Good thing she works so fast," Wals whispered to Rose. "She took the package with her. I'm so excited I almost grabbed it from her hands."

"We've waited this long. I think she wants to talk to us."

Wals made a face. "Yeah, I guess it would be rude to grab it and run."

That earned a chuckle. "Yes, it would. She's probably guarded it for years."

"Shh, the other family is coming over."

The shop was so small that the eight people filled it. Wals and Rose had to shift to the front so the family could get to the back for framing. That put them next to Francine again, which was agreeable to all.

Francine lifted the package off the small table next to her chair. A moment was spent carefully wiping off the dust, as if she was reluctant to let it go. "Did you know Walt hired me himself?"

Rose sank into the wooden chair, already fascinated. "Did he really? You knew him?"

The older woman smiled, her eyes focused on a time long ago. "Oh, yes. He would visit in here now and then. We did portraits of his girls. Then, later, he brought in his grandchildren for their portraits. He was always so kind." Her glance dropped to the package in her lap. "Do you know what this is?"

Wals and Rose could only shake their heads no.

"It is his portrait. He had me do it on a day much like this one." She looked out of the front window, seeing another spring day, other people walking by. "He was older then, having some health problems. Not that he ever complained. Just rumors that went around. But, some of us, we knew."

"How long have you worked here?"

Her eyes turned to Wals, and she refocused. "Oh, since 1962. I was just eighteen then! Didn't know much about silhouettes, but I picked it up pretty quickly. Always was pretty creative. Gosh, I've done thousands of them. It was in 1965, I remember now, when Walt came in."

"Did he say anything about this one? Why it was special to him?"

"No." Francine frowned as she thought back. "No, he didn't. Once it was framed, he asked for a pen and wrote something on the back before I could finish it. It was then he told me to hold on to it until someone asked for it. Just as you asked for it today."

Wals felt his heart speed up. "What did he write?"

"I have no idea! He sealed up the back himself and wrapped it just as you see it. I then put it somewhere where I could keep an eye on it and I knew it'd be safe."

"It's been over forty years. Wow. You must have been curious at some point."

Francine smiled at the way Rose hung on her every word. "Oh, of course I was curious. But, I wasn't told to read it. Just hold it until someone came for it. We all would have done anything Walt asked of us. And he told me to guard it. So, I did. And, now, here you are."

With an understanding smile on his face, Wals held out a hand. Francine still hadn't handed over the treasure. "Are you ready to let it go?"

She gave the package one final pat. "Yes. Now I don't have to worry about it any longer. Whatever it is, remember the man who put it there. He was one of the greats."

"Yes, ma'am. We will."

Rose went to hug the older woman. "Thank you for holding

this for us. Walt would have been so proud of you."

Their eyes filled with tears and Wals gently tugged on Rose so they could leave the shop. "We need to go, honey."

"I know." After one last hug, she wiped her eyes and waved to Francine as they passed the window that looked into the shop.

"**W**ow, all those years and she didn't even peek to see what was written on it."

"I know!" Still emotional, Rose let out a shaky sigh. "I don't know if I could've done that. I would have been too curious."

"Even if Walt himself asked you?"

Waving her fingers in front of her eyes to cool the redness, Rose blinked a few times. "Well, that would make the difference, I guess. She sounded pretty devoted to him."

They had taken a seat in the shady Hub. Wals gazed up at the bronze statue of Walt and Mickey. "Most who knew him personally were." He had to bite his tongue when he almost added Wolf's name to the discussion. Wolf's history with his boss was his story to tell.

"Like that picture in Lance's office."

Wals' mouth went dry as his head snapped round to face her. "Picture?"

"You've never seen it?" Rose looked amazed. "It's right there on the wall!"

"Uhm, maybe I was too busy at the computer?"

"There are three men in the photograph: Walt, Wolf's father, and a man who *really* looks like Kimberly. I figured he had to be her dad."

"Wolf's father?"

Rose shrugged as she watched the Omnibus pull into its parking spot near the entrance to Tomorrowland. "Well, they look so much alike I'm sure it has to be his dad." She gave a light laugh. "It couldn't possibly be Wolf, right?"

As if he had been called, Wolf appeared next to them. "What couldn't possibly be me? Hey, Wals. Lance told me you were…in the Park today."

From the security guard's hesitation, Wals understood Wolf knew their clue search was still ongoing.

Rose looked delighted to see him. "Wolf! We were just talking about you."

"All good, I hope."

Even though they seemed to be casually chatting, she noticed Wolf's eyes never stopped moving as he watched the crowd ebb and flow around them. *Just like Rob.* "Of course, all good. I was just commenting on your father's picture in Lance's office."

Wolf's sharp blue eyes widened as they turned briefly to Wals who quickly lifted one shoulder in a shrug. "My father?" Wolf pictured his father, the Shaman, as he stood on the Rivers of America surrounded by his braves. His answer seemed to be carefully worded. "I didn't know Lance added another picture to his wall."

Rose lightly slapped his arm. "No, silly. The one with Walt and, I'm assuming, Kimberly's father—even though Wals still hasn't answered me on that."

"Oh. That picture. Right. I have a call. Hold on." Wolf grabbed his walkie-talkie out of his belt and put it to his ear. "Sorry. Have to run." Without another word, Wolf turned and melted into the crowd heading into the Castle.

"That was odd. I didn't hear the walkie-talkie beep or anything."

Wals wondered if the expression he had plastered on his face looked innocent or guilty. "Well, you know Wolf. Always busy."

Rose's eyes narrowed. She was starting to realize none of her questions had been answered.

To divert her attention, Wals held up the still-wrapped package from the Silhouette Studio. "Shall we open it and see what we find?"

"Yes, let's." With a resigned sigh, she knew there would be no answers right then. She made a mental note to examine that picture once they got back to the Brentwood's later that night.

Wals looked around the Hub. It was one of the busiest places in Disneyland. With its statue of Walt, a full, picture-perfect view of the Castle, and entries into each of the other lands, guests were everywhere. "Maybe this isn't the best place to open it."

"What do you suggest?"

Her words had come out a little too sharp, causing him to glance into her face. If she had been holding his roses, he was sure two or three of them would have been handed off by now. "How about lunch at the Hungry Bear Restaurant? We can find a quiet table overlooking the River. Great view of the *Mark Twain* and Tom Sawyer Island. And the Canoes, if they're running today."

"That sounds good."

"Did I tell you how cute you look today?"

She had to laugh at that, succeeding in breaking the mood she had created. "Thank you." Not wanting to spend the rest of their day in a pique, she wove her arm through his as they headed for the fort entry of Frontierland. "I was hoping you'd notice. I got this at the Citadel."

Wals had been with her the entire two excruciatingly long days they had spent shopping. He couldn't recall one item she had bought. "Oh, yes, I remember. Looks great."

"Liar."

"No, really. It does look great."

She gave his arm a good-natured punch. "No, I mean you have no idea this is one of the outfits I bought."

"Are you mentally handing away some of my roses?"

Her tinkly laugh drew the admiring attention of two men walking by. Wals tugged her closer. "Yes, and you don't have many left."

"Rats. I thought I was doing so well."

"So, tell me, does this place where you're dragging me have funnel cake?"

Walking along the edge of the River, the *Mark Twain's* whistle sounding in the background. Wals glanced over as the glistening white ship was being loaded. "I think so."

"Then, you're doing fine. The last of the roses are safe."

He patted her hand. "Good to hear."

The Hungry Bear Restaurant was located near the back of Critter Country. The exit of Splash Mountain and the Many Adventures of Winnie the Pooh claimed the far corners of their Land. Just past the canoe dock, its two-story wooden structure held a huge number of tables and chairs for hungry diners.

"Up or down?"

Rose took a moment to watch the flow of traffic. "Most seem to be going downstairs. Let's stay up here."

Wals carried their tray to a table at the far end of the deck. As Rose looked over the edge of the railing, she could see moored not only two large canoes that guests would paddle, but two smaller ones, as well.

"What are those little canoes for?"

Remembering that one of those small utility canoes had taken Wolf and him into the swirling vortex the security guard had created to take them into the past, Wals had to put a tight rein on his memories. It had been terrifying—especially when Wolf had fallen out the back and a wolf suddenly appeared swimming in the maelstrom next to the canoe. He cleared his dry throat. "Oh, just canoes to get cast members to and from the Island if they're needed. Maintenance uses them. Security." Palms sweating, he took a long drink of his cola.

"Nice to know they're there." When his head shot up, she wondered why his eyes were wide. "You know, in case our next clue search takes us somewhere on the River."

Calm down, Wals. She doesn't know. "Right. Right. Yes, they do come in handy. Fries?"

"Yea, thanks." As she munched, she silently wondered what it was she didn't know.

The *Mark Twain* caught up to their location. Rose stopped eating her burger to watch it slowly chug by. "You haven't taken me on that yet." She leaned forward to see better. "Is there someone in there with the pilot? They don't look like cast members."

Wals didn't even glance over. "Yeah, probably. They allow passengers to ride in the wheelhouse, steer and ring the bell and such. It's pretty popular."

"Hmm, I don't know if our *Liberty Belle* does that."

"One up for me."

She laughed. "I said I wasn't sure. That doesn't mean they don't allow it. Can we do that?"

"Ride in the wheelhouse?" At her eager nod, he shrugged. "I don't see why not. Maybe after we eat and find out what our next clue says."

After the last bite of the strawberry-covered funnel cake was devoured and their table had been cleared, Rose scooted her chair closer to Wals. More of the other diners had departed, so their quiet corner was all their own.

"Shall we?"

Wals wiped the last of the whipped cream off on a napkin. He let out a grunt when his fingers remained sticky. "I don't want to touch the silhouette. I'll go wash my hands. You go ahead and unwrap it."

"You sure? I can wait for you."

"No, no, go ahead. I'll just be a minute."

Before he was even out of sight, Rose slid a fingernail under the yellowed tape holding the package shut. Fragile with age, she was amazed it still stuck at all. The edges of the plain brown wrapping paper were peeled back to reveal ivory-colored tissue that protected the oval frame. "The frame looks just like ours. Wow, that is Walt."

Wals slipped back into his seat. A pleased smile crossed his lips as he looked at the portrait. "Yep, that can't be anyone else." He titled his face toward Rose. "Just think. This is the only silhouette of Walt in existence."

"I didn't think of that. You might be right. This is a treasure in itself." Her fingernail hovered over the seam of the backing that hid their next clue. "I don't know if I want to ruin it. It's been like this for over forty years."

"I know what you mean. But, remember, Walt wanted it to be found. He wanted this treasure hunt to continue." Wals stopped for a minute to let his point sink in—for both of their benefits. "If we want to keep going, we have to open it. I don't think it'll ruin the portrait. Only the backing."

"I hope you're right." After a brief moment, she started to slide her nail up from the bottom. The glue, as old as the tape had been, easily gave way. Halfway up the side, she stopped. "Maybe that's enough. Can you see inside to read it?"

Always prepared, Wals tugged his backpack over from where it rested on the deck. Unzipping the largest pocket, he gently moved aside their wrapped portrait and reached to the bottom. "Here, use this."

"My friend the flashlight. I should've known you'd bring it again." After a quick glance to make sure they were still unobserved, she flashed the light into the small opening she had made. "That looks like the same writing as on the other clues. I think I can make it out, not that it makes much sense to me. Again," she added with a light laugh.

"What does it say?"

Rose glanced up. "You're about to rip it out of my hands, aren't you?"

Already behind her looking over her shoulder, he planted a kiss on the exposed skin beneath her ear. "No, I'm not." At her smirk, he shrugged. "Yes, I am. What does it say?"

"**Mike Fink thought it was the best seat on the River**."

"And...?"

"No, that's all it says. Really." She offered him the flashlight, which he waved away as he sat back down.

"No, no, I believe you. It's just..." He paused to look out over the River to the far bend that swept to the right. "If it means what I think it means, we're in trouble. That ride's been gone since 1997."

"The Keelboats, right? We had Mike Fink Keelboats, too. That's the same year ours closed."

Wals didn't hear her. He was trying to recall the history of what happened next. "I remember one of the boats going to auction, the *Bertha Mae*, I think. Someone bought it for $15,000." He looked out over the water. "The other one is out there somewhere."

"Out on the River? What do you mean?"

Wals indicated the forgotten silhouette. "First, why don't you wrap that up and put it into the backpack." He noticed her hesitation. "Or did you have something else in mind?"

Rose's teeth caught her lower lip. "I wanted to take Walt's picture back to show Francine. I thought she might like to see it again."

Pushing aside his eagerness to continue the treasure hunt, he gave her a fond smile. "I think she'd like that." He also anticipated more tears and hugs before he could get back to Frontierland.

He was right.

Chapter 14

Disneyland

Learning they would have to wait over two hours before Rose could experience riding inside the wheelhouse, they decided to just embark along with everyone else.

"My, that wheelhouse thing is popular," Rose commented as they leaned onto the second deck's wooden railing. "I'll have to check it out when I get home. It'd be a blast to steer and ring the bell all the way around."

An unexpected pang jolted through Wals when she mentioned going home. The realization that it had to happen at some point was there, but he wasn't ready just yet. Moving closer, he slid an arm around her slender waist. "Having fun?"

She could hear something wistful in the tone of his voice. Since he hadn't accidently spoken his thoughts aloud for a while, she wasn't exactly sure what was wrong. As the boat slid away from the dock, she snuggled closer. "Yes, I am. This treasure hunt is terribly exciting. And, then, well, there's, you know, you."

"Me?"

"Yeah, well, you're kinda terribly exciting, too."

Comfortably silent with each other, gazing at the scenery slowly slipping by, they listened to the spiel. The ledge man was calling out the depth of the River. "By the mark. Mark one! Mark twain! Half-twain. Mark three. Mark four. Deep four. Ocean Deep." As New Orleans Square drifted past, they could, in turn, see crowds of people in line for Pirates of the Caribbean and the Haunted Mansion, a log plummeting down Splash Mountain and the wet riders' boat ultimately making the bend that extended into the River. Always present on the right, Tom Sawyer Island, all brown and green, had hordes of children running every which way, and Fort Wilderness, tall and silent, nestled in the middle of a thick stand of trees.

"I think the *Gullywhumper* is on the other side of the Island. We'll just have to enjoy the cruise."

Rose let out a contented sigh. "I'll do my best."

The Friendly Village was now off to their left, the Shaman telling his braves the story of how the flute came to their people. Wals bit his lip as his mind's eye brought back the friends he had made in that village, the *real* village, a long time ago in the past. Wolf's older brother Mato, seated there in the middle, had helped Wals, facing a terrifying trip first into this future, and then into the far past to rescue Wolf. Not knowing much, *all right, any*, Lakota Sioux, Wals had a difficult time convincing Mato, and their father the Shaman, what was wrong with Wolf and why he needed help. Wals lips curled into a grin when he remembered Mato riding Splash Mountain with Peter before he opened the final vortex in the Frontierland River to go back home with the injured Wolf. The grin vanished when the unbidden thoughts of the other Rose, Princess Aurora, danced through his thoughts. He had been devastated when she told him Prince Phillip had come back to claim her. Lost and alone, Wals had traveled back with Wolf and Mato to their village. But the dark brown eyes of one of the maidens hadn't held the answer for him.

Rounding the corner of the Island, heading back toward the dock, he now realized it was amber eyes that had truly captured his attention, his thoughts, and, possibly, his future. He glanced down at the slight figure in his arms and wondered when she had moved in front of him so he could hug her and rest his chin on the top of her head. Her body language, her stance was relaxed, not worried about his silence or moodiness. That moodiness, too, would pass.

"Is that it?"

Her soft voice broke through his thoughts. It took a moment to recall what it was they were here to see. The *Gullywhumper* rode too low in the water, dead leaves and twigs littered her deck. The paint looked gray and chipped, and the shutters of the three windows hung at precarious angles. Bruce the Moose stood knee-deep in the water nearby, slowly chewing on a succulent water plant, unconcerned that the once-popular watercraft was on its last leg.

"Yeah, that's her. Poor thing."

"Gosh, do you think that's going to support our weight when we search for the clue?"

Wals let out a low whistle. "Good question. I think we'd better do some research to narrow down our search areas. The less time onboard the better. I can see so many things going wrong."

The *Mark Twain*'s dock was just up ahead, signaling that their voyage was almost over. A marmot whistled across the River as it poked its head out of the old, abandoned Mine Train car. "What do you have in mind?"

"I don't know," he acknowledged. "Somebody I know must know about the keelboats. I'll just have to ask around."

"Would Lance?"

Wals had to laugh. "Probably. Lance knows everyone. And everyone knows Lance."

"Well, that sounds like our starting point. Did you want to go back to the Brentwood's now or spend more time in the Park?" Rose wouldn't have minded going back the Fullerton house right away. She was anxious to take another look at that intriguing picture hanging in Lance's office.

As the *Mark Twain* docked and the exit gate swung back, Wals and Rose joined the other guests as they slowly worked their way down the stairs to the lowest deck. The *swish, swish, swish* of the huge paddlewheel still churning the water could be heard over the soft chatter of guests planning what to do next.

"I wouldn't mind heading back to Lance's house, if you don't. It feels like we have some momentum going and I'd like to keep it."

Rose smiled up at him. "That's fine with me. Let's find out what Walt has in store for us next."

"**W**hat do you mean Adam and Beth have their own keelboat? Really? How'd that happen? There were only two of them."

Lance enjoyed delivering startling news. Arms behind his head, he lounged back in his leather chair, feet perched comfortably on his massive desk. One eye on Rose who was back at the picture on the wall, he gave Wals the explanation. "Adam found the blue-prints online and built it for Beth. Their version of the *Bertha Mae* is happily floating on a rather large river he dredged out of his back-yard." He had one more tidbit to share. "It even runs."

That information brought Rose over to Wals' side. "You're kid-ding."

"Nope. The engine works, the microphone works, and even the delightful banjo-pickin' music works."

"Oh, I have to see this. Can we, Wals?"

Wals knew he'd never be able to say no to that adorable, pleading look in her eyes. "Yeah, okay, I'm intrigued, too. I just don't know them very well. Do you think they'd allow us to come and examine their boat?"

Lance had no problem answering for his friends. "They'd be delighted. Especially since they both had experience with the Hid-den Mickey quests." Lance paused as if a new thought had just occurred. "We just never figured a keelboat would be part of one of the searches."

That last statement hit Rose as odd. It sounded as if Lance expected more to come. How could he possibly know about any future quests? Before she could ask anything, Wals was talking.

"Would you give them a call to properly introduce us? I know we've met briefly at your parties, and I've seen Beth now and then on Pirates, but I don't want to just show up at their door asking to drive their keelboat."

Lance made a face. That was exactly what he had hoped would happen. "Fine." With a resigned sigh, he pushed away from his desk and picked up the phone. Within a few minutes the arrangements had been made for the next day. "Beth," he an-nounced, "as I had previously said, would be delighted to show off her boat to fellow questers. Oh, before I forget. There's one other thing you should know. The *Gullywhumper* is slated to be removed from the River and refurbished. It's going to be remade to look like the keelboats from the Davy Crockett movie."

Wals felt his mouth fall open. "When is that?"

Rose asked at the same time, "How do you know that?"

Wals was answered. "Soon. Within a week or so, if my infor-mation is correct, which it usually is. So, whatever you need to get done, get it done quickly."

Noticing Rose was about to ask her question again, Kimberly distracted all of them by handing Lance their youngest son to be changed. After blowing bubbles into the happy baby's stomach, Lance caught a whiff. "Oh, you meant now. Gotcha. Come on, Mikey. Let's go tease your brother with a dirty diaper."

"Lance."

"Fine. Let's get you changed, Little Man. Mommy's no fun, is she? No, she's not. Daddy is so much fun! Can you say Daddy? Who's a big boy?"

Rose was laughing by the time Lance finally got Michael to the nursery. "I'm the youngest. I can imagine that's pretty much how it was in our house."

Taking advantage of the break, Kimberly had her feet up on the small table in front of the sofa. "Do you miss your family?"

Wals' ears perked up as he awaited her answer, his heart suddenly beating faster in his chest.

"Oh, sure. We're close, but not quite joined at the hip. I'm closest to my older brother Rob. The one you met, Wals."

As if I needed to be reminded of him. "Yes, I recall the name."

"Hmmph, I'm sure you do." She turned back to Kimberly with a huge grin. "Rob is rather protective of me. He was pretty suspicious of Wals at first. But, they worked it out. I'm sure they'll be great friends."

Wals wisely kept silent.

Yorba Linda

The Michaels' spacious house was built in the foothills with a wonderful view of the valley. Adam, a General Contractor, had built the two-story house himself with a certain feisty brunette in mind. After getting her fired from her dream job as the only female keelboat pilot, he felt he needed to make it right after their five-year estrangement. Her engagement present, the *Bertha Mae*, had been bobbing in the water when she saw the house for the first time.

Listening to Beth's story, Rose was close to tears. "And what did you do when you first saw the boat?"

"You mean after I went running down the hill as fast as I could, laughing, crying, and screaming all the way?"

Rose eagerly nodded.

Beth, their three-year-old twins asleep on the sofa next to her, threw a loving look across the living room to Adam. Their huge Golden Retriever, Sunnee, sitting on his feet, also gave him an adoring look. "We climbed up to the roof and sat knee-to-knee, just as the guests used sit, and he proposed."

"Aww."

"Yeah, then I throttled her up and we went for a cruise around the island."

"She always leaves out the part that it all started with a moose."

Not sure if Adam's words were meant for him, Wals took a moment to examine the animation cels that hung over the fireplace. He knew the women would take an inordinate amount of time reliving every moment of that special day, so he had some leisure. The largest of the eight cels was Snow White holding up a dainty finger on which perched a small bluebird. The seven dwarfs were all represented as individual head shots. Dopey held diamonds in front of his eyes, giving him a myriad of eyeballs.

Adam came up next to Wals. "Exquisite, aren't they? They were gifts from Walt in our Hidden Mickey quest. We pulled them out of Walt's office desk. Lance got two larger background cels, one for Snow White here, and one for Pinocchio. I had my set mounted behind special, light-filtering glass when I had them framed."

Now Wals had more information to fit into the partial story Lance had told him. "Ah, yes. That was after you had gone to the Studio in Burbank looking for Walt's office."

Adam gave a brief nod, smiling as he thought back. "Yeah, when we were told the office was long-gone and they wanted to call in Walt's nephew, Roy, to meet us, we lit out of there in a hurry!"

"Yeah, I'd find it hard to share what we have found, too." Wals knew exactly what Adam meant. "How would we be able to explain why we had something signed by Walt that no one else had ever seen and that we had to go places not usually accessed by...well, anyone?"

"Well, having the original introductory letter from Walt helped. It made it pretty clear whatever was found belonged to the finder." Adam noticed a confused look on Wals' face. "Did your letter say something different?"

"No. I didn't get any letter like that with the first clue. Just a container that Lance and Wolf handed to me."

"That's odd. But, then, I didn't even know there was another quest. Doesn't mean they all have to be alike." Adam looked out the front window at their wide, green, front yard. "You know, maybe your first clue wasn't really the first clue. The introduction might be lost somewhere along the line, or is still out there."

"That makes sense. I wonder if I should ask Wolf about it." Adam looked from his host back at the animation cels.

"If you think you need it, you might have to. It appears Lance isn't forthcoming with any extra help for you."

"Which isn't too surprising to anyone who knows him."

Adam had to laugh, drawing the attention of the two women, still deep in their discussion. "Truer words have never been spoken."

"Who are you talking about, honey?"

Adam turned to his wife, a hand resting on Sunnee's broad head. "Lance and his unwillingness to offer help without a long song-and-dance."

"Yep. That's our boy."

Rose almost couldn't contain her curiosity. "So, can we please go out and see the *Bertha Mae*? I'm dying to look her over!"

First, they checked on the twins, Alex and Catie. Still deep asleep, the parents knew they'd have about half an hour. So, glasses of wine in hand, the two couples headed out back to follow the flagstone path that ambled down to their picturesque, manmade river. Tied bow and stern, the light-blue keelboat was secured to a wooden dock.

"Wow, if I didn't know any better, I'd swear we were standing at the dock in Frontierland. You didn't miss one detail."

Adam appreciated Wals' praise. "A labor of love, that's for sure."

"And one of the things that's *really* nice," Beth stressed, "is that I don't have to push the nose out into the River to start the trip. I used to get heckled by the men all the time—until I showed them over and over that I could do it."

"You really loved your job, didn't you? I can tell by the way you describe it. I haven't got that excited working the Dinosaur ride yet."

Beth smiled over at Rose. "You know, I think a big part of it was getting to spiel and having fun with the guests that made it extra enjoyable. There was an interaction you don't get with most rides. Climb up on top and I'll show off for a minute or two."

Adam, Rose, and Wals climbed up the ladder to the facing seats on the roof, sitting closest to the edge near Beth. Picking up the microphone, she flipped a switch and banjo music poured out of the small speaker on the mast at the front of the boat. With a happy smile, Beth turned on the southern charm. "Hey, there, all you sod busters, cow punchers, cattle rustlers, dress bustles, horse wranglers, lone rangers, salt lickers, city slickers, in-laws, out-laws, grandmas and grandpas, you lovely ladies, and all you handsome, handsome men. And all you other men, too. Welcome aboard the Mike Fink Keelboats.

"Now, don't be shy. Just slide on all the way down to the end. That's right. Slide on down. Git movin'." She waved her hand so her three guests would get moving. "Keep sliding. Almost there. Keep slidin'. That's the only way we can keep those wooden seats clean. And if any of y'all pick up any splinters along the way, just consider that a little souvenir of your trip.

"So, I'd like all y'all to keep your hands, arms, feet, toes, fingers, elbows, heads, hats, shoes, purses, and anything else you all might be carryin' inside the boat at all time. I don't want to get this keelboat rockin' 'cause it might just keel over and some of y'all might get keeled.

"Now, as we sail past Fort Wilderness, the last outpost of civilization, and head deep into the wilderness, I'm goin' to let y'all enjoy some of this delightful banjo-pickin' music, guaranteed to make the next few minutes fly by like hours!"

Laughter and applause erupted when she hung up the microphone and flipped off the music. "Gosh, I miss doing that."

Adam gave her a kiss when he descended the ladder. "I'm going to go check on the twins. You go ahead and show them around the boat. I'll be back."

"All right, sweetheart."

"Gosh, they have such a great relationship. Did you see that huge sapphire on her wedding ring?" Still seated on the far edge of the roof, Rose was pretty sure Beth couldn't overhear her.

How in the world would I compete with a huge sapphire and building a keelboat? "Yeah, they seem pretty happy together."

The look on Rose's face turned serious. "Wals, you don't have to compete." She ignored the red stain that appeared on his cheeks. "You're unique in your own right." She waved an arm in the air. "This is great. For them. This works. For them. But, each couple has to find their own special moments." Her smile turned shy. "And we've already made a few of our own."

"Wish I'd quit doing that."

"Thinking out loud? Don't you dare." Rose leaned over to give him a quick kiss on his cheek.

"Everything all right up there? Plotting your next move in your quest?" Beth wondered why her guests suddenly had their heads together and had become more serious than the outing called for.

Rose reacted first. "No, but we should be. Let's get back on the dock. I'd like your thoughts on our clue."

When Adam didn't return right away, Beth figured Alex and Catie were awake and needed something. Turning back to Wals and Rose, Beth stood with her hands on her hips as they looked over her keelboat. "So, what did the clue say again?"

"That Mike Fink thought it was the best seat on the River."

"That has to be one of the keelboats. Which one did Mike Fink drive in the movie? I can never remember."

Wals was able to answer that. "It was the *Gullywhumper*. I looked it up before we came over."

"Okay, that's good. That one is still at Disneyland."

"For now. Lance informed us it's slated for removal and refurbishing."

Beth looked absolutely crushed. "Oh, my poor boats. Well," she tried not to be overwhelmed by news, "I still have my beauty here."

"What do you think is the best seat on the River?"

With an effort, Beth perked up again. "Gosh, everyone had a different idea about that when they got to the front of the line. Most wanted to sit on top to see better. Some liked to sit on the benches inside and enjoy a different perspective—and be somewhat by themselves. And, a select few thought the small bench for two on the bow was the best spot. They couldn't hear the spiel or the music, but they basically had the River to themselves."

"Okay, that covers the whole boat." Wals shoved a hand through his hair. "It doesn't really narrow it down."

"Does it matter that this is the *Bertha Mae* and not the *Gully-whumper*?"

Beth was quick to answer Rose's question. "No, not at all. The boats were basically identical except for the number of windows and the decorative gingerbread trim on the *Bertha Mae*. I don't think that would make any difference."

Wals was trying to eliminate some of their search area. "I don't think Walt would have hidden something up on top. Like you said, Beth, that was where most people sat, myself included. I always forgot about that seat out front. Why don't we look over the benches inside and then that little one?"

"I think you can eliminate that little seat from the equation."

Both heads swiveled to Beth. "Why do you say that?"

"Go look."

"Oh." Wals soon found that the little bench was merely a plank set on two upright boards. The mast went right through the middle. "Okay, that helps. Now let's go over the inside benches."

The keelboat gently rocked as they climbed through the open windows and stepped onto the seats in question.

Beth pointed to the backmost bench. "I would guess that one could be crossed off your list because it's so close to the engine. That leaves only three benches. That isn't too bad."

Wals let out a breath. "Yeah, it's better than having to search all of it out in plain sight. Now we just have to figure out a way to get to the boat. And hope the inside isn't under water by now."

"It's backed next to the Island, right?"

"Yes, but that's No Man's Land. We'd have to hop a fence or two and keep out of sight."

Rose just sat back and let Wals and Beth hash it out. They knew more about Disneyland than she did. While she waited, she ran a hand over the smooth, lacquered wood. Adam had done a wonderful job re-creating the iconic boat.

"There's always the utility canoes."

Wals' eyebrows shot up. He hadn't considered going by water. "It would have to be after dark, when the River's quiet and everyone is getting ready for the *Fantasmic!* show." He looked out over Beth's version of Tom Sawyer Island. "Do you think that'd be better than hiding out on the Island?"

Beth wasn't sure. "Well, even with *Fantasmic!* going, the *Mark*

Twain and the *Columbia* are still used during the show. You'd have to be pretty careful with your timing. There are a lot of cast members lining the rails of the *Mark Twain* in the finale. I don't know how you could hide the small canoe."

Wals grunted as he thought over their sparse options. By land or by water were the only two. "What do you think, Rose? Which sounds better to you?"

"Your Island closes at dusk, too, right? Just like ours?" At their answering nod, she made a face. "If we hid out on the Island, how would we get out when we were done?"

"Good question." Beth pulled an old cloth out of a hidden storage bin and began to wipe off the seats. "You'd have to stay all night and melt in with the crowd in the morning."

Rose stared at her. "By the look on your face, I think you did something similar. Am I right?"

The secret grin widened. "Yeah. Adam and I had to hide out all night to retrieve what turned out to be the final clue. It was on Pirates, not the Island. We had to jump *into* a boat full of guests to get out in the morning."

"Oh, I have to hear that story."

The cloth was stuffed into a pocket for washing. "Another time. You'll come back for dinner some night soon and we can have a proper chat. You and Wals are too distracted right now—which is totally understandable."

"And you really weren't expecting us to stay as long as this."

Rose's objection was waved away. "Oh, that's not a problem. I love showing off my boat. Next time I'll take you on a full tour around the Island. You can drive."

Rose's face lit up. Wals put a hand on her shoulder. "That sounds great, Beth, but we do need to get going. We need to beat the timetable before the *Gullywhumper* goes away. I'd like to be there tonight."

"You've decided?"

Wals could see excitement and dread all over Rose. "Yeah, I think I have. We'll need a few things from my apartment before we go back to the Park."

Adam met them at the back door with Catie in his arms, and Alex chasing after the ever-patient Sunnee. "You're leaving all ready?" He could see Beth was animated about something.

"What?"

"They're either going to steal a utility canoe or hide out on Tom Sawyer Island all night!"

"Well, I wouldn't call it stealing…"

Adam interrupted Wals' stammering. "Did you tell them about the time you stole a canoe and we had a picnic on the Island?"

Beth laughed as she patted his arm. "Next time, honey. Next time they come, we'll all have a picnic of our own on our Island. And, by then, we'll both have some great stories to tell."

Chapter 15

Disneyland

At the Golden Horseshoe for an early dinner, Wals could only pick at his chicken nuggets. One eye on the time, his nerves made eating almost impossible. When their meal was almost finished, the final show of the day for Billy Hill and the Hillbillies began with a roaring start.

Working on her brownie sundae, Rose began to laugh and clap along with banjos and fiddles. "Oh, Wals, this is so much fun! These guys are wonderful." She could see Wals check his watch yet again. "It's all right. We have plenty of time to get over to the Island."

His head snapped around. "Time? Oh, right. I know. You still hungry?" When he pushed his leftover fries in her direction, he saw her shovel in another mouthful of melting chocolate. He then realized he had been preoccupied throughout the entire meal and was now also missing the show. "Just worried, that's all."

Patting his hand, she left behind a smear of chocolate. "I know, but, it'll be all right. We'll do what we have to and go from there. We've done all the preparation we could. Try to relax and enjoy the show." She couldn't help a sigh. "It'll be a long night."

As the opening strains of *The Orange Blossom Special* brought a cheer from the audience, Wals tried to do as she asked. He failed miserably.

Half an hour before the official dusk closing of Tom Sawyer Island, Wals and Rose took the short raft ride across the Frontierland

157

River. Glad to be in the middle of fifteen other people, they hoped they wouldn't be noticed when they failed to catch the last raft back. Aware that cast members did a full sweep of the Island to make sure there were no stragglers hoping to do just what they planned, they needed for get out of sight quickly and carefully.

Exiting the raft and turning right, they ambled around the end of the Island, taking their time to examine the pirate loot artfully displayed into a seating area. Standing at the edge of the guest area, Wals subtly pointed to their goal. The keelboat could barely be seen through the thick trees. "There she is."

Rose tucked her arm into his as they headed to the backside of the Island. "Let's go across the barrel bridge."

"Why?"

She gave a laugh. "Because it looks fun! That's what we're supposed to be doing here, anyway. I want to run across the Suspension Bridge, too."

"We could go back to Dead Man's Grotto. They've added a lot of new elements in there."

"Now you're getting into the spirit."

Just then, one of the cast members started her sweep of the area. "Island closes in fifteen minutes! Please head for the rafts. Last raft in fifteen minutes." She kept moving, her announcement clearly heard by everyone in the area.

"That's our cue." Wals could feel Rose's grip tighten on his arm. Cool as she appeared, he now knew she was as nervous as he. "Let's head behind the Fort. Let me know if you see her coming this way again. That won't be her only pass."

"Okay."

All of her fears came out in that one word. "It's all right, honey. We'll be fine. I know what I'm doing." *I hope.* "Trust me."

Her slight snicker wasn't reassuring. As they neared the path that lead up to the barricaded entrance to Fort Wilderness, Rose paused. "Wow, your fort looks so…so forlorn. Ours is still open and popular."

"Yeah. I used to love running through there, ducking out the emergency exit tunnel. Lots of good memories."

They reached the back of the fort and the small graveyard of the pioneers who had perished, and noticed a family treading up the small hill. Wals, pretending they were lost, pointed over Rose's head. "No, honey, I told you the raft landing is that way! You're all turned around."

"No, that way takes us back to Smuggler's Cove. Come with me. I'll show you."

The father of the family gave Wals a knowing grin as Rose tugged him in the wrong direction.

Once on the opposite side of the Island from the rafts, across from the restrooms, Wals peeked around the corner. "They're gone."

"You're sure you know where the sensors are."

There was longer pause than what would have instilled confidence. "Yes, I'm sure. Lance, for some reason, had a map of them. I memorized it. We need to hurry. Get over the fence...here," pointing at the right spot. "I'll toss the backpack over when you're clear."

"You're sure this is the spot."

"Uh, yes. I hear someone coming. Catch."

The backpack was thrown over the fence in the general vicinity of Rose. Wals made a leap, and, catching the top board, hurtled over to land in a tangle of arms, legs, and tree branches. "Ow."

"Shh! Wals? I'm over here. It's pretty thick."

The dark clothes they had chosen to wear apparently worked since Wals couldn't see her anywhere. When he heard two cast members make their final sweep, he dropped where he was and remained still.

"I thought there were two more guests back here, Joe. I did a count. Thought I was correct."

"Kinda hard to be sure with everyone running in every direction."

"Hey, aim your flashlight over there. I thought I saw bushes moving, but I don't feel a breeze."

As the beam of light scoured the area around his hiding place, he felt like his whole body was shaking from the hammering of his heart. A sigh of relief went unheard when the light kept moving and the two guards decided to continue their sweep.

"Nope, nothing out there. Must've been a cat. Most of them are over on the mainland, but there are a few on the Island."

"Hmm. We'll check with the raft guys. Maybe they have a better idea of how many guests were out here."

"Hey, it's all right. Nobody can get past those sensors, anyway.

There'd be alarms going off if someone was out there. You know that."

"True. Besides, what could anyone do over here? Burn down Fort Wilderness?"

That broke the tension so the first guard relaxed. "Okay, okay, Joe. You know best."

Wals remained motionless for another ten minutes, secure that Rose would do the same. The *Mark Twain* had been closed for the evening in preparation for the first *Fantasmic!* show, so he knew that particular worry had been eliminated. The only thing he hadn't been able to research was the maintenance schedule for the Island.

"Wals?"

He heard the low whisper come from his left. "Rose. Over here. I think we're in the clear."

"You sure?"

"Well, if we're not, you're yelling like that is going to change things pretty fast."

There was a chuckle mixed in with the rustle of branches and leaves. Squatting, she appeared next to his position. "I wasn't yelling. You haven't heard me properly yell yet. They'd probably hear me over in Tomorrowland if I did."

"I'll keep that in mind." He eased into a sitting position, secure that the thick greenery would hide any movement. "I think I heard the last raft take off. We're probably fine, but I'd rather wait for full darkness."

Even in the low light, he could see the excitement in her eyes. "Can we check out the settler's cabin? Didn't you tell me it used to be on fire?"

"Yeah, and a guy with an arrow sticking into his chest sprawled over a fence out front."

"Wow, that's grisly."

Wals didn't want to talk about that cabin, recalling the time he had spent inside of it—with the other Rose from a long, long time ago. "I'd take you over that way, but the train is still running."

She waited a moment, but he didn't elaborate on his reasoning. From what she could remember, she hadn't been able to see the settler's cabin from the train. But, had she been looking for it? Not wanting to argue the point, she shrugged it off. He knew Disneyland. She didn't. "All right. Maybe later." When the Park was closed, there wouldn't be any possibility of a sighting. She'd ask again then. They were going to have a lot of free time on their hands.

"Okay, we need to go north and east to get to the *Gully-whumper.*"

"Aye, aye, Captain. Lead the way."

"You're way too happy, Rose. We still have to examine the boat and hope we don't get soaked or sink it while doing so."

Now that darkness had completely engulfed them, Rose felt more secure and at ease. The flashlights they had stashed in the backpack were small, with a narrow, pinpoint beam of light. She felt their chances of being spotted were almost nil. "Well, as you said, we have all night."

"When did I say that?"

She just smiled. He'd figure it out. "This looks like a path. I wasn't expecting to find one out here."

"There's still maintenance needed for the beaver dam, the cabin, and whatever else is still out here from before. And, they need access to the keelboat, too."

"Just like we do. But, probably for a different reason."

Wals chuckled. "More than likely. Or else we're on a wild goose chase."

Rose's mood perceptibly dropped. "Do you think someone might have found the clue already?"

"I hope not. I'd hate to be going through all of this for nothing." He suddenly came to a stop.

Rose, pondering the possibility that the clue might be gone, ran into his back. "Sorry. Why'd you stop?"

"We're here."

Rose stepped around him to see they had reached the edge of the River. Looking out to the front of the *Gullywhumper,* she could see that it was securely tied to a tree, its nose touching a small jut of land. "Ah, so we are. At least we don't have to wade out to her."

"Yeah, I'm hoping we don't have to get wet at all."

"Gosh. Are we sure that'll hold our weight? It looks lower in the water than it did when we went by on the *Mark Twain.*"

"Well, there's only one way to find out. Go ahead and jump on."

Rose wasn't expecting that. "Me?"

"You weigh less."

"You're joking."

The narrow-beam flashlight that moved up and down her body showed her hands on her hips. "No, I'm pretty sure you weigh less than I do." Her light was then aimed into his eyes. "Well, I was kidding," he admitted with a grimace, "but now I'm blind. You'll have to do it until I can see."

"Oh. Sorry. I can wait."

"Chicken."

"I heard that, Wals. I'm not chicken. I…I just don't want to deprive you of the pleasure of the search."

"You're rambling."

Caught, she let out a light laugh. "Yeah, I am." Looking at the dilapidated boat, she hung back. "I just have a thing about abandoned places."

"And yet you laughed all through the Haunted Mansion."

"Well, it's not ghosts. I just feel like I'm intruding where I don't belong."

"Gosh, Rose, that's the definition of our whole Hidden Mickey search. Starting with backstage at the Carousel of Progress."

Silent for a moment, she tried to figure out another way to describe her reluctance. "It was different with Beth's keelboat. That was all new and shiny. And I worked the Carousel. It was alright for *me* to be back there. You're the one who went onstage."

"Don't remind me."

"But this." She turned back to the *Gullywhumper*. "This is just sad. I want to fix her up, not search for something hidden and maybe have to tear her up some more."

Wals put an understanding arm around her shoulder. "You have a good heart. Even though you did hand off all my roses."

"Hey, you deserved that."

"Yes, I did." After a final hug and a stolen kiss, he shrugged off his backpack. "Now that I can see again, let's get to work." When there was no excited response, he looked back. "You can stay here, if you like. I can handle this."

Appreciating his concern, she shook her head. "No, I've come this far. Two of us can search quicker than one. Then we can get back out of sight."

The *Gullywhumper* sharply listed toward the shore when Wals jumped onto the bow. "Oh, wow, this is worse than I expected. They must have removed whatever stabilizers they had. Hmm, did they even have stabilizers? I don't know. Just watch your footing."

"Drop down inside first. Then the weight will be centered again."

"Good idea. See? That's why I brought... Oh, man. There go my shoes."

Rose could hear the unmistakable sound of sloshing. "How bad is it?"

"I'd say take off your shoes, but I don't know if there are any nails or broken boards."

"Here goes nothing."

The boat tilted again when Rose stepped onto the front. She aimed her flashlight into the cabin before she followed Wals. There was a good eight inches of water filling the seating area. Wals' light wavered as he compensated for her movements. Still saddened, she gingerly climbed onto the nearest seat and got to work.

They could see a few barrels and crates on the back-most bench, apparently used as props at one time or another. While Wals examined the two middle seats, she leaned over the front seat. She knew if she had sat on the wooden bench as the guests used to do, she would have been about eye-level with the Island. It made her even more uneasy.

Not worried about any damage he might inflict, Wals pried up the first seat. The nails easily gave up their grip. "Nothing here." He replaced the light brown perch and lightly tapped in the nails back into the waterlogged wood. They went in so easily he figured he could have just pushed them in manually. "I'll try the next one."

"Never mind. I think I found it."

Separated by the backs of the benches, Wals leaned over the middle seat. "What'd you find?"

"I didn't mean to rip the seat off, but it fell apart in my hands." She held up the soft wood to show him. "The canister is attached to the bottom of the seat. See?"

Wals crawled through the opening rather than risk walking on the deck. "Good work. Wow, this is a flat container. It takes up the whole seat. Hope it's watertight."

Rose shone her light over the gray plastic. "Yeah, I was thinking that, too. Do you want to pry it off the wood or take the whole seat?" She glanced around the cabin that once boasted copper hanging lanterns and pictures of the River. "I don't think anyone would notice it was missing."

"No, let's just take the canister. I'd rather leave the bench just as we found it. I don't know who is coming to claim the boat, but I want it to look like it did before."

After easily pulling their prize off the seat, Rose handed the wood back to Wals. "Watch this." Using his index finger, he shoved the nails back into place. "You'll never see that happen again."

Her response was only a sad smile. "Can we go now? Let's find a place to settle in for the night."

Wals pulled her in for a hug. "All right, honey. You go first. Watch that ragged windowsill."

Once they were back on solid ground, the *Gullywhumper* rocked for a few moments, gentle ripples in the water spreading out into the silent River. When the movement of the boat quieted, the River once again became flat and still.

"I feel like I'm saying goodbye to a dying friend."

Wals understood some of her emotion, but not completely. She hadn't visited Disneyland since she was little and never indicated the keelboats had been special to her. All he could do was be there for her. "She is coming back after they rework her. Maybe she'll look better than ever."

The answering snort was something less than ladylike. "I've seen the movie. She won't look better. But, she'll still be on the River."

"Ready to go?"

"Yeah." She leaned against his side. "Thanks for not calling me stupid over the boat. I guess I'm just sensitive."

"It's all right. Hey, it's almost time for the fireworks show." He looked around their small cove. "There's some flat rocks over there. Might be a good viewing place."

"One that certainly isn't in any of the brochures."

"That's for sure. Oh, shoot. I forgot about *Fantasmic!* We need to get out of sight behind those trees. The *Columbia* should be going by any minute now."

"Is that why it was parked on this side of the Island? I wondered about that."

Wals peered out from behind their tree. "She'll be all dark when she comes around again. Then the *Mark Twain* will pull up behind her. After the second show and the Park is closed, they'll probably put the *Columbia* back in Fowler's Harbor. The *Mark Twain* will be left at the dock to run again in the morning."

As the tall schooner silently slid past their spot with the actors onboard relaxed and chatting, Rose asked Wals, "Did you ever go into Shows and Entertainment?"

"Me? No. Two left feet and can't sing to save my life. Sounded like it'd be fun, though."

"It is." At his questioning look, she smiled. "I've played Tinker Bell in parades more times than I can count. They wanted me to do the Meet and Greets, too, but I didn't want to give up working the attractions."

"You must have looked adorable."

"Well, I can't answer for that." She let out a laugh, and then quickly covered her mouth. "Oops. Not sure how far sound can travel." Her voice dropped back to a whisper. "I started the training to be a face character, but didn't think I could handle it well enough."

"What do you mean? You have a wonderful personality."

"Oh, I could handle the kids all right. It was their dads I figured I'd have a problem with. I'd have to stay in character when I'd probably want to punch them in the nose."

"Yeah. I've heard Kimberly say that they can get grabby sometimes."

"The parades are different. We're separated from the crowds while we dance, or else we get perched on a float."

They could clearly hear the crescendo of music from the finale. "Okay, time for the *Mark Twain*, then the fireworks, then we can find a place to settle in."

The fireworks weren't nearly as magical as Wals had imagined. With the *Mark Twain* and the *Columbia* parked right there waiting for the second show, they could only watch random bursts of color through the thick trees.

"Well, that was disappointing."

Leaning back against Wals, Rose merely sighed. She didn't mind. There had been plenty of fireworks shows before. She was just content to be with Wals on another adventure.

Once the last rocket of the finale had rained down a waterfall of blue sparkles, Wals nudged his comfortable companion. "Let's sneak away."

"To Las Vegas?"

Wals did a doubletake. "What'd you say?"

Realizing she misunderstood, Rose blushed deeper than her namesake. "Sorry, what did you ask? Mus not have heard you right."

"I said we need to get away from here. The second show is going to start and these ships will light up like a firework."

"Uh huh."

Crouched down, they relied on their dark clothing and the thick brush to hide their movements. Going inland, Wals chose to stop on the edge of the worn trail. It would be smoother than sitting out in the middle of the brush. "You hungry?"

No, just mortified. "Yea, what'd you bring?"

Wals dug through his backpack. After smoothing down the blanket he pulled out, he handed her a granola bar and a banana. "Take your pick."

"Oh." She handed him back the banana. "Anything to drink?" She had to put a hand over her mouth to keep from laughing at his offering. "Juicy boxes? Oh. My. Word. How long have you had those? Or is there something you're not telling me?"

"Very funny. Yeah, I'm addicted to them. Especially the Cheery Cherry ones. Lance must have put them in there." He had to chuckle. "Probably in anticipation of just that reaction, I might add."

Around five in the morning, Rose awakened to find her head in Wals' lap. His head was leaning back against a tree trunk. "Wow, can't believe we slept through the night."

At the sudden voice, Wals' head attempted to snap back, but met a sturdy barricade. "Ow! What happened?"

"Sorry. Thought you were awake."

Rubbing his eyes and then his sore neck, he stifled a yawn. "Am now. Can't believe we slept through the night."

"That's what I just said, Wals."

"Must've been where I heard it."

"What time does the Park open this morning? I'm getting hungry."

"Want another juicy box?"

That earned a laugh. Rose stood and arched her back to ease her aching spine. "Quit staring."

"Just admiring the view."

"Men."

Having slept in a sitting position, it took a moment for Wals to get his legs working. "Yeah, and I'm good at it. Gosh, I haven't slept out like this in a lot of years. We used to go camping, back… before…I went to live with my grandparents."

Rose came over to hug his waist. "Did you enjoy camping? We never went."

"Well, glad I could be there for your first time."

She glanced around with a wry look. "Hope there's more to it than this."

Wals dug around inside his pack. "Hey, here's a bag of granola I missed. Well, we usually went camping up in the mountains with tents, sleeping bags, and a roaring campfire."

"And probably not having to hide out from security guards."

"Not usually, no." When she didn't accept the granola, he dropped it back in the pack. "Yeah, breakfast at the River Belle Terrace sounds better than this."

"Since we have some time, why don't we open the canister? It's light enough to see now."

"Good idea. Do you want to do the honors?"

As she eagerly took the canister, a big grin spread over her lips. "This one is so flat. I wonder what's in it."

Still in shock from what they discovered at Walt's Barn, Wals couldn't even guess. "We shall soon find out."

Rose gave a small gasp as she separated a clear sheet from between two waxy ones. "It's Mickey and Minnie. Wow, look at the style. They must have been drawn a long time ago. Is that Walt's signature?"

Wals examined the clear animation cel. Mickey and Minnie were dressed in an older version of their typical clothes. Hand in hand, they gazed adoringly at each other while standing in a field of blue flowers. "Yeah, that is Walt's signature. He quit drawing

Mickey a long time ago... Well, even before he died in 1966, that is. He was so busy with movies and Disneyland and the World's Fair and everything that the drawing was given over to his animators. This is pretty special."

"So's this."

The second piece of art had been folded twice. Once opened, it revealed a different Disneyland than the one they were hiding out in. "Hey! This is Mickey Mouse Land! Walt originally wanted the Park to be next to the Burbank Studio. See? These streets are Buena Vista and Riverside Drive."

The water-colored drawing was roughly rectangular with one end being significantly wider than its opposite edge. All the parts of the Park were labeled: The Castle, Granny's Farm, Railroad, Train, Boat House, and the picnic area. There were buildings, parks, railroad tracks, a car track, a circus tent, and a large lake with an island in the middle.

"Wow, it has so many elements like Disneyland."

Wals was fascinated. "Yeah, but as he worked on the concept, Walt found his Park kept growing bigger and bigger. His plans quickly outgrew Burbank and the restrictions of the Studio land. That's when he started the search for more land."

While Wals held onto the concept art, Rose found one more piece of paper. "Here's our next clue, Wals. It says '**Don't go up the brass pole. That was already done. Maybe Jess can help**.' Who's Jess? That's not from *Toy Story*, is it?"

Wals carefully refolded the map and put it back in the canister. "It can't be. That was way after Walt's time. Where is there a brass pole?"

"The Carrousel?"

He made a face. "That's a lot of brass poles. Sounds like we have more research to do. Let's get that animation safely out of sight. That's going to look great framed. I'll ask Adam where he had his done."

Rose's head suddenly snapped up. "Do you hear the sound of a motor?"

"What? Where?" Wals hurried to get the canister stashed into his backpack. It was a tight fit with the blanket and the rest of his supplies. "What direction was it coming from?"

"The cabin you still haven't taken me to."

Before they could head in the other direction, there was the unmistakable sound of breaking branches. "Wals! Rose!"

"That sounds like Wolf." Wals still wasn't sure if he should head in the opposite direction. Wolf didn't sound happy. But, then, he usually didn't.

"Wals!"

"Ooh, that sounded angry. You'd better answer."

"Wolf, over here." Wals and Rose started toward the River. "Hey, Wolf. I thought you could move through the forest without making a sound."

Wolf's blue eyes narrowed into a glare. "I can. I wanted you to hear me. Next time you decide to spend the night in the Park, don't leave your car in the parking lot."

Wals' mouth dropped open. "Oh. Right. Shoot. Forgot about that. Did anyone else notice?"

Wolf tilted his head to the side. "What do you think? I had to move it to keep it from getting towed off. It's in the security lot right now."

"Thanks, buddy." Wals attempt at cheerfulness didn't help. "Hey, wait a minute. How'd you get the keys to my car?" When there was no response, which didn't surprise Wals, he asked instead, "Fine. Can you give us ride to the mainland? We're starved."

Rose had kept silent during this interchange. She didn't figure it was a good time to again ask about the picture in Lance's office. "We'd really appreciate a ride."

Wolf held out a hand to indicate she should head over to the utility boat. "Did you get what you came for?" The barely-audible words were aimed at Wals.

"Ah, Lance must have called you. Yes, thanks. It was quite interesting."

"Lance didn't call me."

It took a moment for it to sink in. Rose had already reached the clearing and was waiting. "Right. I'll fill you in later. Quite a find. By the way, do you know who Jess is?"

"Yes. Get in. The Park is almost open for early admission, so you don't have to hide. We'll just walk together toward the entrance, or wherever else you need to go."

"But…"

"Up front, Wals. Rose, you in the middle. I'll steer."

"Thanks, again, Wolf. I was getting really hungry waiting."

"That's all right, Rose. Glad I could help."

"Speaking of helping," she started, ignoring Wals' effort to stop her, "do you know who Jess is? Walt mentioned that name, but I don't know who she is."

"Fire horse."

"Fire hose?"

"I said fire horse." Put on the spot, Wolf couldn't refuse to elaborate. "Jess and Bess were the original horses that pulled the fire engine down Main Street."

Rose looked blank, but Wals knew exactly what Wolf meant. "Thanks, buddy. Much appreciated."

The small boat pulled into the slip next to the Hungry Bear. Wals jumped out first to secure the line to the waiting pole. After Rose was helped onto the deck of the restaurant, Wolf pulled Wals aside, his voice low. "I appreciate the excitement these searches bring, but you need to plan a little more carefully, Wals. Leaving your car like that in the parking structure was a big mistake. Mistakes can lead to unwanted questions."

Wals had known Wolf long enough not to be affronted by the criticism. They had gone through too much together. "I understand. And, you're right. Thanks for not making it a big deal in front of Rose."

Wolf nodded toward the waiting woman. "She's a good one, Wals. Don't mess it up."

"You'd like her brother."

"Rob? Yeah, nice guy."

"How... You know what? Never mind." Wals waved off what he was about to ask. "I don't even want to know how you know about Rob. You already know where we're going and what we're going to find, don't you?"

A rare smile played across Wolf's lips. "Yes. And, you're going to love it."

Wals put a hand on Wolf's arm to delay him a moment longer. "Next time you see Walt? Tell him thanks for us."

CHAPTER 16

Disneyland

Using the information they had received from Wolf—however unwillingly it had been given—Wals led Rose to the Firehouse on Main Street.

"In Florida, ours is called Engine Company 71."

"71? Why is that?"

Rose couldn't believe he asked that. "That's the year when Walt Disney World opened."

"Oh, sure, I should've known that. Are you going to tell me how much bigger yours is, too?"

"Well, it is. So much more brick and gingerbread. Quite impressive. As are the rest of the buildings in Town Square." Her head tilted back to see the upper window. "Why is there a little light on in that window?"

"Why? Is your light bigger?"

With a light laugh, she playfully whacked his arm. "I didn't mean it that way. Well, at least, this time I didn't. Is someone up there?"

"That used to be Walt's private apartment. The light is always left on in his memory."

"Oh, so that's where it is. I heard rumors about a secret apartment and a secret dinner club, but never knew the exact locations. Can we go see it?"

Wals' mouth twisted to the side. "Well, a few years ago I would have said yes. But, something happened during a Park-wide race at least five or six years ago. Someone tore up a piece of furniture inside the apartment and it's now off-limits to the general public. Special guests and family are the only ones allowed in right now."

"I'm special."

He pulled her in for a hug. "Yes, you are. But," he drawled out the word, "I don't think that'll gain us entrance."

"Why in the world would someone damage something like that? Some people have no respect."

Wals merely nodded. Her question had suddenly brought back a long-forgotten partial conversation he had overhead during one of Lance's epic parties a few years ago. Adam and Lance had been quietly chatting when Beth came to join them. She mentioned Walt's apartment, much the same as Rose had done. Wals recalled that Adam and Lance instantly changed the subject. No amount of teasing from Beth could get them to answer her question. Now he wondered why they had been so uneasy. At the time, he had the impression Beth knew exactly what it was about, but the men's conversation didn't seem to want to go there. Maybe Wolf... He suddenly snorted. No, Wolf would probably be the last person to ask.

"What's wrong? You look a million miles away."

The distant look on his face vanished as he glanced up at the glowing tribute. "Not quite that far. So, even though this charming building is such a disappointment when compared to your magnificent one, shall we go in and see what we can find?"

"Fine. I'll try to do my best in such inferior surroundings." She gave an aristocratic sniff. "But, it will be difficult."

"Sometimes we must bear the worst of things."

"See? You do understand, Wals."

With a shared laugh, they entered through the wide-open, dark red folding doors of the Disneyland Fire Department.

Instead of heading directly to the well-marked stall that had housed Jess, the pair wandered around looking at all the vintage firefighting apparatus on display. There were a couple of kids climbing over the bright red firetruck parked inside facing the street. It looked as if it was ready to answer the next call that would sound the huge bell over the wooden desk. The brass pole Walt had mentioned was tucked away in the far corner on their left.

"So, did someone actually climb the pole? Wouldn't that have put them inside the apartment?"

From his position at the bottom of the pole, Wals could see the huge round hole was effectively stoppered at the top by solid wood painted black. "Well, rumor has it that a young kid did climb the pole to see where it went. Supposedly Walt was sitting inside and was startled to see a redheaded boy pop up from the floor. But, like I said, it's all rumor. I don't think it was ever really verified, like so many legends. But, I did hear that Walt's daughter said Fess Parker and Buddy Ebsen slid down it on a dare from Walt."

"That must have been something to see."

"That was in the early days of the Park. Walt was standing over at his window watching people come and go on Main Street. He saw Fess and Buddy on their way to an appearance and called them up to the apartment. That's when he suggested that they slide on down."

Rose let out a sigh. "Wouldn't it have been something to have been here back then? To possibly see Walt in his own Park?"

"Yeah, it would have. Wolf once said…" Biting his tongue for his slip, Wals tried to figure out some way to end what he had inadvertently started. He drew a blank.

"Wolf said what?"

"Wolf heard stories, uh, about the early years." His grin didn't quite look right.

Rose waited, but nothing more came. "Okay, I'll have to ask him myself if I want to hear the stories he heard, I suppose." One side of her mouth turned up a half-smile.

"You just gave away another rose, didn't you?"

Her smile extended. "Two, actually. They're getting rather low in numbers."

"Rats. Thought I was doing better."

"You were," she conceded. "But, I'll just have to go to the source for Wolf's obviously fascinating stories about the Park. Maybe they're concerning his father and Walt. They must have been good friends."

"Wolf's father? The Sham… I mean, the same one you think is in the picture in Lance's office?" *Quit talking, Wals*, his mind was screaming.

"Yes, that picture." Noticing Wals' slip of tongue, that the picture wasn't what she thought, Rose again filed away her curiosity. Determined to corner Wolf at some point during her visit, she was going to pointedly ask him about that intriguing photograph. For now, though, because Wals had become tense, she knew to change the subject as if she had forgotten all about it. "So, tell me about the horses Bess and Jess." She led him over to the empty stalls.

The small stalls, decorated with the same green Victorian wall-paper and stained wainscot as the rest of the interior, were next to each other with Jess's being closest to the entry of the firehouse. Various pieces of leather and silver tack were hanging on the back walls. A large, ornate letter 'D' decorated each side of the bit. A wide, thick leather collar hung on its own peg. This important part piece of the harness had been used to distribute the load around the horses' necks and shoulders when they had to pull the heavy fire truck loaded with guests.

Wals couldn't answer her question. "I have no idea about them. Thanks to you, Wolf answered the clue telling us to come here, saving us a lot of research, I might add. I just see that the clue pointed to Jess, and this was his—or her?—stall. And, under a window, I see," he sighed as he looked out on the busy Main Street.

The two boys who had been noisily climbing over the fire truck were now replaced by numerous families taking pictures of their children sitting on the high seat. Others wandered through the miniature museum looking at the brass extinguishers and nozzles. There were log books that dated back to the turn of the century. The walls displayed axes, picks, and helmets from various eras. Attached to one wall was an ancient checkerboard and two wooden chairs for those quieter moments.

"It looks like it's going to be busy in here all day. Do you think we should come back later?"

Rose had been wandering around the room as if looking at the artifacts. Alternately dropping and picking up a brochure she had in her hands, she watched the reactions of those around her. No one seemed to take any notice. She even tried stumbling against the large wooden wheels of the engine. Nothing. Returning to Wals' side, she grinned. "I don't think we need to come back. Hand me one of the flashlights. It should roll nicely."

As he dug it out of his pack, he became wary. "What do you have planned?"

"Watch and learn." She took the flashlight and rolled it under the half-gate into Jess's stall. Feigning surprise, she put her hands on her face. "Oh no! Look what I did. I'll go get it, Wals."

Glancing surreptitiously over his shoulder, no one even looked in their direction. "Go ahead. You were right. I'll keep watch. Not that it seems to be needed. Besides, this slat wall covers half of the stall."

Rose turned out to be very clumsy when retrieving the flashlight. While bent over to pick it up, she would examine the wooden walls, looking for a telltale W E D. When none was found, the flashlight would be kicked a little further on. "Oops. I'll get it. Ouch. Don't worry. I'm fine." The only reply she heard was Wals amused snort.

She managed to roll the abused flashlight around the entire stall without finding any indicator of anything hidden. Her last attempt was truly accidental when her foot connected a little too strongly, sending the light all the way under the feeding trough. "Oh, shoot. Now I'll have to go under for it."

Noticing the firehouse was currently empty of other guests, Wals glanced over the short entry gate. "Everything all right in there, honey?" All he could see was the bottom her shoes and her rear end.

"Yeah." Her voice was muffled. "I kicked it too hard. I'm under the feeding box thingy."

"So I see," as he briefly admired the view. "Well, take a look while you're there. I think you've managed to search the whole place."

"Hey!" Wals could hear excitement in her tone. "I think this is it. There's a small box under here. I think it's painted and vanished like the feed thing."

"Shh." Wals let out a warning hiss as a family entered and passed close to their location. When the youngest child again began to whine about wanting popcorn, the group gave up and left the building. "Okay, you're clear for now. Any chance you can hurry?"

There was a grunt and the unmistakable sound of screws being pulled out of wood. "Oops. I think I may have damaged it a little." A moment later she stuffed something into the backpack he had conveniently turned to face her.

"Damaged what? The trough or the clue?"

"Yes. Let's get out of here." She latched the half-gate closed behind her and headed out to Main Street. Going into the Town Center, near the flagpole, she threw herself down onto one of the green benches. "Whew. That doesn't get easier with practice. My heart is beating out of my chest."

"I know what you mean. You did all the work, but I feel the same. So, do you think you got what we came for?"

Rose snuggled next to his side. "Well, I didn't see any initials anywhere, but I could've missed them. If this *isn't* what we wanted, I just ripped a hole in that feeding box thingy."

"Trough."

"Fine. Trough thingy. Let's just hope I'm right. Do you want to leave? I could really use a shower."

Wals tugged her closer when she made a move to rise. "Well, that's what you get when you stay up all night partying on an island."

He could feel her chuckle. "If that's your definition of a party, we need to talk." She managed to extricate herself from his grasp, not that she really wanted to. "So, where did Wolf say he parked your car?"

Wals put his head on the back of the bench. "Oh, my car. I forgot about that." There was an audible *crack* from his neck when he raised his head again. "Ow. Remind me not to do that again. It's in the security lot. With Wolf. And all the security guards."

"How do we get there?"

"Well, the fastest way would be to steal something from the shops, or mug a guest."

Rose snickered. "Why don't we keep that as a backup plan. We can't just walk there?"

"Let's go ride the Monorail."

That stumped her. "Okay." Drawled out, it sounded like it had three syllables. "Then, can we take the Omnibus up Main Street? I'm getting somewhat tired. From my all-night party."

Wals stood and held out a hand to help her to her feet. "You're funny. Sure, the bus is loading. Let's sit on top and enjoy the view down Main Street. It'll be nice not having to search for something and just enjoy ourselves."

As they rolled along, the *ooga* horn sounding when an inattentive guest threatened to walk in front of the huge vehicle, Wals and Rose took time to read some of the upper window tributes that honored past Disney greats. Rose gave an unseen wave to the Silhouette Studio window when they neared the end of their ride. Disembarking near the entrance to Tomorrowland, Wals led her past the backside of the Matterhorn, the Submarine Lagoon that had housed Nemo and his friends for almost two years, and up the far ramp to the Monorail station. After a five-minute wait, the sleek, new, blue Mark VII Monorail pulled into the station.

"Blue is my favorite color."

"I'll keep that information in mind. We're getting an orange one any day now."

"Is that your favorite color, Wals?"

"Orange? Hardly. Hmm." Wals had to think. "I'm not sure I have a favorite color. I am partial to brunette."

A hand went up to her messy hair. "Is that an official color? Not brown or mousey?"

As the train smoothly pulled out of the station with a double blast of its horn, climbing a short incline, and crossing over the train tracks in Tomorrowland, it headed over the berm that separated Disneyland from the real world. After traveling along Harbor Boulevard for a short distance, the train curved to the right to head through Disney's California Adventure and onward to the Disneyland Hotel. Once they unloaded guests at the Downtown Disney station, they were on their way again.

Wals had slid over to the far right window when he got the chance. "Okay, once we finish with this turn, we're going over the Security area. I want to see exactly where my car is."

"There it is."

"Figures. He parked it right next to the main door. Hmmph."

The Monorail curved back toward the Park. "So, what's that building with the palm trees?"

"Indy."

"Part of the ride?"

Wals had to pull himself back from thoughts of revenge on Wolf. "What? Oh, no. It's the whole ride. Not too many people realize how far they have to walk when they get into the queue. That's one of the reasons it's decorated so thoroughly. Diversion."

They were silent most of the way back into the Park as the Monorail hummed quietly over its special track.   Wals did rouse himself to point out the Monorail barn and the train's roundhouse building behind Fantasyland. Rose could barely see the nose of an orange Monorail before the trees hid it from their view.

As they left the Monorail station, Rose wanted to know how they would reach the car.

"Well, if we go back to my original plan, we'll be escorted to Security and not have to walk."

"Wals, I'm not mugging anyone." She had to smile at a woman who overheard her. "Just kidding." Eyes wide, the woman hurried on past them. "Gosh, some people have no sense of humor."

"Imagine that." Wals stopped walking and looked around while trying to decide what to do. "We could get back on the Monorail and exit at Downtown and walk across the street. Or we could walk through Downtown Disney and enter Security that way."

"Which is shorter?"

"Crossing the street."

Rose tugged him back to the Monorail's entry ramp. "Up you go. Maybe we'll get to ride in the red one this time."

"Maybe we'll catch…"

The double blast of the horn as Monorail Blue headed out of the station ended his sentence.

"The next one," he finished with a grin.

Just as Wals quietly tried to slip into his 300ZX, the door to Security opened. A smug Wolf came out and leaned against the doorframe, two other guards behind him. There were a few whistles and some applause when Wals slammed his car into gear and jammed out of their parking lot.

"They seem like a nice bunch of guys. Rob would love them. Maybe he'd like to transfer to California."

"Yeah, Rob would fit right in…" Wals caught the last part of her statement. "Wait a minute. Is he thinking of moving here?"

Rose helpfully pointed out the front windshield. "Light's green."

Wals bit back his next comment and pulled out onto Disneyland Drive. "Thanks. So, you didn't answer me. Is Rob thinking of moving?"

"Not that he mentioned." She shrugged. "But, you never know with Rob. He loves seeing new things. Going to new places."

"What about you?" Wals found he was holding his breath as he awaited her answer. Had she been thinking of moving here? To be with him? Did he dare ask? Would it spoil things if he moved too fast? Could he stand it if she was gone out of his life? All of these thoughts whirled through his mind, but that last question was the one that stuck and kept repeating. He already knew the answer.

"Do I like going to new places? Yes, I do." She knew she was teasing him. Their relationship was new, but it had strengthened so much throughout this Hidden Mickey quest. She was fully aware of where her heart was leading. However, she also knew it was warring with what her brain told her was too fast. But, one question kept echoing in her head: Could she stand to go back to Florida without Wals?

"Would you…" He broke off, his heart pounding again, his mouth suddenly dry.

"Would I what?"

He didn't realize her symptoms were the same as his. "Would you consider transferring to California?" In a hurry to get back to Fullerton and continue this conversation without the distraction of driving in traffic, naturally Wals hit every red light down Harbor Boulevard. He felt a warm hand cover his on the shift knob.

"Yes, I would."

A loud honk broke his gaze into her eyes. Not realizing the light had turned green, he waved an apology to the driver behind him, hoping it didn't look like a rude gesture through the back glass.

"I've heard Sacramento is a nice city." Her eyes got wide. "Red light!"

Wals stood on the brakes. Tires smoking, the car screamed to a stop at the crosswalk. "Sacramento?!"

"Gosh, I was just kidding! You about gave that guy on the bike a heart attack!"

"Then it would match mine! Gosh, don't kid around like that when I'm driving."

The hand came back to cover his. Now it was cold and clammy. "I'm sorry. I was just teasing." Her voice went from shaky to shy. "I would love to move to California, Wals. To be with you."

Overly cautious, Wals checked in every direction before he moved through the intersection. "We'll finish this when we get back to Lance's." He took the barest of moments to look over at her before putting his eyes back on the road. "I'm really happy to hear you say that, by the way."

Rose headed up to her guest room for a much-needed shower and change of clothes.

With a cocked head, Kimberly watched the retreating figure bound up the stairs. She turned to Wals as he tiredly dropped into the nearest chair. "Why is she glowing? I can tell you both look totally exhausted, but she...she's positively glowing about something." Her green eyes narrowed. "Anything you care to share with the class?"

"You're being nosey, Sweetheart." Lance, settling onto the sofa, was just as curious as his wife. Even though he mildly criticized her, he was incredibly interested to know what had happened. "Did you find your clue on the keelboat?"

Wals ran a hand over his face. He wasn't sure who to answer first. He chose Lance, much to Kimberly's disappointment. "Yes, and also another one in the Fire Station." At their surprised looks, he nodded. "Yeah, Wolf came to the Island last...no, this morning and picked us up. He ignored my question..."

"I know the feeling."

Wals clearly heard Kimberly's mumble, but kept going. "But, he did answer Rose when she asked about one part of the clue. Once we knew where we needed to go, all we had to do was find the next capsule."

"What was in it, if you can tell us?"

"The first one or the second one? Sorry, but I'm really tired. Haven't slept against a tree in... well, ever."

Lance grinned. "That can be a story for another time. Or did you want to wait for Rose to come down? If she falls asleep, we could be here for a while."

"Or if I do." Wals looked up at the ceiling as if that would show him what Rose was doing. "We'll wait." Wals frowned and looked away, lost in thought. "We might be engaged."

Kimberly happily screamed and rushed over to hug Wals. "Oh, that's so..." She backed away, nose wrinkled. "Sorry. Hate to be blunt, but you could use a shower, too." She pointed to a room off of the back hallway. "Why don't you use the downstairs guest room? Lance will get you something to change into." It wasn't a question.

"I will?"

"Yes, you will. Just a fresh shirt would do." She shooed both of the reluctant men out of the room. With Michael and Peter both down for a nap, she contentedly sat back, put her hands behind her head, and started to plan a wedding.

Wals, wearing a fresh T-shirt with a large arrow pointing upward toward his head that read 'I'm With Stupid,' sat next to Rose on the sofa. Lance had to take a phone call and Michael started to cry, so they were alone for a moment. "Um, I need to tell you something."

"That bad?" Trying to tear her eyes off the hilarious shirt, she smiled at the serious look on his face.

"No, I don't think so, but you might. Not sure. I might have told Lance and Kimberly that we're engaged." Her reaction wasn't what he expected.

"Are we?"

"Would you like to be?"

"Are you asking me?"

Wals let out a nervous laugh. "I think you just handed away all the next roses I'll get for you. Yes, I'm asking you. I don't think I could stand being alone any longer. If you went back to Florida, I don't know how I'd manage. Don't go back to Florida."

Their foreheads touched. "I don't want to go back to Florida. But I have to."

His eyes fell. "Oh. Is it something I said?" He tried to pull apart, but she wouldn't let him.

"Yes, it is something you said. You asked me to stay in California."

"Oh. That's what I thought." Deflated, he looked away.

"Wals." She waited until she had his attention again. "I have to go back to Florida to quit my job, transfer here, pack my things, say good-bye to my family, and invite them to a wedding."

"Oh, that. Need any help?"

"Yes, I could use some help."

Unseen, Kimberly had come to the door, saw what apparently was happening, and shooed Lance away into the kitchen.

Wals smiled as they continued whispering. "What kind of help do you need?"

"You can talk to Rob."

There was a loud groan. "Can't I just pack all your clothes and furniture?"

"Oh, you'll do that, too."

"That's my girl." Wals chuckled. "How big a wedding do you want? It's all up to you."

She turned shy again. "I wouldn't mind Las Vegas like you suggested."

"Hey, don't put that off on me. *You* said Las Vegas."

"Yeah, I guess I did. Have you ever done that?"

"Gotten married in Las Vegas? No, can't say I have. You?"

She laughed out loud and sat back against the sofa cushions. "Well, it is comforting to know you don't have another wife stashed somewhere. I meant have you ever attended a wedding in Las Vegas."

Wals had to shrug. Now that the serious issue of actually becoming engaged was over, they had relaxed and could tease each other again. "No, can't say I have. Wouldn't you rather get married in front of Sleeping Beauty Castle?" Wals was surprised that name could come out of his mouth without even the slightest twinge of emotion. He knew, at that moment, that he had found his future and had made the right decision.

"Is that allowed?"

"No."

"Well, I guess that answers that."

"Yeah, I guess it does. Vegas it is. Will your family fly out for Vegas?"

Rose threw her head back and laughed. "Oh, my. You should see them in Atlantic City. They'll have a blast."

"Then, is it settled?"

Rose leaned in for another kiss. "Just tell me when and I'll be there."

"White dress and all the trimmings?"

"Only if you're in a tux."

Wals pretended to mull it over. "A tux? Man, is that what I

have to look forward to for the rest of my life? Can't I just go casual?"

She glanced down at the T-shirt carefully chosen by Lance. "Only if it's that shirt."

"Deal." He held a hand out to shake on the deal.

"Let's go tell Kimberly. Now I know why she looked ready to burst."

"Not just yet." His hand on her arm kept her from jumping up from the sofa.

"Why? What is it?"

He leaned in for a soft kiss. "I just wanted to tell you something."

"I love you, too, Wals."

After the phone call to Florida to share their surprising, but happy, news, Wals and Rose finally remembered the capsule Rose had uncovered in the Fire Station.

All together in the living room, an excited Peter had been handed the small plastic container. It had already been discussed that he wouldn't be told what it was or how it had been obtained. He just thought it was something Uncle Wals had brought for him to open.

"There's something banging around inside, Auntie Rose."

That was news to her. "There is? I didn't notice before. What do you think it is, Peter?"

"Sounds like a marble I put it in the..." He broke off, eyes wide as he glanced at his parents. "Uh, never mind. I don't know. Can I open it now?"

"Sure, go ahead. Pull on that end part."

"It's too hard. It won't come." A vein in Peter's neck stood out as he strained against the hold of the endcap.

"Want me to help, buddy?" Lance held out a hand to his son.

Defeated, Peter handed him the container. "Stupid plastic thing."

"Peter, that's not necessary. It's just tight, that's all. Help your dad by holding on to it."

"Okay."

With Peter's help, Lance managed to pop the cap off. A small gold key immediately fell onto the carpet.

"I'll get it!" Peter dove under the coffee table to retrieve the key. "Got it! What does it open, Dad?"

"I have no idea, Petey. Let's give it back to Uncle Wals. It is his, you know."

"Oh, right." After one last, longing look at the new, intriguing item, Peter handed it to Wals.

Wals had to smile at the forlorn look. "Don't worry, Peter. If it opens anything fun, I'll let you know, okay."

"Can I watch TV?"

Used to the ever-changing attention span of their five-year-old, Kimberly gave him a light pat on his behind. "Sure. You have a little time before bed."

"Thanks, Mom." Without a backward glance, Peter hurried from the room.

"Ah, youth." Lance upended the capsule to knock it against his hand. "I think there's a piece of paper stuck in here."

"Another clue?"

"Not sure, Rose. Got it." He handed it to her as she was closest.

Rose unfolded the paper and found something else inside. As she scanned the first lines, her eyes became wide. "Oh, my. Listen to this:

'Since you're already here, come on up and say hello! I'd love to meet the person who figured out my little Hidden Mickey Quest. I appreciate the work you went through to see it to the end, and hope you enjoyed the journey. As I said in my first note to you…'

"What note?" Rose looked confused. "Was there something else in the first container, Wals?"

Shrugging, he shook his head. "No, you saw it all. But, when I talked it over with Adam the other day, there might have been another capsule before the one found in Schweitzer Falls. I guess we'll never know. Keep reading."

"All right. It continues:

'I would like you to appreciate what you have seen and the places you went. Some of those attractions were special to me. Some of the people even more so. I always hope that my legacy will continue long after I'm gone. People like you can help that happen. Remember me and remember what I have created for everyone to enjoy.

The extra card I enclosed, well, it's not open yet, but it will be. You'll love it! Maybe we can go together and share a table. Then you can tell me what you had to do to solve the clues Wolf put into place with me.

If no one is home when you come, just let yourself in with the key. It's yours to enjoy whenever you want.

Best wishes, Walt.'"

"What's the card he mentioned, Rose?"

Her mind reeling, Rose stared at Wolf's name written in Walt's hand. All the unanswered questions she had asked flooded back. Wals last question caused her to bite her tongue. This wasn't the time. Once she moved here, she would have all the time in the world. With an appeased smile on her face, Rose handed Wals the embossed golden card.

Wals noticed her odd expression, but it was forgotten when he read the elaborate writing. His mouth opened and then snapped shut. It was something he had always wanted but never thought he could get. "It's a lifetime membership to Club 33. Wow." That word seemed so insufficient to cover all that Walt had given them during the course of this Hidden Mickey quest. He glanced over at Rose, his new fiancée.

Walt had given him more than he could possibly have known.

CHAPTER 17

Fullerton

Wals arrived early at the Brentwood's house. Excited. Nervous. Determined. Confident. And, most importantly, incredibly happy.

All of the plans that had been worked out with Rose's family when they were finalizing matters in Florida ran through his mind. First on the agenda was to pick up Rose, then, convoy with the Brentwoods on the four-hour drive to Las Vegas, and finally, meet up with her family at their hotel. Arrangements had been confirmed at a nearby chapel for the ceremony that evening, then they all would return to the hotel for a small celebratory dinner. The newlyweds would then quietly slip away to begin their honeymoon at a nearby, unnamed resort.

Fingering the small velvet box in his pocket, Wals took a moment to marvel at the speed in which he had been able to procure a custom wedding ring. Knowing Rose had admired Beth's sapphire ring, he had gotten in touch with Adam before leaving for Florida to find out where he hopefully could find a similar stone. Adam surprised him by inviting him over that evening and presenting him with a small array of gorgeous sapphires. Not exactly forthcoming about their origin, Adam merely stated that they were an inheritance from an uncle. Deciding on an oval Burmese sapphire, they quickly arrived at an incredibly fair price. Living so close to the Los Angeles jewelry district, Adam had also been able to steer him to a jeweler who not only specialized in custom rings, but also owed him a favor. And now all Wals had to do was slip the diamond and sapphire filigree creation onto her finger as he said his vows.

When the front door flew open and Rose jumped into his arms, he was brought back to the present. "I heard you were here."

"I didn't knock yet."

Rose indicated the camera aimed right at them. "Dad saw you."

"Lance." Wals shook his head as he glanced upward. "Is he watching now?"

"Probably."

"Let's give him a lesson on how it's done right."

Their kiss was long and thorough. Wals gave the unseen Lance a thumbs-up behind Rose's back.

Rose was a little breathless when she stepped back. "My. I should marry you more often."

Wals tucked an arm around her waist as they entered the house. "Once will be sufficient. I anticipate a lot more of that in our future."

All of Wals' and Rose's carefully-made plans seemed to evaporate once they stepped into Lance's office.

Lance set his phone face down on the desk. "We're going to need to stop at Disneyland for a few minutes before we hit the road."

Wals glanced at his watch. "Lance, I know I'm early, but what on earth could be that important? We have a four-hour drive ahead of us. Rose's family is waiting."

He was waved off. "I know. I know. Wolf called in a problem on Main Street."

Wals looked at Rose for her reaction. Apparently, this was news to her, as well. She appeared as baffled as he was. "When has there ever been a problem Wolf couldn't handle by himself?"

That stopped Lance for a moment. "True. It did seem odd, but he was insistent. He said it has to do with Walt's apartment."

Rose immediately went from confused to intrigued. Even though Walt had left them a key to 'come visit' whenever they wanted, their wedding plans had overshadowed everything else. Anxious to get her settled in California, they hadn't had time to check out the fascinating gift. "Well, we could take a couple of minutes..."

"Rose! I thought we wanted to get on the road. Your parents

are waiting for us."

"And Rob." Lance, as always, tried to be helpful.

Wals bit the inside of his cheek. His private interview with her brother had been tense, to say the least. "And Rob," he added with a smile that didn't manage to reach his eyes. "Thanks," was thrown at Lance.

"Any time. Look, Wals, it'll only take a few minutes." He pointed at the torn Rose. "See? Your ever-loving is open to it. We'll be on our way before you know it." Unobserved by the others, Kimberly had silently waved at Lance from the doorway before disappearing. At her signal, he got up from his desk before there could be any more arguing. "Kimberly already has the car packed. The sitter is here for the children. Just follow us to the Park, and we'll go from there." Without a backward glance, he strode from the room and headed for the garage.

"Is it always this difficult to get married?"

Rose slipped her arm through his. "No clue. I've never gotten married before. But, we do have a few extra minutes. Mom and Dad aren't expecting us until the middle of the afternoon. Plus, I've been dying to see Walt's apartment ever since we found the key. Is it all right, honey?"

There was that adorable pleading look in her eyes. "All right. I'm just anxious to get to where we need to be, that's all. I don't want you slipping through my fingers at the last minute."

"Not going to happen, Wals. Not going to happen. You're stuck with me for the rest of your life."

Wals reassured, they left the house and tried to follow Kimberly's Aston Martin to Disneyland. That proved to be more difficult than it sounded.

"My word. Lance must think he's driving at Le Mans. I don't want to take the corners that fast. We know where they're going. We'll meet up there."

Relieved, Rose let out a sigh. "Oh, thank goodness. I couldn't believe he took off like that. They'd better be careful. My dress is in that car."

"Yeah, so is my tux. I might not have a trunk, but I'd like it to arrive in one piece."

Following at a more sedate, legal, speed, Wals silently hoped Lance wouldn't be driving like that all the way to Las Vegas.

Once they arrived at the Security lot, Kimberly had already disappeared inside the Park. "She's visiting some of her Princess friends while she has a few minutes," was all the explanation they were given.

"Okay." Wals again checked his watch. The prospect of this trip being delayed only half an hour vanished into thin air. "Do you want us to go on ahead, Lance? The way you were driving, I'm sure you'd catch up rather quickly."

"But I thought we were going to see Walt's apartment, honey." Rose leaned over to kiss his cheek. "We have plenty of time. Mom and Dad are probably already having fun in the casino. They'll never notice if we're late."

He looked into her eyes. "You're sure?"

Bouncing up and down on her toes, she nodded. "Yes. Let's go see."

Nodding his agreement, Wals checked back with Lance. "So, where's Wolf? I thought he'd be here to meet you."

Lance merely shrugged as he led the way through the berm and backstage behind New Orleans Square. "Hey, it's Wolf. What can I say?"

The route they were on was used by the Main Street vehicles when heading into the Park for the day. As they walked by, Wals pointed out their storage units to Rose. One of the Omnibuses was still under cover. Stepping over the tracks for the streetcars, they rounded the back of the Jungle Cruise, the distinctive sound of the boat motors clearly heard. Two shots rang out.

"I think they got the hippo in the trees." Rose tugged on Wals' arm. "You never took me on your Jungle Cruise."

"Want to go now? I think we have plenty of time."

"Don't pout, Wals. We'll get to Las Vegas soon enough. I'm not going anywhere."

"Apparently not going to Vegas right now either."

"I heard that." Rose instantly forgot Wals' moodiness when they reached the metal stairs that led up to Walt's hideaway. "This is it, Wals."

Lance, who had been uncharacteristically quiet, affably slapped Wals on the shoulder. "Yep. This is it." He bounded up the stairs before there could be any reaction, leaving Wals and Rose to follow at a more sedate pace.

"I did some research on the Internet once we found the key. I'm expecting a lot of red and white and gold..." Whatever else Rose had been expecting to see died on her lips.

Just as soon as they stepped over the threshold and walked through the short hallway, they were greeted with a loud "Surprise!"

Wals and Rose were instantly engulfed by her parents Monica and Steven, Rob, Adam, Beth, and Kimberly. Off to the side, Wolf smiled at the confused looks on the couple's faces. A man and a woman, both strangers, sat quietly in two of the brocade chairs.

"What are you all doing here?" Rose was the first to recover her senses.

"We came for your wedding, honey."

"Yes, Mom, I know. In Las Vegas."

Her mother waved an airy hand. "Oh, this is so much better. We'll go on to Vegas when we're done here."

Rose pulled back from her dad's hug and glanced over at Wals. "What's so much better?"

Not having a clue what was going on, Wals only shrugged.

Kimberly came to Rose's side and whispered for her to follow. Still in a daze, Rose went with her, hoping her friend would fill her in on what was going on.

Kimberly led Rose to the other side of the apartment to the small bathroom. Rose's mouth fell open when she saw her wedding dress hanging from the shower enclosure. Kimberly nudged her into the room. "You need to change."

"But..."

"No buts. Lance and I wanted to surprise you with a Disney wedding." Kimberly hugged the woman who had become one of her best friends. "This is our wedding gift to you, sweetie. Wals should be changing by now, too. I'll help you get dressed."

"No, I'll do that, Kimberly. This is my darling little girl." Rose's mother, Monica, stepped into the small bathroom and put a gentle hand on Rose's pale cheek. "I've been looking forward to this since the day you were born."

Kimberly quietly slipped out of the room to go and join Lance.

"Did you tell her about the honeymoon?"

She shook her head, her eyes misty. "No. She's having a moment with her mom." Kimberly's mom had been gone since she was a young girl and hadn't been there for her big day with Lance.

Understanding his wife, Lance pulled her close. "I love you," he whispered.

"Mom would've loved you."

In the other hallway, Wolf was almost to the point of physically forcing Wals into his tux. The groom was having a difficult time wrapping his head around the abrupt change of plans. "Wals, if you don't start doing this yourself, I'm going to have Rob hold you down while I dress you."

"But..."

"No buts. This wedding is a present from Lance and Kimberly." Wolf flashed a smile. "My gift is something else." The smile instantly vanished. "Get dressed. Now."

It took Rob poking his head around the corner. "Need some help, Wals?"

"I've got this. Thanks." All his questions and objections were pushed aside. Rose hadn't come running for him to save her from whatever was happening to her. Everyone else appeared to be in on it. His wedding was going to happen and it was going to happen now. "Should've known Lance had something up his sleeve."

A grin spread over Wolf's face while he made sure Wals was dressed properly. "We've been planning this ever since you mentioned going to Las Vegas. I called Monica and Steven myself. They were all in favor of it."

"Steven Tyler."

"I know, right?" Wolf reached over to adjust Wals' bow tie. "There. Perfect. Now, come out and mingle with your guests. I need to check on Rose. She's probably having second thoughts by now."

No one saw the panic come and go over Wals. Heart pounding, he went out to the main area of Walt's apartment. Now that he accepted what was about to happen, he was able to look around.

The antique crystal vases that decorated the room were filled with red roses. As his gaze swept over them, he briefly nodded to the two strangers, figuring they were somehow related to Rose. The chairs they were in, usually in the center of the room, had been pushed back to the far wall. The music box was in its place on the stand nearest the patio. Monica and Rob sat together on one of the red velvet-covered daybeds that Walt used to sleep on. When he realized Steven wasn't with his wife, Wals heart sped up. It must be time. Steven must be ready to walk his daughter down the aisle, short as that aisle was.

On some unseen signal, the woman in the brocade chair leaned forward to unzip the black leather case at her feet. Pulling out a violin, she tested a few strings and then rose to her feet. The instrument tucked under her chin, the hauntingly beautiful notes of the *Sleeping Beauty Waltz* drifted over the guests. All talking ceased and a Park photographer stepped from his spot in the entry hallway, camera ready.

As best man, Wolf came over to pull Wals into position in the center of the cleared room. "Ring?"

"What!?"

"I need the ring. It's my job."

"Oh." Wals pulled the velvet box out of his inner pocket and handed it to Wolf. They both saw the box waver from nerves.

"You'll be fine. Just repeat whatever that guy says to you and say yes if he asks you a question."

'That guy' was a justice of the peace who appeared to be enjoying himself. Usually performing ceremonies inside the courthouse, he had been thrilled to be asked to come to Disneyland—and especially to Walt's apartment. On signal, he, too, rose to stand in front of Wals. At the sound of the opening strains of Mendelssohn's *Wedding March*, the audience came to their feet and all eyes turned to the hallway.

A vision of white and lace floated on her father's arm as Rose came to join Wals in the middle of the room. The full, lace-covered chiffon skirt stopped at an empire waist. The sweetheart-neckline of the bodice was covered with a sheer netting of lace and pearls, the shoulders capped by a hint of lace. On her head was a Juliet cap and short veil. Her lips curled into a happy smile, Wals thought she was the loveliest vision he had ever seen. As he took Rose's hand from her father's, he placed a tender kiss on the back of her knuckles. Rose handed her red rose bouquet to her matron-of-honor, Kimberly.

"Dearly beloved."

A shower of red rose petals was hurled after the newly-married couple as they carefully made their way down the metal steps of Walt's apartment. The Main Street Horseless Carriage, decked with roses and tulle, stood waiting at the base of the steps. For the occasion, the double doors that usually blocked off the backstage area from Main Street had been thrown open. After Wals and Rose climbed onto the black leather seats, the carriage began its slow, chugging way down Main street. The Fire Engine immediately pulled into place to load the rest of the wedding guests.

"This is so surreal. I love it!" Rose, with an armful of roses, was throwing them off the sides of the Carriage as they went their way up Main Street. Cameras were snapping pictures and people rushed to collect the fallen flowers. "I can't believe they did this for us."

"I can't, either. I can't even imagine the number of strings that had to be pulled."

"Does this mean we aren't going to Las Vegas?" Rose handed three of the roses to Francine from the Silhouette Studio and waved a happy good-bye as the carriage reached the Hub and turned left.

Wals sat back against the tufted cushions. "Well, we can cancel the chapel, that much I know. We still have our room at the resort."

Not really listening to Wals, Rose was looking all around. "Where are we going?"

The yellow Carriage passed by the entrance to Adventureland and, with a honk of its rubber horn, turned left to enter the wooden gates of Frontierland.

"Maybe we're going to ride Big Thunder."

Rose handed off the last of her roses. "Oh, Wals! You're too much. But, that would be fun."

Their answer came moments later when the Horseless Carriage stopped in front of the closed doors of the Golden Horseshoe. The uniformed driver came around and offered a hand to help Rose down.

"I guess we're here." Wals heard a ringing bell and the Fire Engine pulled in behind the carriage. Lance waved from the rear seat, Rob holding a hand over his ear nearest the clanging bell.

The two drivers went over to the wooden boardwalk and removed the crimson-velvet rope that had blocked the entry to the Horseshoe. The ornate leaded glass doors were then opened and the serving staff welcomed the newlyweds with a round of applause. As soon as the couple stepped around the corner into the main room, four fiddlers began playing a lively rendition the *Wedding March*. Billy Hill and the Hillbillies were on stage, huge grins on their faces. To the side of the stage was a five-tier wedding cake adorned with red roses and topped with a porcelain Mickey and Minnie.

More applause sounded as the dazed couple made their way to the front of the room, followed by family and friends. Inside were all the friends and cast members Wals had worked with on the Canoes, Pirates, and Casey Jr. More security guards were there, the ones Wals had gotten to know while he worked at the Park. Several princesses in costume had come to round out the festivities. Even Tinker Bell and the fairies from Pixie Hollow were enjoying the party.

"Why is he dressed like Elvis?"

"Who, honey?"

"The Billy on stage in the middle."

Wals tore his eyes from all his friends and looked up on stage. There, in deed, the head Billy was dressed as Elvis. Lance slid next to Wals and guided him to the center table nearest the stage. "I see you spotted one of your surprises. We didn't want you to miss your Las Vegas plans too much, so we invited Elvis to the party."

"Lance, you well know we weren't going to the Elvis chapel."

Wals was waved off. "No matter. Adds a little class to the proceedings. Monica! You and Steven over here."

While the wedding party was getting settled, the Bllies began a medley of Disney songs. The cast members came and went as their schedule allowed. Once everyone was seated, the rest of the wooden tables and chairs were pushed out of the way.

Elvis Billy called out for the couple to have their first dance. Leaning on his left hip, Elvis began crooning *Love Me Tender* as Wals and Rose swayed to the music and shared another kiss. Soon everyone was dancing and the tempo of the music quickly altered.

"I didn't remember *Love Me Tender* as rock and roll."

"Just go with it, Wals! This is awesome."

A huge pile of presents was on the end of the food service bar. The servers, dressed as can-can dancers, had to work around them to make the rounds with trays of hors d'oeuvres and drinks. Elvis Billy acted as emcee for the party which was destined to become the talking point of every cast member in the Park.

Wals and Rose were called up to cut the wedding cake so the cast members who had to get back to work could still have a slice. Wals ignored the calls to 'smash it' and held out a small piece so Rose could take her first bite.

"Thank you, honey. I appreciate not having to wipe icing off my face."

Wals snorted. "Never did understand that custom. You look too beautiful to smear with chocolate."

"Aww." Rose leaned closer to Wals so no one could overhear, impossible as that was with the fiddles and guitars that were now entertaining the party. "You know, this is a little different from the casual party we had planned—not that I'm complaining. It's just... I was looking forward to what you had originally planned to wear."

With a grin, Wals took a step back and unfastened two of his shirt studs. Pulling the sides of his bright white shirt apart, a black arrow pointing up at his chin and the words 'with stupid' were clearly seen.

Wondering why Rose had collapsed against Wals laughing her head off, Kimberly took over the cutting of the cake. As a precaution, she decided to also serve it to keep some of the rowdier canoe guides from just grabbing a hunk out of one of the tiers. Still chuckling, Wals and Rose headed back to the dance floor as her parents were called up on the stage. Elvis handed them a microphone.

A grating screech made everyone cringe when Steven tried to say his opening words. A loud "sorry!" was heard from the back upper balcony where the sound guy quickly adjusted the squelch to fix the problem.

"As I was about to say," when Steven was able to continue, "Rose's mother and I would like to welcome Wals into our family. We couldn't have picked a better fit for our little girl. While we'll miss her terribly in Florida, now we have a wonderful excuse to come visit California. Often," he stressed ominously, and then grinned as he handed the mike to his wife.

Wiping a stray tear, Monica echoed her husband's sentiment while the Billies played *There's No Place Like Home*. "Wals, Rose, come on back up here. We have a little something for you that we'd like you to open when you get back from your honeymoon." After handing Rose an embossed envelope, Monica turned to scan the audience. "And, speaking of honeymoons, Wolf, will you please come up here, too?"

"No."

A confused look passed between Wals and Rose. What in the world did Wolf have to do with their honeymoon? *Hopefully nothing,* Wals sincerely thought to himself.

On the floor, Lance accepted something from Wolf, hid it, and bound onstage. It was done so quickly that most of their friends missed the interchange. Once in place, Lance took the mike with his usual flair. One would have thought he was ready to burst into song. He raised his sparkling cider-filled champagne flute in a toast. "To my good friends Wals and Rose. May you enjoy many, many years of wedded bliss."

Everyone there who knew Lance held their breath, waiting for the other shoe to drop. They were disappointed.

"Wolf, shy creature that he is, wanted to help make this day special for you."

"All of you already have, Lance."

Lance acknowledged Rose with a tip of his glass. "Ah, but the party isn't over yet." With the panache of a magician, he pulled a long envelope from his inner jacket pocket. "This is a little something from Wolf."

The Billies managed a drum roll with their fiddles and the audience laughed.

Envelope in hand, Wals and Rose stood on the gas-light-lit stage, its tall red curtain closed behind them. Glancing into the box on the side of the stage, they could see Rob sitting in there with one of the princesses. "What is it, Lance? You all have done so much already. Thank you seems so insufficient."

"Oh, just something he thought you'd enjoy."

Wals turned to the audience. "Okay, now I'm truly worried."

There was full-out laugh. "You should be," was called back to him.

Wals handed the envelope to Rose. "You want to do the honors?"

Rose pulled out a document and what looked like tickets. Her scream caused the microphone to squeal again. "Sorry. Oh! It's a seven-day cruise on the Disney Magic! We're going to the Caribbean, Wals!" Flying off the stage, Wolf was engulfed in a chiffon and lace hug. Wals followed, to shake the hand that could be seen through the folds of the dress. "Thank you." Her smiling, teary face turned to include the whole group. "We can't thank all of you enough!"

Wals and Rose were driven back to their car, holding their regular clothes and as many presents as could safely fit. The newlyweds would spend their first night in Wals' apartment and, early in the morning, head to the airport for their flight to the East Coast and the cruise ship.

Soon after the bride and groom left, the party in the Golden Horseshoe, out of necessity, began to break up. The Billies had their regular shows to perform for the rest of the evening. What was left of the wedding cake was taken to the cast member restaurant, the Inn Between, for everyone's enjoyment.

Monica, Steven, and Rob headed back to Adam and Beth's for one last night. They still fully intended to go on to Las Vegas for the next three days.

Kimberly, after everyone had gone, tiredly leaned on Lance's shoulder in the back of the Horseshoe. The Billies had just swung into *The Devil Went Down to Georgia*. She gave a contented sigh.

"Happy?" Lance put his hand over hers.

"Yes. That was a beautiful wedding. I'm so happy they found each other."

"I still don't think Wals is over the shock of having his wedding in Walt's apartment instead of Vegas. You'd think, with all he's been through, that he'd adapt to change a little better."

Kimberly softly chuckled. "Perhaps it's because of what he went through that he'd rather be in control." She could feel Lance's shrug.

"Maybe. Do you think they opened Steven and Monica's present yet?"

"I would have," she admitted, a grin playing over her lips. "I wouldn't want to wait until I got back. Think they'll like it?"

"A hefty down payment on a new house with an ocean view? Yeah, I think they'll like it a lot."

Still nestled against her husband, Kimberly thought back to her own wedding, not far from where they now sat. The Victorian gazebo at the Disneyland Hotel had been a beautiful setting. All of Lance's security guard friends had made an arch with their Mag-lights under which they had run. Her chuckle aroused Lance from his own daydreams.

"What? I heard you laughing."

"Just remembering our wedding. I hope they have as much love and fun as we've had in our years together."

"I wholeheartedly agree."

Epilogue

Two Years Later

"**A**re you all settled into your new house?" Kimberly glanced over at Rose who was busy arranging a cheese tray.

"Don't know why I'm fiddling with this. Once the hoard descends, it'll be gone in a minute." A veteran of two Security Guard and Princess parties, Rose well knew what would happen once the guests started to arrive. After centering a tomato carved into a large rose, she moved on to the next tray. "And, yes, to answer your question. Finally. Between moving and the continual practice for the new Soundsational Parade, it's been pretty hectic."

"What's your character, again? Lance told me, but, well, you know Lance."

"If he said Dancing Piñata, then he's correct." She could see Kimberly's amused look. "Yeah, I know. I'm one of the three dancing piñatas in front of The Three Caballeros float." There was a stifled snort. "Hey, I tried to get on the Peter Pan's Neverland Buccaneer Blast float, but I didn't have seniority. It's all right. I could have ended up on roller skates over in California Adventure."

"Well, as long as you're happy. And, I can see that you are." Kimberly had been quietly observing her friend since her move from Florida. Having worried about the quickness of their marriage, it turned out that Rose and Wals were ridiculously happy together. They were a good fit. "Are you enjoying Huntington Beach?"

"Well, we're not on the beach, but, as you know, we can see it from the balcony on the second floor. I know the recession's been difficult, but we sure got a fantastic price on our house. Wals said something about a 'buyer's market.'"

"It was good you waited a while. Hey, could you check the oven? I think the cookies are done."

As Rose pulled out the chocolate chip cookies, they were engulfed with the heady fragrance of chocolate, butter, and vanilla. "Ooh, I could eat the whole batch."

Wolf, just then walking in through the back door, grabbed the first cookie off the tray. "Save some for the rest of us." The whole treat was popped into his mouth, a look of pure contentment spreading over his face. Once his eyes opened, he reached for another only to have his hand slapped.

"You're as bad as Lance."

"Speaking of whom, your slightly-deranged husband just finished setting up the polo field."

"Polo?" Rose did a double-take. "You're bringing in horses?"

Using the diversion, Wolf grabbed another hot cookie and headed for the bathroom. "No. I'll be right back."

"Not exactly horses." Kimberly tried to figure out how to explain Lance's complicated game that would probably cover a good solid mile of playing field. "We borrowed Peter's and Michael's stick horses, got a few more, some mallets, and a whiffle ball." She had to shrug. "You'll figure it out with everyone else. Hello? Rose?"

No longer listening, Rose was staring at the doorway through which Wolf had disappeared. "Yeah, sounds fun." Distracted, she dropped the towel she was holding onto the granite countertop. "I'll be right back."

Kimberly watched her follow Wolf and heaved a sigh. "Rats. I was hoping she'd forget what Walt wrote." She turned back to the vat of potato salad. "Guess not. And, I need to quit talking to myself."

"**G**osh, can't a man have a private moment to himself?" Wolf emerged from the bathroom and ran into the waiting Rose. Arms folded across her chest, a frown on her face, he knew what she wanted. Moving around her and escaping like he had done for two years wouldn't work this time.

"We need to talk."

"Words that no guy ever wanted to hear."

When he tried to feint a move and get past her, she stood her ground. "Not this time, Wolf. You've evaded me for too long. At first, I wondered why we never saw you anymore. Then, I figured it out."

"I knew you were too smart for Wals. Where is he, by the way?"

She grabbed his shirtsleeve. "Quit stalling. Come with me."

"Doesn't look like I have a choice."

They both knew he could easily pull from her grasp. Marching him through the hall to Lance's office, she chuckled and let go of his shirt. "Sorry, but I've been waiting long enough. Wals won't tell me. He says it's your story. Lance, well, I think I could get it out of him, but I'd rather hear from you." After the door to the office closed behind them, Rose went over to the picture on the wall. "Why did Walt mention you by name in the last clue Wals and I found? Is this you?" She stabbed a finger onto the glass protecting the black-and-white photograph.

"Yes."

"Okay, I can see you're going to make me work for it." Rose settled onto the leather sofa and patted the cushion next to her. "Sit, and tell me how that's remotely possible. And please don't treat me like I'm an idiot."

"I wouldn't dare." A resigned sigh filled his broad chest. "Fine. You're a persistent little thing, I'll give you that." He took a moment to gather his thoughts and could feel her ready to let loose another salvo. "I'm not stalling. This goes back farther than you realize."

Rose's eyes narrowed. "Back beyond Walt? How old are you?"

His head turned slightly to face her. "If I said over two hundred, would you believe me?"

Her mouth opened to reply, but there were no words.

"I see that's not what you expected." At her vague nod, he continued. "But, it's true. I was born in a village along a River. My people are Lakota Sioux. That's the language I've been teaching Peter. Anyway, when my mother was pregnant with me and about to give birth, a gray wolf began to stalk her. A wolf with bright blue eyes." He paused to see her reaction.

Torn between enthralled and skeptical, Rose remained silent. She secretly hoped he would break out in a laugh and tell her he was just kidding.

"My father, the Shaman, knew about the rogue and tried to track him down. But, he was too tricky. This wasn't an ordinary wolf." He had to stop as images of his capture by the evil fairy who had sent that wolf came screaming back into his mind. He thought he had banished all that. "He succeeded in getting my mother off by herself and bit her. Whatever it was in the spell that infected him traveled through my mother and got to me, as was intended." When Rose's mouth started to form a word, he held up a hand. "It'd be best if you'd just let me finish. There'll be a question period after the lecture."

The humor relaxed her. "Fine. I feel like I should be taking notes."

"My mother didn't survive, and neither did the gray wolf. My father's arrow shot straight through him. And, the Shaman still wears the wolf skin as a reminder of what he lost. I can see it in your eyes that you're picturing a scene at Disneyland along the River. That scene represents my family. The Cooking Woman stirring the pot helped raise me.

"Whenever I want, I travel back in time to that time period and visit them. Don't interrupt..." Looking away, he felt the centuries of torment every time a jump was made. "Just as that wolf traveled through time to get to my mother, I can travel through time, too. And, no, I don't know why or how. I just do.

"Wals has gone with me. It's rather...terrifying, to say the least. But, it happens. And, just so you know, I turn into a wolf when I go back. Yes, a real wolf. A talking wolf."

"This just gets better and better."

Wolf had to chuckle. "After all this time, I still can't figure it all out. Let's just flash forward to the 1940's when I first had contact with Walt Disney. Well, I was a wolf then, so let's just say introductions weren't possible. Then, in the mid-1950's, I looked him up again. He was busy with the little Park he called Disneyland and I needed a job. We hit it off and he hired me to be on the security team."

"Did he know you...you...do whatever it is you do?"

"Eventually." Wolf nodded back at the photograph. "That blond-haired man in the photo is Kimberly's father, as I think you know. He and I became a special team to help Walt achieve his goals. We mostly worked behind the scenes to make sure everything went as it should. Most of the time we succeeded. Sometimes, not so much."

When Wolf paused, Rose hoped he would fill in some of that story, but he had another route in mind.

"It was Walt who came up with the idea for those Hidden Mickey quests. He wanted to make sure his legacy would continue."

"Well, that seems unnecessary. Look at what his company became."

"Yes. Now. The Studio was successful back then, but, at first, there was no certainty that Disneyland would catch on. Walt was a genius, and he had a sure vision of his future. But, he wanted to make sure it would all continue."

"So, he set up the quest Wals and I were doing?"

Wolf nodded, glad to see she seemed to be beyond the shocked stage. "And we helped him. Walt was an incredibly busy man, so we took on the task of setting most things in place. And, after all these years, it fell on me to make sure they remained in place."

"Why is that?"

"Well, Walt expected those quests to be found right away. But, most of them weren't. Here we are, all these decades later, Walt's gone and Kimberly's father is gone, and there are still some Hidden Mickeys out there."

"Wow."

Wolf tried to stand to leave, but she put a restraining hand on his sleeve. Resigned, he dropped back to the sofa. "I assume you have some questions."

"You said Wals went with you on a trip?" At his brief nod, she frowned. "Did that have to do with the other Rose?"

"He had quite a time of it. I'm proud of what he did. Wals is quite a hero to me."

She had to smile at the praise. "To me, too." She ran a hand over her face. "Wow. What a story. So, you're like a werewolf?"

Wolf let out a disgusted snort and rolled his eyes. "No! I'm not a werewolf! Why is that the first thing everyone asks? And, no. I don't have a tail. Gosh, I went through this with Wals."

"Sorry. Sheesh, Wolf. You tell someone you turn into a wolf

when you travel back through time and you don't expect that question?"

With another snort, he turned his head away.

"Can you show me what you do?"

"Gosh, Rose, I'm not a pony in the circus—though sometimes it feels like I am. I'm used to the process, but it's somewhat scary for everyone else. It takes a certain howl to call the storm that opens the portal so I can jump. There's usually a lot of thunder, lightning, and water involved. I don't think Kimberly would appreciate her house being messed up."

"Ah, they do know. I knew it!"

"They've seen the process, but haven't gone with me. There are dangers involved. With them being a family, we'd all rather not take the chance. Even though Lance does pout a bit when I leave."

Feeling Wolf staring at her, Rose pulled her mind back from his incredible tale. "What?"

"Can I go now? There's a lot to be done before everyone arrives."

"Oh, the party!" Rose jumped to her feet. "I forgot all about it." She put a hand on Wolf's arm. "I can't say I totally believe everything, but, thanks for confiding in me. I need to chat with Wals."

"I would assume you do. But, please keep this just between us. If anyone outside of our circle were to learn…"

"Yes, yes, I know. That's understandable. But, thanks, again." She watched him stride from the room as if he had been a condemned man released from prison. "Time will tell if I believe you or not," she muttered to herself.

December, 2016

The winter storm pounded against their balcony. Nestled together behind the security glass, Wals and Rose watched the waves pound against the shore two blocks away. Usually they sat there to watch the day end, but there would be no sunset that evening. A different pounding reached their ears.

"Is that the front door? Who'd be out in this weather?"

Wals groaned as he contemplated leaving his warm companion. "I'll go see. Maybe it's import…"

His words were cut short by the sudden appearance of Wolf at their bedroom slider. "I tried knocking."

Wals' eyes narrowed. Wolf had other ways of entering a room. "Is everything alright?" The usually placid Wolf seemed upset.

Wolf nodded a hello to the surprised Rose who had followed, quietly sliding the door shut behind her. "No, something's happened."

"Has there been an accident?"

The question confused the security guard. "Accident? No... no. It's Star Wars Land."

Since all three of them still worked at Disneyland, they were well aware of the new land that was about to break ground behind Fantasyland and Frontierland. "And?"

Wolf's eyes shot to Wals. "And, they are going to drain the River. Months earlier than they planned. My family, Wals."

Realization hit Wals. "What will they do without the River, Wolf? They depend on it."

Rose stepped between the two men. "Wait a minute. I'm assuming this has to do with what you told me a few years ago, Wolf. But, why are you concerned about your family? They're... they're..."

"No, they aren't gone, Rose. I can still get back to them." Wolf tried to figure out what he hadn't told her before. "You don't understand. There's a link to Disneyland and my past. The River is my usual portal to go visit them. The Village, to put it simply, is in the same place."

"I still don't see why you're upset."

Wals knew. "Rose, honey, whatever happens at Disneyland now, in our time, affects the past. When I went with Wolf the first time, it was when Tom Sawyer Island was being converted to Pirates Lair. That meant, in Wolf's family's time, there would be pirates coming to their area. We had to rescue two people and warn his family. I told you about Dr. Houser and Briar Rose."

Still trying to piece the puzzle together, she merely nodded.

Wolf took that as a sign of acceptance. "And now that the River is going to be drained, the Friendly Village on the River is going to go away. The train—and the River—is going to be rerouted. I have to go back to my family and help them prepare. I have to get them moved before it happens here. Wals, I need your help. You know them all. You'll have to help me convince them to leave."

A look of terror passed through Wals' eyes. The passage was never easy. "I need to have something with me so I don't lose my memory again."

"Your nametag inside your shirt worked when you went for Mato."

"I'm going, too."

Wolf and Wals didn't seem to hear her as Wals went over to their dresser to find an extra nametag. "What else do we need, Wolf? Food? Supplies? Are they going to face a drought?"

"I said I'm going, too. I want to help."

Both men turned to her. "No, you're not. It's too dangerous, honey. If all goes well, we'll be back before you even know we were gone, however that works."

Arms folded, she didn't accept that. "I'm going with you. If I'm expected to accept this as a fact, I need to see it. Plus, it sounds fascinating." She slapped a hand over her mouth. "Oh, Wolf, I'm sorry. I didn't mean it like that. If there is trouble for your family, I want to help. I am going."

Rather than argue, Wals quickly found her nametag and handed it to her. "This needs to touch your skin at all time. Just a precaution." He watched until it was secured inside her blouse. "Wolf?"

"We'll know more once we get there. You ready?"

Wals mouth fell open. "We're leaving from here? What about the River?"

"No time for that." Wolf turned to Rose for the final instructions. "Grab ahold of my shirt, and, whatever happens, do not let go. Wals, you know what to do."

The three friends huddled together in the center of the room. Her fingers digging into Wolf's shirt, Rose closed her eyes and pressed her other arm protectively across her still-flat stomach.

Between one breath and the next, the room was empty as the storm raged against the house.

—THE END—

Next book...

HIDDEN MICKEY MERCHANDISE

HIDDEN MICKEY ART
ON CANVAS
LIMITED EDITION PRINTS
© 2015 DOUBLE R BOOKS

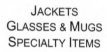

HIDDEN MICKEY
BASEBALL CAPS
&
T-SHIRTS
FOR GROUP QUESTS

JACKETS
GLASSES & MUGS
SPECIALTY ITEMS

THE LIMITED EDITION
HIDDEN MICKEY HEART NECKLACE

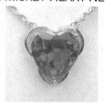

© 2010 NANCY RODRIGUE

AND MUCH MORE...
AVAILABLE AT:
HIDDENMICKEYBOOK.COM/MERCHANDISE.HTML

THE HIDDEN MICKEY FAN CLUB BLOG
LOG IN AND GAIN ACCESS TO OUR ARCHIVED NEWSLETTERS WITH BEHIND-THE-SCENES ARTICLES WRITTEN BY PAST AND PRESENT CAST MEMBERS WITHIN THE DISNEY PARKS. FANS ALSO RECEIVE ADVANCE ANNOUNCEMENTS ON BOOK SIGNINGS, SPECIAL EVENTS, AND SPECIAL OPPORTUNITIES TO BUY BOOKS AND MERCHANDISE BEFORE THESE ARE RELEASED TO THE PUBLIC.

BLOG.HIDDENMICKEYBOOK.COM

JOIN THE FACEBOOK HIDDEN MICKEY FAN CLUB
LOG IN TO FACEBOOK AND "LIKE" THE "HIDDEN MICKEY FAN CLUB" TO BE ENTERED IN THE BOOK GIVEAWAY CONTEST. EACH TIME A 100 "LIKES" MILESTONE IS REACHED, A HIDDEN MICKEY ADVENTURES QUEST & GAME BOOK IS GIVEN AWAY IN A RANDOM DRAWING. JOIN TODAY TO WIN!

WWW.FACEBOOK.COM/HIDDENMICKEYFANCLUB